"I'd have know[n] ... Anna. You sti[ll] ... eighteen-year-old girl—"

"Don't bother, Jake," she interrupted. "As you ought to know, I'm not eighteen anymore. I grew up. Did you?"

"Tongue's sharper," he noted appreciatively.

"Eyes are open." She marched out the door, and he followed her to her ancient pickup. It had once been a bright, cheery red, but the relentless Texas sun had baked it to a muddy rust, and Anna gave thanks for each day that passed without her having to replace another part.

Wanting to end the encounter, she flipped a strand of long blond hair back from her face and said, "Why don't you do what you do best and get lost."

"Guess that means you haven't forgiven me."

Anna wished violently that the Palo Duro Canyon would open up a new fissure right where Jake Rollins stood and gulp him whole. But with her luck, good old Mama Earth would belch him back out, none the worse for wear.

She knew she was overreacting. But she couldn't be reasonable when she thought of what his coming back could mean. Jake didn't know it, but he could tear her world apart even more completely than he had the day he'd called her from Las Vegas and told her he'd married someone else.

Dear Reader,

Do you believe in second chances? As I sat down to write this letter it occurred to me that my publishing career has something in common with the theme of this story. After writing several books for another publisher, the line I wrote for suddenly folded. This is my first book from my new publisher, Harlequin Superromance. A second chance, if you will, for me to share my stories with readers.

Cowboy Come Home is about second chances. A second chance at love, a second chance for family. A chance to change not the past, but the future. And what better place to set such a story than a town in west Texas called Happy? Yes, Happy, Texas, is a real place, although I've fictionalized nearly everything about it. And while the characters are fictional, I like to think I might meet people like them when I go back to visit.

Eve Gaddy

P.S. The sign is real, too, but I don't have a clue how it lost the frown.

I love to hear from readers. Please write me at P.O. Box 131704, Tyler, Texas, 75713-1704. Or e-mail me at egaddy1@ballistic.com

COWBOY COME HOME
HOME
Eve Gaddy

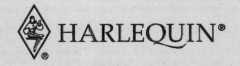

HARLEQUIN®

TORONTO • NEW YORK • LONDON
AMSTERDAM • PARIS • SYDNEY • HAMBURG
STOCKHOLM • ATHENS • TOKYO • MILAN • MADRID
PRAGUE • WARSAW • BUDAPEST • AUCKLAND

ISBN 0-373-70903-X

COWBOY COME HOME

This edition published by arrangement with Harlequin Books S.A.

® and TM are trademarks of the publisher. Trademarks indicated with ® are registered in the United States Patent and Trademark Office, the Canadian Trade Marks Office and in other countries.

Visit us at www.romance.net

Printed in U.S.A.

This book is for Rosalyn Alsobrook, who knows I couldn't
have done it without her. Thanks, Roz, for critiquing, for
listening, and particularly for talking on the dreaded phone.
Also, many thanks to my guide to Happy, for taking a day out
of your busy schedule to show me around and patiently
answer my questions. And thanks to Kathy Cowan for being
my guide to the mysterious ways of horses, and for teaching
me about fence mending, among other things. Last and most
important, thanks to my family for all the love and support
you give me.

CHAPTER ONE

RUMOR HIT town before he did.

The theories about why Jake Rollins had returned to Happy, Texas, ran every bit as wild as he had. Some claimed he'd come back to finally make peace with his father, Wes Rollins. They swore he was back to stay and he planned to take over running the Rollins ranch. Others discounted that idea, since Jake had never been one for cattle ranching. No, if he was there to stay, they figured, it would be to raise horses. He'd always had a thing for horses.

But most folks believed he'd only come back for a visit—about time, too—and had no intention of sticking around. After all, what could a man like Jake find to keep him in Happy?

To tell the truth, nobody really knew, but every last one of them had a theory.

Except, that is, Anna Leigh Connor. Anna didn't know and didn't care what had brought him back. She just thanked God she'd had warning before she walked smack into a past she'd never thought to see again.

Jake Rollins. The man who'd given her her greatest heartache. And her greatest joy.

Still, she admitted to curiosity. What would Jake look like after all this time? He couldn't possibly be as sinfully good-looking as he'd been at age twenty. Surely that dark-blond hair had dulled to a lackluster brown, those knock-'em-dead-blue eyes had faded to a boring shade, without a wicked gleam in them.

And if there truly was a God, that sinewy plane of hard-muscled belly had been replaced by a paunch. His face would reveal every line of dissipation, his body every excess he'd committed in the sixteen years of wild living he'd no doubt indulged in since he left home. Anna devoutly hoped he felt—and showed—every bit of it.

Fortunately, she didn't see any unfamiliar vehicles parked outside the Hitching Post, Happy's one convenience store and home to much of the ever present gossip. Having forgotten her coat, as usual, she dashed inside with gritted teeth. Right now the grouping of dingy white Formica-topped tables and orange plastic chairs near the entrance stood empty, waiting for another group of folks to gather to drink coffee, talk and pass the time.

A reprieve, Anna thought as she headed for the refrigerated units at the back of the small wooden building, but she had a feeling the calm wouldn't last long. She would run into Jake sooner or later. Though never would suit her just fine.

Becky Swenson's voice, bursting with news, drowned out the tinny sound of country music issuing from the battered boom box behind the counter. The decor suited the place, with various cattle brands from the area's ranches adorning the beige walls, along with a few Western landscape pictures.

As Becky talked, Anna grabbed a carton of skim

milk, a loaf of bread, a couple rolls of toilet paper and stuffed a box of chocolate sandwich cookies— Leigh's favorite—under her arm before carrying them to the counter.

"Wes came in here day before yesterday," Becky said, patting a hand over her mousy brown curls, "and I swear, I'd as soon try to get words from a dying frog as him. But—" she paused significantly before continuing "—he did admit that Jake is back in town."

"He did?" Anna asked, curious in spite of herself. Somehow the picture of crusty Wes Rollins gossiping with Becky Swenson wouldn't quite come clear. He usually didn't even drink coffee with the rest of the men, though he did show up from time to time.

"Well, he grunted when I asked him, and he bought an extra gallon of milk. Jake used to drink a lot of milk, didn't he?"

Anna doubted milk was his favorite drink now, but she let the question ride. She had no desire to get into a speculative discussion of Jake Rollins's interests. Especially since she'd once been one of them. She'd bet Becky, who'd gone to school with them both, and had known her since they were all in diapers, remembered that fact nearly as well as she did herself.

"And speaking of good-looking devils," Becky continued, her voice turning sticky-bun sweet. "Look who just walked in. Why if it isn't Jake Rollins, as I live and breathe."

Half suspecting Becky of pulling her leg, Anna turned around. Shock hit her in the chest like the kick of a horse, as chill and bitter as the winter wind that whistled through the open doorway. She couldn't breathe. Her head whirled, her stomach plunged. For an endless moment she could do no more than stare at the man filling the doorway.

Life, she thought, sucking in air again, was terrifically unfair. He didn't look dissipated at all. Older, mature, not a boy any longer but a man. And oh, Lord, what a man. Same dark-blond hair, same sky-blue eyes, same lady-killer dimple winking in one lean cheek. Six feet plus of pure, hard male. A white T-shirt, visible beneath his black leather jacket, stretched across his muscled chest and flat abdomen. So much for the paunch he deserved, she thought. Faded denim hugged his long legs just tightly enough to inspire wicked fantasies. Some picture. Enough to make a strong woman's knees buckle and give a weak one a heart attack.

He nodded at Becky, but his eyes were for her. "Anna Leigh," he said, in that midnight-sinful voice she remembered all too well.

Had nothing changed about the blasted man? "Anna Connor," she corrected, and met his devilish gaze with a bland look of her own.

He grinned at her, acknowledging the pointed remark, but he didn't look away. No, he looked her over like he had all day and then some, and like he for durn sure approved of the view.

A tingle of sensual awareness started in her belly and spread. She cursed herself and swore she wouldn't let him affect her, wouldn't let him get to her. But it was too late, he already had. Along with the undeniable attraction, and just as unwelcome, a finger of fear shivered through her.

She turned back to Becky and said sharply, "Would you mind ringing this stuff up, Becky, or are you going to stand there gawking for the next half hour?" She couldn't really blame her friend. If he hadn't been the last man on earth she wanted to see, she'd have been gawking, too.

Obviously shocked by her curtness, Becky stared at her with rounded eyes. "Well, sure, Anna. I didn't know you were in such a hurry." She sniffed, and Anna knew Becky would give her the cold shoulder for at least a week. She'd endure an ice age, though, if she could just get out of there and away from Jake.

"Where do you keep the picture?" he asked her, lounging against the counter while Becky rang each item up as slowly as an armadillo crossed the road.

Sixteen years since Anna had seen him and he still surprised her. That wasn't the sort of question she'd have expected him to ask her. "What picture?"

"The one that ages while you never do."

She cast him a withering glare—one that had made other men pale. "Still have that charm, I see. Don't bother wasting it on me, cowboy."

He smiled, a slow, wicked smile guaranteed to make a woman melt. Well, dammit, not her. She had dry ice in her veins when it came to him.

"Charm is never wasted on a beautiful woman. How have you been, Anna?"

Becky's eyelids had stretched so wide by now that it was a wonder, Anna thought, her eyeballs didn't fall out of her head. She ignored both Becky and Jake, hoping if she didn't respond he'd go away.

He didn't.

"I'd have known you anywhere. It's downright spooky how much you still look like the eighteen-year-old girl—"

"Don't bother, Jake," she interrupted. "As you ought to know, I'm not eighteen anymore. I grew up. Did you?"

"Tongue's sharper," he noted appreciatively.

"Eyes are open." Thank God, Becky had finished totaling up her purchases. She slapped her money down and held out her hand, palm up, aware of Jake's knowing smile and Becky's goggling eyes. Thankfully closing her fingers around the change, she said, "This has been fascinating, Jake, don't think it hasn't. But I have business to attend to."

He stepped to the door with her. "I'll walk out with you."

"No, you won't."

Disregarding her order, he held the door for her and walked with her to her ancient pickup. Once a bright, cheery red, the relentless Texas sun had baked it to a muddy rust, and Anna gave thanks for each day that passed without her having to replace another part.

Her palm itched to smack the dimple right off his cheek. She quelled the urge, rather than give him the satisfaction of knowing he'd provoked her. Flipping a strand of long blond hair back from her face she said, "Why don't you do what you do best and get lost?"

"Guess this means you haven't forgiven me."

"Sharp as a barb on a wire. What was your first clue?"

He laughed. "Oh, I don't know. Might have been some of those killer glares you've been aiming my way."

She didn't answer, but stalked toward her truck.

Laying a hand on her arm, Jake stopped her. "Come on, Anna, sixteen years is a long time to nurse a grudge."

She froze, willing herself to feel nothing, willing herself to ignore the jolting current that sizzled up her arm and through her bloodstream from that simple contact. Dammit, it wasn't fair that he could still affect her with a casual touch.

"I'd have to care to hold a grudge," she said, slicing him with a sharp glance. "And I don't. Now get your hand off my arm."

Instead, he slid his fingers down to feel the wildly galloping pulse at her wrist.

"You want to keep those fingers intact, you'd best move them," she said, damning him for evoking a reaction from her. And not just any reaction. Dislike, disgust, a response like that would have been fine. But no, even after what he'd done he could still make her pulse race with excitement and pleasure like a filly's at the starting gate.

He dropped her wrist and gave her a rueful smile. "Damn, Anna, you're even more beautiful now than you were as a girl."

Thinking she ought to yank that silvery tongue right out of his lying, sexy mouth, she jerked open the truck door, slid in, and slammed it closed. He stood there smiling at her through the window. Anna wished violently that the Palo Duro Canyon would open up a new fissure right where Jake Rollins stood and gulp him whole. With her luck, good old Mama Earth would belch him right back out, none the worse for wear.

She rolled down the window for a final pithy comment. "Like I said, Jake, save it for someone who cares."

Naturally, the window jammed open. Jake didn't say a word as he opened the door, turned the handle, and rolled it back up. He didn't need to. His smart-ass grin said it all.

She knew she was overreacting, knew that seeing him again shouldn't have thrown her so much. But she couldn't be reasonable about the fear that hammered in her pulses, the pain that squeezed her heart when she thought of what his coming back could mean. Jake didn't know it, but he could tear her world apart now as easily, and even more completely than he had sixteen years ago.

The day he'd called her from the National Rodeo finals in Las Vegas and told her he'd married someone else.

JAKE WATCHED Anna leave, not bothering to go back into the store. He'd only gone inside in the first place because he'd seen Anna dash inside and decided it was too good an opportunity to miss. For a man with a plan, he thought, climbing into his own truck, he wasn't doing too great. He headed to his father's ranch, surprised to find how easily the habit of driving home came back to him.

Seeing him again had rattled Anna, though she'd

done her best not to show it. Those jade-green eyes of hers had sizzled with anger, but something else had blazed in them as well. He'd bet one of his championship belt buckles that she felt the chemistry that still flared between them. Just as he did.

He'd expected her reaction, her anger. No surprises there. Wincing, he recalled how he'd broken the news of his marriage to her. Not a very smooth move, he had to admit, even if he had been hardly more than a kid.

But what really jerked his chain was his reaction to her. He'd had one purpose in mind for Anna Leigh, and one purpose only. A swift and instant rekindling of the old fire between them hadn't been in the plans.

He should have been prepared. After all, he'd seen her daughter, her spitting image, only a few weeks ago. But who would have imagined that Anna would still look so young, or be every bit as blond, slim and pretty as he remembered her? No, that wasn't quite it, he thought. The girl had been pretty. The woman was drop-dead gorgeous.

Even so, sixteen years was a long time. He shouldn't have had such a strong reaction to her, no matter how beautiful he still found her.

But the fact remained, seeing Anna Leigh Connor in the flesh had blown him away.

That thought still plagued him, when fifteen minutes later he pulled up to the Rollins ranch. He'd only been in town a couple of days and the reunion with his father had been both easier and harder than he'd expected. Wes had taken Jake's call that he wanted to come see him, and stay a while, in stride, even though it would be the first time they'd see each other face-to-face since Jake had left home so long ago.

That had been his father's choice, as much as his. The old man had never made the attempt to see him ride—no big shock, given his disapproval of Jake's choice of profession. And Jake had never come right out and asked him, either. It was simpler to think he wouldn't come than have to face the rejection if he'd asked and Wes had turned him down.

So neither had asked and neither had given. Until Jake had showed up early one morning after driving all night and caught Wes coming out of the barn. Unsure of his welcome, Jake had gotten out of his truck and waited for his father to reach him.

Wes was older, was Jake's first thought. Still a big, powerful man, he'd aged well. But sixteen years had taken their toll, on both of them.

For a long moment, they'd simply stared at each other, then Wes had stretched out his hand and Jake met it with his own. Gripping it tightly, with an emotion he hadn't expected to feel, Jake could have sworn he saw moisture in the old man's eyes.

But Wes Rollins didn't cry. Not even on the day they'd buried his wife. Jake couldn't imagine him breaking down now, and sure as hell not over the son he'd never gotten along with paying him a visit.

Jake still hadn't told him of his plans to settle near Happy, to buy a place of his own where he could breed and raise cutting horses. They had both carefully avoided the topic of how long Jake planned to stick around. Would his father be glad when he found out? Or would he even care?

JAKE DREW UP a chair across from his father at the kitchen table. The same scarred wooden table he remembered eating at all through his childhood and until he left home. For a minute it infuriated him that Wes so clearly had no use for the money he'd sent him over the years. At least he could have bought himself a damned new table.

Wes, never one for unnecessary talk, merely grunted in answer to most of his questions. Though it had been years since Jake had talked to his father much, he still recognized the tone of his answers. A deep sound meant no, yes came out slightly higher, and a snort meant he had no use for the question.

Jake decided beating around the bush would get him nowhere, so he opted for the direct route. "When did Carl Connor die?"

Wes looked up from his sandwich and pinned his son with a speculative stare. "Carl?"

"Yeah. Carl Connor. Anna Leigh Connor's late husband." And once upon a time, Jake's best friend, though he didn't repeat that thought aloud.

"'Bout four, five years ago." Of course, being Wes, he didn't elaborate.

Jake remembered his father telling him about it in one of their rare phone conversations, months after the fact. Wes had been no more forthcoming then than he was now. "Did he get sick? What happened?"

"Like that, is it?" Wes said, and nodded.

If Jake hadn't known him to be incapable of it, he'd have sworn he smiled. His father's brown hair might be liberally sprinkled with gray, but age, apparently, hadn't dulled his wits a bit.

"Won't do you any good." Wes took a bite of his sandwich and chewed it slowly before adding, "She won't have anything to do with you."

Despite his best efforts, Jake flushed. Damn, the old man always had known how to pick his most vulnerable spot. "I didn't ask your opinion, I asked how Carl died."

His father nodded again. "I know what you asked. Got a good idea why you asked it, too." After a pause he said, "Drunk driver hit him. Rolled his pickup. He went into a coma." His gaze met Jake's, his eyes, like his son's, a sharp, piercing blue. "Died about three days later."

Three days. His appetite deserting him, Jake pushed his plate away. Familiar feelings of guilt and regret hit him. He'd walked away from Carl, who'd been his best friend, as completely and finally as he had Anna and his father. Another more cynical side figured that Carl wouldn't have wanted him around anyway—not once he'd married Anna.

But to die like that... So damned young. "Must have been hard for Anna."

"Yep. He was a good man. Did his duty, lived up to his responsibilities."

Unlike you. The implied words hung between them. Frustrated, Jake shoved a hand through his hair and ground his teeth together to keep from speaking.

A knock saved him from uttering the words that had been threatening to spill. Wes pushed his chair back and rose stiffly, as if it pained him to move. It probably did, Jake thought. The old man was too stubborn to admit he had arthritis. Tall, powerfully built, and tough as boot leather, he didn't take kindly to aging.

Wes swung open the door and stood stock-still. "Mary?" He sounded bewildered. "What are you doing here?"

"I came to welcome Jake home, of course. Don't just stand there, Wes. Let me in."

Standing, Jake smiled at her tone. He'd recognize Mary Gallick's voice anywhere, even though he hadn't heard it in years. It seemed his high school English teacher still had the habit of command. Even funnier, Wes obeyed her instantly, scrambling to get out of her way. Mary, a small sparrow of a woman, made Wes look even larger—and extremely ill at ease. Jake wondered why.

"The prodigal returns, I see," she said, nailing him with a critical eye. "It's about time."

He couldn't help grinning. She'd always been his favorite teacher. Only ten years or so older than he, her youth had made her more accessible than most of his teachers. "Yes, ma'am. How have you been, Mrs. Gallick?"

"I'd be better if you called me Mary. I don't need to feel any older than I already do and being called Mrs. Gallick by somebody your age makes me feel positively ancient." She turned to Wes. "Did you ask him?"

Shooting Jake a quick glance, his father shook his head. He mumbled something that sounded like "Back to work," jammed his hat on his head and shot out the door seconds later. Jake didn't recall ever seeing his father move that fast.

Mary watched his retreat, a smile lifting one side

of her mouth. "I didn't think so," she murmured before taking a seat at the table. She patted her short, dark hair into place and eyed him sharply. "Are you just here for a visit or are you planning on sticking around?"

At the blunt question, Jake's eyebrow lifted. "As a matter of fact, I'm thinking about staying."

"Good." She smiled. "Your father will be happy about that."

Would he? Jake wasn't so sure, especially since he had no intention of running cattle. He started clearing the table. "What is it you wanted to ask me?"

"Well, it has to do with the library."

The dishes clattered into the sink. Jake turned around and looked at her. "What library? Happy doesn't have a library."

"Exactly." She beamed at him, clearly pleased he'd caught on so quickly. "But it's going to."

Light dawned. "You want me to donate money to build a library?"

She looked startled. "I didn't realize you—" She stopped, shaking her head. "I'm sorry, it's none of my business."

"Does everyone think I came home because I'm broke?"

"Well…" Her lips quirked. "Nobody knows. It's all speculation. You know how Happy is. And you know how little your father talks."

Jake smiled cynically. "You can tell the curious that I'm not broke. And while I can't fund the entire building, I might be persuaded to donate a respectable amount."

"That would be wonderful, Jake. But what we really need—" she hesitated then finished "—is you."

Needed him? How long had it been since somebody needed him? He couldn't remember. Equal parts pleased and wary, he waited for her to go on.

"We have a grant, but it won't cover all the expenses. So we want to host a charity rodeo with the proceeds going to the library fund. We need someone who knows what he's doing to run it." Enthusiasm sparkled in her brown eyes. "So naturally, when Wes said you were coming home, I thought of you."

He frowned, leaned back against the counter and folded his arms across his chest. "But Mrs. Ga— Mary, I've never put on a rodeo before." And it sounded like a lot of work he wasn't at all sure he wanted to do. He had his plate full enough with his own plans. "I'm a bronc rider. I've never been involved in the production end of things."

"Oh, come now, Jake. You've got connections. You know people on the circuit. You could pull in some big names if you wanted to. And with you as the organizer, we'd get instant recognition."

"I think you're making too much of my fame. I'm old news."

She stood, jamming a hand on a slim hip, reminding him of her determination when she wanted something. "Horsefeathers. You could do it if you wanted. Admit it."

He supposed he could. A library was a good thing, a good cause. And he liked thinking that he could be instrumental in bringing Happy something lasting and worthwhile. Besides, he was used to lending his name, not to mention his money, to various charities. This involved more than that, though. It meant spending a lot of time and effort to make sure it was done right.

But he'd need help. Someone else who knew what they were doing would be nice. Someone, he realized, beginning to smile, who already ran a riding school. Someone who already hosted play days and who knew all about barrel racing.

"I can't do it alone."

"Everyone would pitch in. It would be a community project."

"More than that. I'd need a cochair," Jake said. "And I know just the person."

"She won't do it," Mary said flatly. "Forget it, Jake."

"How do you know who I'm thinking about?"

"Honey—" she smiled indulgently "—I'm not that much older than you. And I'm not senile yet." She patted his arm. "I remember as well as everyone else that you and Anna Leigh Connor used to be sweethearts. And she's even prettier now than she was all those years ago."

She had that right. "You get Anna to cochair this rodeo with me and I'll do it."

"And how am I supposed to do that? You're not exactly one of her favorite people. Good Lord, Jake, you practically left her at the altar."

"Yeah, and she married Carl Connor soon enough after that, didn't she? Doesn't look like she wasted much time mourning my loss." It still stung that she'd managed to get over him so quickly. And with Carl, his supposed best friend. Jake had always suspected Carl had a thing for Anna. He'd proved it, too, when he moved in on her as quick as a rattler with dinner in its sights.

"Tell her it's her civic duty," he suggested.

"Anna's had it rough, Jake. She doesn't need you making it rougher."

He shrugged. "No Anna, no dice."

"You're up to something. I can see it in your eyes."

Jake gave her an innocent smile. "Let me know what happens." He had faith in Mary Gallick. She wanted the library, which meant she wanted the rodeo to take place. Somehow, she'd get Anna to agree.

He'd have a chance to get to know Anna again.

Because one way or another Jake intended to find out if Anna's pretty little girl was Carl's daughter.

Or his.

CHAPTER TWO

INSIDE THE BARN, Anna turned her head at the slam of a car door. Moments later Leigh entered at full tilt, with her mouth running to match.

"Mom! Mom, are you in here?"

"In Promise's stall," she called, then bent to sift through another forkful of shavings. She stifled a sneeze at the chaff and dust of the hay. "How did cheerleader practice go? And where's your jacket?" she asked in exasperation as Leigh clumped into the stall beside her, blowing on her hands. "It's thirty-five degrees outside."

"Left it at school. Guess what? I got the pictures back!"

"What pictures?" Grateful for the respite, Anna leaned on the handle of the manure fork as the acrid odor of soiled shavings wafted upward. Mucking out the stalls was her least favorite chore. Leigh would help her, though, as soon as she changed into something warm.

"The ones from that rodeo in Houston a few weeks ago. You know, the one me and Blaire went to with Mrs. Nelson when you couldn't go."

"Blaire and I," Anna corrected automatically. She'd hated to miss seeing Leigh race, but with a clinic scheduled for that weekend, she'd had no choice. Fortunately, Suzie Nelson didn't mind taking Leigh along with her own daughter. "Are they any good?" she asked skeptically. Suzie's strong points didn't include photography.

"Super," Leigh said, holding them out to her. "See for yourself." She wrapped her arms around herself and shivered. "Brr, I'm going to find a coat."

"Don't get on the phone." Like most fifteen-year-old girls, Leigh wanted to live with the phone permanently attached to her ear from the time she came home until she went to bed. "I could use some help here. Luis and José are out checking fences," she added, referring to her ranch hands.

"Sure, Mom." Her grin flashed, quick and blinding. "Back in a sec."

Stepping outside the stall, Anna thumbed through the stack of snapshots, pausing to study the good ones. Candid shots of the two girls, Leigh as fair as Blaire was dark. A couple of Leigh on Promise, her barrel racing horse, obviously taken before the competition. Another one, surprisingly good, of Leigh and Promise on the straightaway home. Gazing at it for a long moment, Anna sighed, pride for her daughter's success warring, as always, with uneasiness about Leigh's future.

If only Leigh saw barrel racing as a hobby, rather than a career. Anna wanted her to finish school, go to college, have a more stable life than a career in barrel racing could ever give her. But Leigh was young. Stubborn. And she wanted to rodeo—professionally. Still, Anna didn't intend to panic yet.

Teenagers were notoriously fickle. Something else might strike Leigh's interest.

Smiling at the sight of Leigh receiving her prize for second place, she realized Leigh's features were blurred in that picture. But as Anna took a closer look, the face of the man awarding the prize became heart-stoppingly clear.

Jake Rollins.

She closed her eyes, shook the picture and opened them to stare at it again, praying it had been an hallucination.

It was real, all right.

He wore that same smile, that dazzling, knee-weakening smile that she remembered seeing on his face the first time he won the saddle bronc event in a local rodeo. And that night after the rodeo had been the first time Jake danced with her, when he finally realized she wasn't just a pesky kid who lived on the neighboring ranch.

"Mom, what's wrong? You look like you're about to throw up."

Anna turned glazed eyes to her daughter, holding the photo out to her. "This is— This man is—"

"Yeah, isn't it cool?" Her fingertip touched his face. "That's Jake Rollins. He's a five-time saddle bronc World Champion. Didn't I tell you he presented all the prizes?"

"No," she choked out. "No, you didn't mention it."

"Sure I did, Mom," she said impatiently. "You just weren't paying attention. Right after I came home, I told you all about it. You were doing the books."

That explained it. If Anna's attention had been on her finances, then she probably hadn't been listening that closely. Now that she thought about it, she did remember Leigh mentioning "a cool guy" had given out the prizes. But she hadn't mentioned him by name. Anna would have reacted if she had.

"He said he used to know you," Leigh continued.

"He—did?" Apprehension kicked up her pulse. Oh, God, what else had he said? Surely he hadn't mentioned their past relationship or Leigh would have brought it up already.

"Mmm-hmm," Leigh mumbled, leafing through the remaining photos and selecting one. "Here's another picture of him. Blaire made her mom take it." Leigh's nose wrinkled as she laughed. "Blaire thinks he's really hot."

Hot, Anna thought, dazed. Leigh's best friend thought Jake was hot. And dammit, she realized, gazing at the photo as an almost forgotten ache invaded her heart, Blaire was absolutely right.

"He's nice, too," her daughter continued. "He talked to me for a while later on, after the rodeo. Isn't he Mr. Rollins's son? That's what Blaire's mom said. Why hasn't he been around before now?"

Leigh chattered as she took over mucking out her mare's stall. Anna answered her questions vaguely, her mind racing with questions of her own. Jake had seen Leigh. Met her. Found out she was Anna's daughter. Taken the time to talk to her. And he'd obviously had a strong impact on an impressionable young girl. Small wonder. Leigh, crazy to rodeo, to win a circuit championship, would find a five-time national rodeo champion fascinating. Oh, Lord, what did it all mean?

Much to Anna's relief, Leigh finally changed the subject. But worries continued to churn in Anna's mind.

An hour later with the chores finished, she still hadn't sorted things out. Counting back the weeks, she realized that rumors of Jake's return had started circulating shortly after that ill-fated rodeo. Then he'd put fact to the rumors and come back to Happy. Coincidence? she asked herself as she entered the small, whitewashed wood frame house that had once been Carl's parents' home. Not hardly.

No one had seen as much as Jake's shadow in Happy in sixteen years. Not until three weeks after he'd first set eyes on Leigh. What was he up to?

Anna had an uneasy feeling she knew.

Unlike everyone else in town, Suzie wouldn't have thought to go out of her way to mention Jake to Anna. Since Suzie hadn't grown up in Happy, she hadn't known him, or Anna's history with him. Not that it would have made a difference if Anna had known about the meeting, except she might not feel as blindsided as she did now.

Maybe she was reading too much into this, given her guilty knowledge. Jake's return didn't have to hold a sinister significance. With any luck it didn't.

The phone rang, interrupting her worries, as she and Leigh cleared the supper dishes from the table. Leigh answered it, chatting for a few minutes while Anna finished up.

"It's Grandma, Mom," Leigh said, handing her the phone.

"Homework," Anna reminded her as she took it and Leigh left. "Hi, Mom. How are things? Is Edward any better?" Her mother had remarried and moved to California several years ago, after Anna's father's death. Though she and Anna kept in touch regularly, they only saw each other a couple of times a year.

"The new medicine is helping," her mother said. "He's doing a lot better. When are you and Leigh going to get out to see us?"

"Oh, Mom, this isn't a good time. I'm not sure."

"Well, whenever you can manage it, let us know. Anything new going on there?"

"As a matter of fact, yes." Though they'd never questioned her decision, Anna had always wondered just what her parents had suspected about her hasty marriage and pregnancy. "Jake Rollins is back in town."

There was a long silence before her mother spoke. "Jake Rollins? Good Lord."

"It surprised a lot of people."

Another pause. "Any particular reason he came home? It's been years, hasn't it?"

"Sixteen. And I have a feeling I know what's brought him back."

"Leigh," her mother said. "Does Jake know he's her father?"

Anna let out her breath in relief. "No, I never told him. How long have you known?"

"Honey, your father and I weren't stupid. We figured it out pretty quickly."

"You've never said a word."

"What was the point? You'd made your decision and we had to trust that it was the right one."

"It was. It's not marrying Carl that I'm questioning. But not telling Jake..." At the time she'd been so certain she was right to keep it from him. "He met her at a rodeo three weeks ago and suddenly he comes home. I can't help but think he suspects. Mom, I don't know what's going to happen."

"Do you want me to fly out there? I can get a flight tomorrow if you need me."

"No, it's sweet of you to offer, but Edward needs you there. We'll be all right. It's probably nothing." Her doorbell rang just then. "Let me call you back, okay? Someone's at the door."

"You know that you can call me whenever you want to talk."

"Thanks, Mom. I will." She hung up the phone feeling oddly cheered. At least there was one person she could speak to frankly. Even if her mother couldn't do anything to help her, she could listen.

Mary Gallick, Leigh's English teacher, stood on her doorstep. "Is this a bad time?" she asked. "Do you have a minute?"

"Sure." Anna suppressed a groan. She liked Mary, and had since she'd been her student years before. But nearly every time Mary came over, Anna ended up involved in yet another school project. And at the moment, she didn't have the time, much less the inclination. "What can I do for you, Mary?" she asked, leading her into the living room.

"I have a proposition for you," she said, taking a seat on the well-used blue twill sofa.

"About school?"

Mary shook her head, smiling mischievously. "Not exactly. Come sit down, Anna, and let me explain."

Anna sighed, eyeing Mary warily, but she took a seat and politely waited for her to begin.

"You know we've been trying to raise funding for the new library in Happy."

Anna nodded. Having been to quite a few town meetings, naturally she knew about the plans. "I'm sorry I missed the last few meetings. I never heard if the grant came through." And she'd been too busy to ask anyone, she thought guiltily.

"Yes, it did. Except that the funds we've been promised won't cover everything, and we need to match them. So we decided to...that is...we think..." Uncharacteristically, she fumbled for words. "The, uh, the city council decided to host a charity rodeo to raise the rest of the money."

Puzzled, Anna looked at her. What was she so nervous about? "That sounds like a fine idea, Mary. What is it you want me to do?" she asked, thinking that she could surely swing taking charge of an event or two.

"Would you consider—could you—"

Anna continued to look at her, wondering when she'd get to the point. And what was taking her so long to get there.

"We need someone to chair it," Mary said in a rush.

This time Anna did groan. Her riding school demanded her full attention, even now in the winter, the off season. If Anna was going to succeed, and as the sole support of herself and her daughter she fully intended to, then she had to work, and work hard, year-round. Just keeping her head above water wasn't enough. She wanted more, a lot more.

"I know it's a lot to ask," Mary continued, a pleading note in her voice, "but we really need your help."

Just say no, Anna told herself. *Yeah, right. When Mary Gallick asked, no one said no.* Her heart sank at the thought of the extra work. Besides, she'd never put on a rodeo. Just play days and clinics, not the same thing at all. A rodeo was a much bigger proposition. "Mary, I want to help, but I just don't see how—"

Mary interrupted. "You wouldn't have to do it all. We've found someone to cochair it with you. An expert, as a matter of fact."

An expert. Foreboding pricked her nerves like tiny needles. The apprehensive expression on Mary's face all but confirmed Anna's hunch. Nevertheless, she asked. "And who is this expert?"

"Jake Rollins."

Anna sprang to her feet. "Are you out of your mind? I wouldn't cochair a dog fight with that man."

Mary straightened and glared up at her. "Now, Anna, I know you have a history with him, but think of the town. We could generate a lot of publicity if a five-time World Champion helped chair the event. You have to admit, he's perfect for the job."

"Oh, I'm sure he would be. If you can convince him to stick around long enough to do it."

"He says he's back to stay. I believe him, Anna."

Great. Just great. She paced a few steps, whirled

to face Mary again. "Let him do it all, then. Or if he needs help, someone else can provide it. It's not going to be me."

"That's just it. He won't do it without you. His exact words were, 'No Anna, no dice.'"

That sounded just like the jerk. Anna crossed her arms over her chest. "Tough."

"Think of the school."

"No."

"Think of the town."

"No."

"Think of your daughter's education."

Anna winced. That last one hurt. "Mary, I can't. Honestly, I can't. I don't have the time. I can't afford to."

"If you'll pardon me for saying so, Anna," she said acerbically, "you can't afford not to. Think of what this event could mean, economically, to you—to the whole town. And if you cochair it, why, with that sort of publicity, you'll gain no telling how many new students, new boarders. This could put your school on the map, draw in new people from miles around."

The worst of it, Anna thought, was that Mary was right. The rodeo would be a godsend of an economic boost to the whole area. Including, and especially, Anna's riding school.

But she couldn't. Plan a rodeo with Jake? Spend time with him? See him, talk to him, work with him?

No way in hell.

THE NEXT MORNING Anna dropped Leigh off at school and then drove immediately to the Rollins's place. She had to have lost her mind. How she had ever let Mary talk her into coordinating a rodeo with Jake Rollins, she didn't know.

Yes, she did. Leigh's intervention had swung her. She'd heard them talking and decided that having Happy host a rodeo would be awesome. The most awesome thing that had ever happened, according to Leigh. How could Anna resist those glowing eyes, the sparkling enthusiasm that filled her with motherly pride? She couldn't, of course.

But the bottom line was that she'd be a fool not to take every chance possible to increase her school's success.

So, rather than continue to be hammered at by both her daughter and her friend, she'd said yes. But by damn, if she had to work with Jake Rollins she meant to lay down some rules. Rules to keep her— and her daughter—safe.

As she drove along the gravel drive to the Rollinses' one-story beige-brick ranch house, she saw Jake walking a good-looking blood bay toward the stables, cooling him down after a ride, she assumed. No horse of Wes's, she thought, familiar with the older man's stock. Switching off the car, she sat watching Jake a moment. He moved the way she remembered, with a long-limbed, carelessly graceful stride.

He wore faded jeans, scuffed boots, a battered black Stetson and a faded red flannel shirt. Nothing special, nothing different from what most men she knew wore every day. So why did it look so good on Jake?

Disgusted, she wondered again why Jake couldn't

have lost those damnable good looks. But she should be well past the age that she reacted so strongly to someone's physical appearance. Why wasn't she? Why did this one man still have the ability to send her into sensory overload simply by touching her?

Shock. That must have been it, she decided. The surprise of seeing him had made her lose control. It wouldn't happen again.

That settled, she slid out of the truck, shutting the door with a determined bang. A stray piece of metal fell off with a clatter, strengthening her resolve. She thought she saw Jake grin as she walked toward him, but at the distance couldn't be sure. It didn't improve her mood.

"Hello, Anna." Smiling at her as she approached, he tipped his hat back, revealing a shock of mussed dark-blond hair. His warm breath came out in puffs of cloud in the frosty morning air. The dirt beneath their feet sparkled with the glimmers of moisture crusting the ground. Behind him, the green of winter wheat waving in the field presented a striking backdrop for man and horse.

Infuriated by the ever present shiver of fear at the thought of what his return to Happy might mean, she parked her hands on her hips and glared at him. "I'm sure you know why I'm here."

"You mean this isn't a friendly social call?" He managed to look hurt and cocky at the same time.

"Not by a long shot, buster. What do you think you're going to accomplish by forcing me to work with you on the rodeo?"

"C'mon, Slick," he said to the horse. He shot her a speculative glance and started leading the horse toward the barn. "World peace?" When she snorted he smiled again and asked, "Forcing's a bit strong, don't you think? But I expect to accomplish a hell of a rodeo."

"You don't need me to do that."

Once inside the spacious barn, Jake tied the bay's reins to the freshly painted white wooden door of a stall. She caught the whiff of leather and healthy sweat as he lifted the saddle and pad from the horse's back. Then he tossed her a brush, taking it for granted that she'd groom one side of the horse while he did the other. A chore they'd done a thousand times when they were kids, she remembered, as he must have known she would. It didn't amuse her how easily they fell into the rhythm again.

"If you weren't so busy being prickly and defensive," he said after a few moments, "you'd see that your involvement would be a good thing."

"All I see is you manipulating things—" she ran the brush down a long flank "—especially me, to suit your purposes. And I want to know what those purposes are."

"Anna, having a rodeo, one with all the usual events, will help everyone." He spoke patiently, as if explaining something to a child, which yanked her chain even more. "The library fund, the town, even your riding school stand to gain. And your daughter has a good chance of placing in the barrel racing event."

It took all her willpower not to blurt out "stay away from my daughter!" The last thing she wanted to do was draw his attention to Leigh. "You don't need my help."

"Sure I do. I need someone who knows which end is up when it comes to organizing things." He stopped grooming the horse to look at her over its back. "You already host clinics and play days. Setting up a rodeo won't be much of a stretch for you. Besides, I'll be helping, too. You won't have the whole thing on your shoulders and neither will I."

"You're missing the point."

He came around his horse's head, standing so close she smelled the clean, fresh scent of the outdoors on him. "Which is?"

"I don't want to work with you," she said gritting the words out through her teeth. "I don't want to be around you. I don't even particularly want to see you."

He leaned over, his arm reaching around behind her. For a minute she didn't know what he intended and felt a brief flare of fear. No, not fear, she realized, but...excitement. What the heck was wrong with her? She was long over this man.

Jake straightened up and she saw the horse blanket in his hands. He bunched up the material, holding it so the bay could stick his head through the opening, then smoothed it over its back and hindquarters.

"Get that strap for me, will you?" he asked, motioning at the leg strap on her side.

Anna complied automatically. A moment later he stood beside her again, looking down at her with amusement dancing in his eyes.

"What are you afraid of, Anna?"

"I'm not afraid of anything." She lifted her chin, daring him to prove her wrong, but the skeptical look he gave her said he wasn't buying it for a minute.

Irritating, aggravating—

"If you're so dead set on not having anything to do with me, why did you agree to work on the rodeo? Because you obviously did agree to it."

No way would she tell him she needed the business it could generate. She had her pride, after all. Besides, she wasn't destitute, just anxious to improve her school's success. "Mary said you wouldn't do it if I didn't agree to cochair it. And she was practically drooling at the idea of having you involved. What was I supposed to do? If I'd refused, I'd have come off looking like the Grinch." Not to mention, she wasn't about to let him know how much he affected her.

Jake grinned and lifted an eyebrow. "No way you could ever look like the Grinch. He's nowhere near as beautiful as you are."

To her shame, and fury, she felt a flash of pleasure at his words. "Stop it! Stop—flirting with me, or whatever it is you think you're doing. If you think you can waltz back here and—and— Well, it won't work. Don't forget, I know the real Jake Rollins. And he lost his charms for me a long time ago."

The next moment he had her backed up against the wall of the stall, his face inches from hers, strong hands on either side of her face. He smelled like the elements, earth, sky and wind, and her imagination added the smoky odor of fire. Like freedom. Like danger. Her heart pounded at racehorse speed as she gazed up at him. Up close and way too personal.

My God, she'd forgotten just how blue his eyes

were. Deep, vibrant blue, like a clear Texas sky after a passing thunderstorm. Deep enough to drown in. She felt dizzy, disoriented.

He intended to kiss her.

Her chin came up as the realization hit, and she glared at him, daring him to do it. If Jake thought a stroll down memory lane would have her mooning over him again, he had another think coming. She was a grown woman, not a teenager in love for the first time.

But he made no move to touch her. Instead, he spoke very softly, asking, "What do you think of him?"

Anna stared at him blankly. "Think of who?"

He jerked his head toward the bay. "Slick. My stallion."

"I don't know. I can't see him," she said breathlessly. And at the moment her memory wasn't kicking in.

He moved aside and she began to breathe again. A pang shot through her, which she assured herself was relief, certainly not disappointment.

"So, what do you think?" he repeated, his voice soft, deep, dangerous.

Dangerous? Don't be ridiculous, she told herself. Cursing her overactive imagination, she looked at the horse. "He's nice," she admitted. "Well-behaved for a stallion."

He backed off, glaring at her like she was nuts. "Nice? A cool drink on a hot day is nice. A warm fire on a cold day is nice. A stud like this is—"

Irritated, she interrupted. "Fine. He's gorgeous and you know it. What's your point?"

"*He's* the point. Slick is what I'm doing back here. I'm going to breed and raise cutting horses."

Mary was right. Anna's stomach felt like lead. "You're staying? Here, in Happy?"

His smile said it all. "Back for good."

"On your father's ranch? And he agreed to that?"

"I didn't ask him. I'm looking for a place of my own."

He'd obviously forgotten what life in the small Panhandle town was like. Ordinary, dull. And Jake had never been either of those. Nor, if his past actions were any indication, could he tolerate those things on a daily basis. He'd always lived for excitement. He couldn't have changed that much.

"You'll be bored silly within a week," Anna said, putting her thoughts to words. "You're not serious."

"As a heart attack, darlin'," he told her with a devilish grin.

"Maybe that's what you think right now, but let me give you the most likely scenario. You'll get everyone in Happy excited about this rodeo, have them counting on you to do your part, and then you'll leave town before it's even planned. And guess who that leaves holding the bag?"

Anger flashed in his eyes, intensifying the blue. "And you base this conclusion on something that happened sixteen years ago. I was twenty years old when I left home, Anna. Not much more than a kid. I don't suppose it's occurred to you I might have changed."

"Not in this lifetime," she said.

He took a step closer, not quite touching her but

close enough she felt his body heat. She didn't like that smile; it was entirely too knowing.

"I see what it is. You're scared. That's why you don't want to work with me on this rodeo."

"Scared? Of you?" Tossing her hair back over her shoulder, she gave him a wintry smile. "Fat chance. The only fear I have is that you'll duck out."

He touched her then, just his fingers lingering on her cheek. "You can't deny there's chemistry between us still, any more than I can."

She laughed. "Your ego is so inflated, if I stuck a pin in you, you'd pop."

"Yeah?" His gaze focused on her mouth. "Then I guess you won't mind giving me a demonstration of how indifferent you are."

As soon as he spoke she knew what he meant to do. Stepping quickly out of his reach she said, "I don't think that will be necessary."

"Afraid to put it to the test?" he asked. And smiled again.

The wicked, wicked smile that had always made her melt hadn't dimmed with age. Nothing about the man had dimmed with age. *Show some backbone, Anna,* she told herself.

"Give it up, Jake. I'm not taking the bait," she said, and strolled out of the barn. Her life would be a lot easier if she didn't wonder exactly what it would be like to kiss Jake again.

His laughter followed her and she gave a fleeting, if satisfying, thought to turning around and smacking that laughter right out of him. Lucky for Jake she wasn't a violent woman.

Lucky for Jake she decided indifference would spike his guns better than anger.

But Anna knew she hadn't fooled him. And she damn sure hadn't fooled herself. Jake Rollins still got to her. He always would.

CHAPTER THREE

WES ROLLINS didn't enjoy being a fool. But sitting in his truck parked in front of Mary Gallick's house, he felt like a lovesick kid about to ask a girl on his first date. He had to be crazy to think she'd want anything to do with him. Why, he was old enough to be her— No, he wasn't that old, but he had to be ten or fifteen years older than Mary, at least.

His wife, his first love, had been gone for over seventeen years. Since her death he'd seen a few women here and there, but not many and not often. The past few years, well, he hadn't even wanted to be with a woman in longer than he cared to remember. And then Mary Gallick had charged into his life. She'd always been there, but he'd never taken much notice of her. Until this library thing started.

He'd had his eye on her for a while. Ever since she'd marched up to him in the Hitching Post and demanded that he show up at the first library fund meeting. Before that, he couldn't remember exchanging more than a few words with her. But she'd been so earnest, so determined, so…alive. She made Wes feel like he'd been seeing everything in shades of gray. Mary brought the colors to life.

He fumbled with the pearl-covered snaps of his brand-new dress shirt and cleared his throat. Too bad he didn't have some of Jake's famed way with women. Not that it seemed to be doing Jake much good with Anna Connor, he thought. The boy was going to have a long row to hoe with that one.

Wes didn't doubt that Jake had plans for Anna, and he had a strong suspicion that a large part of those plans involved Anna's daughter, Leigh. There'd been a lot of talk when Anna had turned up pregnant so soon after marrying Carl. Wes had always wondered just exactly how things stood, but he'd never felt it was his place to question the girl. Not after his son had left her flat. He didn't imagine Anna wanted anything to do with the Rollins family after that, and he couldn't much blame her.

Still, Wes didn't think Jake had realized he might be leaving a child behind. Nothing could make him believe that his son would have shirked that particular responsibility if he'd known. But Jake had to suspect, at least now that he'd come back and seen Anna—and Leigh.

Whether Jake would stick it out this time, Wes didn't know. And he was leery of asking—since he'd just as soon not hear that the boy planned on taking off again. He wanted, more than anything, to forge a relationship with his son. Though it wouldn't make up for the sixteen years they'd missed—his own fault, as much as Jake's—it would go a long way toward making the future brighter.

He glanced at the house again to see Mary standing in the doorway waving at him. No backing out now, he thought, and climbed out of his truck to meet her.

"Wes? What are you doing outside in this cold?

You've been sitting there for fifteen minutes. Did you think I wasn't home?''

She led him into her kitchen as she talked, pulled out a chair and plopped a plate of cookies down in front of him. ''You're in luck. I just took these out of the oven.''

Chocolate chip. The mouthwatering scent of them had his stomach rumbling. Wes couldn't remember eating homemade cookies since his wife had died. He still hadn't said anything, mainly because he'd lost his voice. Sweat popped out on his brow and he wondered what in the hell had made him think he was ready to sweet-talk Mary Gallick into going out with him. He was no ladies' man. He'd never be ready.

To cover his edginess, he reached for a cookie and almost moaned when the taste of it exploded in his mouth. Sweet heaven, the woman cooked like an angel.

Mary perched expectantly on her chair across the table from him. Pretty as— Well, he was no good with words, never had been. But if he was, he'd have said that Mary, with her soft brown hair and big brown eyes, was pretty as a sunset.

''You know that Jake said he'd chair the rodeo, don't you?'' Mary asked after a moment. Wes nodded. ''And Anna's chairing it with him,'' she added.

He choked on his cookie. ''Anna agreed? To help Jake?''

''Well, he said he wouldn't do it without her. So I didn't give her much of a choice.'' Her eyes danced mischievously. ''Did you think I couldn't pull it off?''

Shaking his head in wonder, he said, "I think you can do anything you set your mind to."

She blushed. Maybe he wasn't as hopeless with women as he'd thought.

"Is that why you came by? To talk about the rodeo?"

"Uh, no." In search of something to do with his hands, he picked up the worn cowboy hat he'd set on the table and shifted it from hand to hand. "I, uh, I wondered if—" His tongue tangled in his throat. Furious with himself, he stood. "Dad-blast it, I'm too old for this. I don't remember how to do this fancy, or smooth, so I'm just going to say it. Mary, would you have dinner with me tonight?"

She stared at him like he'd lost his mind. "Are you asking me on a date, Wes?"

Crossing his arms over his chest, he glared at her. "I'd say that was pretty obvious. Will you go?"

A smile broke out, spreading over her face like sunshine. "I'd love to. Give me ten minutes to change."

After she'd left the room, Wes pulled a red kerchief from his pocket and wiped his face. Surely to God this business got easier with practice. He didn't think his heart would take the strain.

LEIGH SAT FORWARD in her chair, forearms propped on the table in front of her. If Blaire could see her now she'd turn pickle green and stroke out. There sat the famous Jake Rollins, at her kitchen table. Talking to her and listening to what she said, not ignoring her like adults usually did. Of course, he'd come to see her mother, but she wouldn't tell Blaire that. No, she'd let Blaire think he'd come to see *her.*

All her friends thought he was really fine. Leigh did, too, and she thought his rodeo career was even cooler. He'd been the saddle bronc World Champion five times. World Champion. What she wouldn't give to be the barrel racing World Champion even once.

"Are you sure your mother won't mind you letting me in when she isn't here?" he asked, leaning back in his chair, getting comfortable.

Long legs stretched out in front of him, he seemed relaxed but also like he was waiting for something. Her mother, maybe?

"I wouldn't want to get you in trouble," he added, his blue eyes twinkling.

He really does have pretty eyes, Leigh thought. She gave him one of the sultry smiles she'd been practicing in front of the mirror. "She won't care. It's not like we don't know you or anything."

He stared at her a minute. "Are you okay? I can come back later if you don't feel well."

So much for sultry. "I'm fine," she said, abandoning the pose. Besides, he might be cute but he was still kind of old. "And Mom will be back in a minute."

"All right, I'll wait." He glanced around before his gaze came back to her. "You've heard about the rodeo we're planning, haven't you?"

Leigh nodded enthusiastically. "Mrs. Gallick was talking to Mom about it the other night."

"Do you think some of the kids from school would like to help with it?"

"Would they!" Most of the kids she knew were rodeo crazy. "Doing what?"

"Fixing up the arena, helping with promotion, things like that, for now."

"Will we get out of class if we help?"

He laughed. "I doubt it. But maybe we could arrange to give you some kind of credit. Community service or something. We'll take it up with Mrs. Gallick. I'm not sure exactly what needs to be done yet. That's one reason I came to talk to your mother."

That made sense. "Mom's real good at that kind of thing. Everybody says her play days and clinics are the best around. We draw in people from all over." A surge of pride swept through her when she thought about what her mom had accomplished, and what she'd accomplished, too. Her mother always made Leigh feel as if she had a big part in the riding school's success.

Some of her friends thought their parents were dweebs, but Leigh and her mom had always been close. Even more so since her dad had died, when she was ten. The only real problem, as Leigh saw it, was her mom's refusal to let her rodeo, to try to make the circuit finals. Leigh still had hopes of talking her around, though.

And if she couldn't get her mom to change her mind, well, she'd be sixteen before too long. All she had to do was win one good race and the prize money for that would be her stake for the next. Leigh indulged in a brief daydream of money, trophies, belt buckles, and not rubbing it in too much when her mother admitted she'd been wrong.

"Do you help her with the play days?" Jake asked, zapping her out of her daydream. "And with the riding school?"

"Sure, most of the time I help her with the daily classes, and when I can, I help with the clinics. Sometimes I miss, though, when I go to a rodeo and Mom can't."

"Like the Houston rodeo. Your mom wasn't with you there."

"No, she had a clinic that weekend." Before they could get into another discussion about her mom, she changed the subject. "Say, Mr. Rollins, can I ask you something?"

"Only if you call me Jake."

Leigh smiled. That would kill Blaire. "Okay, Jake." Hesitating a moment, she fingered the sleeve of her sweater. "Some of the kids, well, we were wondering…why did you quit rodeoing? You were still winning when you quit, weren't you? You don't have to tell me if you don't want to," she added in a rush. His expression didn't give her a lot of hope that he would, either.

He was quiet so long she didn't think he'd answer. When he did speak he looked older, much older than he had only a few minutes before. The lines in his face deepened, his mouth turned grim. His eyes looked tired. "I guess I got fed up with it. Rodeoing is—" He shrugged and bent forward. "You have to not mind never being in one place for long, living in hotel rooms, being on the road constantly, hurting all the time from injuries." Pausing, he rubbed a hand over his jaw. "After a while it gets old."

"But you were winning! You were a champion. How could that get old? Wasn't it exciting?" He made it sound boring, even depressing, but Leigh didn't see how it could be, especially if you were a winner, and a world-class winner to boot.

"Sometimes it's exciting. When you win. When you lose, though..." Leaning back, he clasped his hands together on the table. His eyes held a faraway look, an unhappy look. "A lot of it isn't much fun at all."

"I still think it would be cool." She spoke defiantly, waiting to see how he'd take it. If he'd try to talk her out of rodeoing, like her mother always did.

He tilted his head, considering her. "Is that what you want, Leigh? To rodeo? To barrel race?"

She nodded enthusiastically. "More than anything. I want to make the finals. First the circuit championship and then—" she drew in a deep breath and said reverently "—the nationals." He didn't say anything, just looked at her with a funny expression on his face. "But Mom, well—"

The door slammed loudly, cutting Leigh off in midsentence.

"What are you doing here?" Anna snapped the words out so abruptly and angrily that Leigh turned to stare at her in amazement.

Rising, she tried to explain. "Mom, we've been waiting for you. Jake was just—"

"Leigh, go see to your homework. I'm sure *Mr. Rollins* will excuse you."

"But, Mom, I don't have any—"

"Now, Leigh," Anna said, in a tone that Leigh knew better than to argue with.

"Okay, okay, I'm going," she said, as sulkily as she dared.

What's bugging her? Leigh wondered as she left the room. At the doorway she paused and looked back to see the two adults staring at each other. She didn't think her mother was mad at her. The look she gave Jake said that he was the one in deep trouble. Poor Jake, she thought as she reached her bedroom. Her mom didn't get mad often, but when she did— Watch out! Still, she had an idea Jake could take care of himself.

Watching Anna's face darken with anger, Jake suppressed a grin. Ticked her off again, he thought. This time without even trying. He admitted he shouldn't have baited her the day before, but he hadn't touched her, after all. Even though he had damn well wanted to.

That go-to-hell look in her eyes and her sharp-tongued taunts had been impossible to resist, daring him to see if she would still heat to full boil when he kissed her.

Too bad she hadn't let things reach their natural conclusion. He'd bet next month's oats bill that the old sizzle was alive and kicking between them, no matter how much she might want to deny it.

"Don't be mad at Leigh for letting me in," he said, not wanting to make trouble between mother and daughter.

"I'm not." She shrugged out of her worn navy pea jacket and hung it on a peg by the back door. "I save my anger for those who deserve it."

Meaning him, obviously.

Instead of taking a seat at the table, she came to

a halt nearby and stood staring down at him. A dark-green cable-knit sweater deepened the jade of her eyes. Faded jeans hugged long, shapely legs that went on forever. Her face innocent of makeup, long blond hair pulled back in a ponytail, she looked almost as young as her daughter, and so damned beautiful it took his breath. *Get a grip, Jake. You've seen pretty women before. What is so special about this one?*

"I'd appreciate it if you didn't encourage Leigh in her pipe dream of fame and fortune."

His eyebrows drew together in a frown. "It's not exactly a pipe dream. I've seen her race. You have to know she's damned good, and so is her horse."

"Of course I know she's good. And I raised Promise from a foal, so I know exactly how good she is, too. But that's beside the point. I don't want my daughter to rodeo. Not that hard, not as much as it would take for her to win a championship. It's not the sort of career I've got in mind for her. Or the kind of life I want for her."

"Then why let her race at all?"

Anna spun around and paced the floor for a few steps. "I can't stop her." Halting, she picked up a dishrag and wiped savagely at the faded yellow countertop. "For heaven's sake, I run a riding school, and barrel racing is a huge part of it. Naturally, she's interested in the rodeo." She tossed the rag down and turned to glare at him. "But just because I let her go to rodeos and enter some races doesn't mean I'd agree to anything more intensive."

"If it's what she wants, what she really wants, you may not have much say in the matter."

Anna folded her arms across her chest and leaned back against the counter. "She'll get over it. She's too young to know what she wants for a lifetime, for a career." After glaring at him a moment, she continued. "I'm sure you didn't come here to talk about my daughter. I'm simply asking you—no, make that telling you—not to encourage her fantasies of world championships."

Jake plowed a hand through his hair, wishing he knew how to approach her. He didn't want to make her madder, but he wanted to get through to her. For her sake and for Leigh's. Because he knew from experience where a stand like Anna's could lead. "I wouldn't encourage her against your wishes. I want you to know that. But I think you're making a mistake with her."

"Based on your no doubt vast knowledge of teenage girls?" she asked, sneering pointedly. "Thanks for the advice. I'll be sure to give it just as much attention as it deserves."

He shoved his chair back, rising to face her. "Anna, you used to rodeo. And you were good, damned good. Don't you remember what it was like?"

"Yes, I do. And I remember what happens to people when they're exposed to fame and money too young. People like you, Jake."

He winced, knowing he deserved that shot. "What I did—the choices and mistakes I made—Leigh won't necessarily make the same ones. Don't let your own experience with me prejudice you against your daughter's dreams."

She dropped her arms, her hands clenching into

fists before she gripped the edge of the countertop behind her. "You dare say that to me? After what you did? After you ran off and left me and everyone else you knew behind? Do you think I want that for Leigh?"

He didn't know how to explain to her that the rodeo—and his ambition—hadn't been the only problem. The major problem had been his fear that if he stayed in Happy he'd never even get the chance to attain any of his dreams.

"No, I can see it isn't," he said. "But you also don't know Leigh will react like I did."

"This is none of your business. You've talked to her for a few minutes and suddenly you think you know everything there is to know about her. Well, you're wrong. You don't know anything about my daughter."

Yes, he did, but she obviously wasn't ready to hear it. He'd seen Leigh race, seen the drive and desire, heard the hopes and dreams in her voice when she spoke of barrel racing. Leigh had it bad, and he was very much afraid that nothing her mother did would change that. And nothing he said would make an impression, because Anna couldn't let go of the past.

"You still hate me, don't you?"

"This isn't about you, Jake. It's about Leigh and the fact that I want you to butt out of my business."

Anger flaring, he gripped the back of a chair with white-knuckled intensity. "What the hell do you think I'm planning to do? Seduce her away with tales of glory?"

Anna flushed. "She's young, impressionable. She

romanticizes everything, especially the rodeo circuit. You have no idea the harm you could do.''

His hands tightened on the wood, then let go. "By telling her the truth? That it's not all fun and glory? That most of the time it's hard and lonely and you never know whether you'll wake up a winner or yesterday's news? How is it going to hurt her to know that?"

"Is that—" She hesitated, shock and surprise filling her eyes. "Is that what you told her?"

Irritated by her reaction even though he should have expected it, he shrugged. "I didn't have time to say much. But yeah, that's more or less what I said.''

"I'm—I'm sorry. I didn't realize—"

"No, you didn't." Struggling with his temper, he turned his back on her.

"Jake—" He felt her hand on his shoulder and turned to look at her.

Leigh made a production of clearing her throat loudly. Anna's hand dropped away like she'd been scalded.

"We need more firewood. Don't mind me," Leigh said, smiling cheekily as she walked through.

The door closed behind her and Anna sighed. "What did you want, Jake?" she said after a moment.

Leigh's entrance had broken the spell. Whatever Anna might have said, she wouldn't now. "I came to talk about the charity rodeo." Though after the conversation they'd just had, he'd almost forgotten what he'd come to ask her. "What all needs to be done to the arena? That seems the logical place to start.''

She plucked a sweater off the back of a chair and hung it on the Peg-Board by the back door. ''It needs painting. Enlarging it would be even better. And the stands are in bad shape. I doubt we can even get the insurance we'll need until they've been repaired.''

''How about getting the high school kids to contribute some time and energy to fixing it up? I can probably get supplies donated.''

''Good idea.'' She walked around the small kitchen, tidying up, though Jake hadn't noticed anything that looked out of place. ''It will give them something useful to do and help us out, too. I'll talk to Mary tomorrow. What else?''

''I've got a stock contractor in mind. We need to set a date and then meet with him. May or June would probably be best.''

''May is prom, graduation and Memorial Day, don't forget. Early June might work better.''

''All right. I'll set up a meeting with him. What's a good time for you?''

''Mornings. Afternoons I'm usually busy with my classes.''

He didn't want to leave, but he was running out of things they needed to talk about. And Anna didn't appear to be in a talkative mood. ''I'm on the trail of some sponsors.''

''Good, we'll need them.''

''Yeah. I'll let you know about the meeting.'' She couldn't wait to get rid of him, he thought. He remembered a time when neither could stand to let the other go. A long time ago.

She used to wait for him after football practice so they could snatch a few more minutes together, a few more kisses before going home and doing chores. And whenever he'd finish up early, he'd head to her place, because if he helped her with her work, that meant more time for them to be together.

But those were just memories now.

"I'll walk you out."

Grinning wryly at the pointed dismissal, he grabbed his coat and slid it on, then held hers out for her. Her back to him as she struggled into the jacket, she stood close enough to get a whiff of her perfume. Something light, airy, feminine. A fragrance with a sexy punch that made his stomach clench. Damn, he had to quit letting her get to him so easily. *He* was supposed to get to her, not the other way around.

He followed her out and stood by the back steps while he watched Leigh pile wood onto a canvas carryall. Tall, slender and graceful. Like her mother. Her youth apparent mostly in the roundness of her face.

Leigh passed them with her load of wood. "Bye, Jake. See ya." Her grin hit him dead center between the eyes. Just like it had the first time he saw her smile, more than three weeks ago at a Houston rodeo.

The same smile that he saw when he looked in the mirror.

He turned to Anna. "Leigh doesn't look much like Carl."

Anna glanced at him and he could have sworn he saw a spark of panic in her eyes. Yet her voice didn't waver when she spoke. "No, she looks like me."

"Funny," he said, his gaze holding hers, "I thought she looked like me."

CHAPTER FOUR

ANNA'S HEART contracted with a sickening lurch. Jake said nothing; he simply waited. Icy fingers of fear paralyzed her voice. *Oh, God, he knows. He knows.*

Their gazes locked and though she tried desperately not to show it, she knew he could read the panic in hers. But still, he said nothing, and neither did she. His eyes narrowed, hardened against her, and then he turned his back and walked away.

Anna had no rational explanation for the emotion that clogged her throat, threatening to choke her. No explanation for the urge she fought to run after him and tell him the truth. With her heart beating rapidly, unable to face Leigh yet, she retreated to the barn. To her horses—her work, her solace. To her reason, other than her daughter, to live.

What right did he have to the truth? None, she thought, swiping angrily at her tearing eyes. He had no rights here. No right to bring turmoil to her life yet another time. Wasn't it enough that he'd broken her heart sixteen years before? She didn't owe him anything. Jake had given her nothing but heartache.

Nothing…except her daughter. Her one true joy. And she'd be damned if she'd hand him Leigh's heart on a platter so he could trample all over it, too.

Inside Promise's darkened stall Anna wrapped her arms around the mare's neck and the memories swamped her, washing over her in an inexorable tide.

God, she'd loved him so much. Been so naive, so…stupid. It hadn't occurred to her that Jake's calls had grown less frequent for a reason. Just as it didn't occur to her that the last time they were together she'd get pregnant, despite using protection. She wasn't even nervous about telling him. Not much, anyway. They'd intended to have a family, though not right away. She simply assumed they'd get married a little sooner than originally planned. Have their kids a little sooner…

But then Jake called and her world exploded. Anna closed her eyes. Snippets of static-filled conversation echoed in her mind as the pain of the present blended with that of the past.

"When are you coming home, Jake?"

"I'm not."

"You mean there's another rodeo so soon after the finals?" She tried to keep the disappointment out of her voice, but she wanted to see him so badly she thought she'd die.

"Yeah. No— Listen, Anna, something happened in Vegas."

"You won the finals," she said, her heart bursting with pride. "I know, we heard. That's wonderful."

"No, something else. Anna…" He hesitated for a long, soul-wrenching moment then said, "Anna, I got married."

Her heart stopped beating, blood roared like a

prairie fire in her ears. He had to be joking. "That's—that's not funny, Jake."

"I'm serious, Anna. I'm married."

He kept talking, but the rest of the conversation came to her as gibberish, her mind focusing on the only words that mattered. Jake was married. Married to some rodeo groupie, though he'd never admit it. Anna knew the type, she'd seen them often enough. And she'd suspected Jake had women crawling all over him from the time he left home. But she'd trusted him.

Anna didn't tell her parents, didn't tell anyone about Jake's call. For days she existed in a mind-numbing no-man's land of despair. Every day she pushed herself physically, hoping to become exhausted enough to sleep without hearing that last conversation echoing over and over in her mind.

Four days later, alone in the barn, she began mucking out her barrel horse's stall. Bend, shovel, bend, shovel. She hadn't eaten that day, unable to face food even if she could have kept it down. She kept shoveling, telling herself the dizziness came from lack of food. It didn't bother her, not really. It was a welcome distraction from her thoughts. Black spots began to dance before her eyes and the world turned gray.

She came to with her head in Carl's lap and his worried eyes watching her.

"Anna, my God, you scared me to death." His eyes, she noticed inconsequentially, had deepened to a dark hazel with his concern. His light-brown hair fell over his forehead and she reached a hand up to push it back. He pushed her hand away impatiently, a gesture of worry that wasn't like him. "You just flat keeled over. Lie still and I'll get help."

"No. Carl, don't." Anna grabbed his hand and held on tight. "I'm okay. I just overdid it."

His sharp eyes missed nothing, looking her over steadily. "I've never known you to faint before."

She'd never had her world destroyed before, either. "I'm fine," she insisted, struggling to sit. She gave him a weak smile, which she didn't think deceived him for a minute. "Why did you come over?" she asked, though she had a feeling she knew.

He was still eyeing her skeptically, but he answered. "I wondered if you'd heard from Jake lately. When is he coming home?"

Tears welled in her eyes, threatening to spill. She turned away, grasping for control. She might as well tell him. Everyone in town would know soon enough. "He isn't."

Carl looked confused. "Sure he is."

"He's not coming back." She spat the words out, anger and hurt fueling them. "He got married in Vegas."

"Married? But he's engaged to you."

She laughed harshly. "Not anymore. Now he's married to another woman." And she was pregnant. And alone.

Carl took her hand, squeezed it consolingly between both of his. Large hands, comforting hands. "I can't believe he'd do that. He's nuts about you. Are you sure, Anna?"

"I'm sure. He told me himself." She started crying then, great gulping sobs of misery. Carl gathered her close and let her weep against his solid chest until she finally ran down.

"I have to tell my parents," she said, ashamed that she was clutching his shirt like a lifeline, but she couldn't seem to let go. He was the only sane thing left in a world gone mad. "I don't—I don't think I can."

"Jake's the jerk here, Anna, not you. Just tell them. They'll understand."

"No, they won't. Carl—" She looked at him then, at his dear, kind face. Not a handsome face, like Jake's, but so comforting. Strong, dependable, steadfast—that was Carl. She knew she could tell him anything and he'd always be her friend. "I'm pregnant."

His mouth turned grim, but his gaze on hers didn't falter. "Did you tell Jake?"

She shook her head. "I was going to and then— he told me he'd gotten married." She shifted away from him, put her face in her hands. "I have to tell my parents," she repeated. And she didn't want to think about how they were going to react to the news.

"No, you don't." He turned her face up to his and repeated, "No, you don't."

"Of course I do. How am I supposed to keep it a secret? I'll be showing in a few months. Maybe sooner." She fought back useless tears. "Then everyone will know how stupid I was."

"You weren't stupid. You loved him."

"Yes." And she still did. "I believed him, Carl. I thought he loved me. Oh, God, what am I going to do?"

"Marry me, Anna."

She stared at him, unable to believe what she'd heard. He didn't look as if he'd lost his mind, but he must have to say such a thing. "Carl, that's crazy. I can't marry you."

"Yes, you can. I know you're in love with Jake. But, Anna, I've always loved you." His gaze, earnest and compelling, forced her to believe him. "Let me—let me take care of you. You and the baby."

"You can't want that."

He smiled at her then. "I want you more than anything. I always have. I swear I'll make you happy. Marry me, Anna."

And she had.

The town of Happy had buzzed with speculation when Anna and Carl married a week after the news of Jake's marriage came out. When she started to show the whispers began anew. But Anna never told anyone else, not even her parents, the truth about her pregnancy. Her silence, she felt, was the least of what she owed Carl.

Carl, of course, had been rock solid, and his behavior had put much of the gossip to rest. Most folks had decided that if he wanted to claim another man's child as his, that was his business. Besides, it was just possible they were wrong and the child really was Carl's. Eventually the scandal had been, if not forgotten, at least buried.

But now Jake Rollins had come home.

"Oh, Carl," she whispered. "What am I going to do?" It comforted her that she could almost hear his reply. *Just do the best you can, Anna. Whatever is best for you and Leigh.*

"Mom!" Leigh's voice, calling from the back door, brought her full circle. "Mom, can you help me with my math?"

"Coming," she managed to call out, not wanting Leigh to come looking for her.

Anna wiped away her tears, squared her shoulders and left the barn. *Whatever it takes,* she vowed. Whatever she had to do to ensure Leigh's continued happiness, she would do.

Jake had ruined her life once. He wouldn't get the chance to ruin her daughter's.

JAKE RIPPED OFF his coat and pitched it onto the washer, slamming the back door shut behind him. He strode into the kitchen to the refrigerator, jerked open the door and cursed, long, low and fluently. One lousy beer. Typical. He yanked it out, gave the top a savage twist, and downed a quarter of it in a single swallow. It didn't help much.

He wasn't a big drinker, at least not since his youth when he'd discovered that for him, drunk equaled stupid. Now he intended to make an exception. Of course, he'd already done an incredibly dumb thing tonight without the benefit of liquor. Confronting Anna at this stage—even if it had been only implied, and not stated—had been suicidal, not just dumb.

He wanted to slam his fist into something, kick something. Instead he flung himself into a chair, wincing at the protesting creak. Great, all he needed was to break his neck in one of his father's ancient wooden chairs.

Tilting the bottle up, he let another long swallow

of beer slide down his throat. He might be a fool, but dammit, Anna Leigh Connor was a liar. He'd given her the perfect opening, and she'd stood there without saying a word.

When he'd met Leigh in Houston he'd known her immediately for Anna's daughter. Even before he'd seen her name on the program, he'd recognized her. It wasn't until he watched Leigh prepare for her race, though, that it hit him she could be his daughter, as well.

She'd been laughing at something, pushed her hat back and turned toward him, full-face. For an instant, a split second, it had been like looking in a mirror. Except the face that looked back at him was younger, blonder…and female. He'd known then, with a deep, gut-wrenching certainty. Leigh Connor was his daughter. His and Anna's.

Of course he'd checked into it. Her age fit. Sure, she could have been Carl's, given that Anna had married him a bare week after Jake had told her of his own marriage. But that just made him all the more suspicious. He'd always thought Carl had the hots for Anna, but to take another man's child—his best friend's child—and raise her as his own? Without so much as a word to the child's real father?

Jake admitted he hadn't been blameless. Blameless, hell—he'd been a total jerk. Marrying Cookie had been unbelievably stupid, not to mention, just plain wrong. He still regretted not only the marriage, but the cruel way he'd broken the news to Anna—though seeing him face-to-face wouldn't have made it any easier for her to hear.

No matter his regrets, he couldn't change the past.

He'd been wrong and he'd hurt her badly, but none of that negated the facts.

Anna should have told him about the baby. He'd had a right to know—both then and now. He'd have taken care of her. Hell, he'd have gotten a divorce and married her, and saved himself a miserable few months married instead to a woman who couldn't have stayed faithful on a bet. *But Anna couldn't have known that,* he reflected, before shoving the thought brutally aside.

Anna and Carl hadn't given him a choice.

So Anna had married Carl. And Jake's child carried Carl Connor's name.

Every fact he'd gathered, each time he'd seen Leigh since that rodeo, had convinced him more strongly than ever that she was his daughter. His flesh and blood, though Anna might never admit it.

What had he expected? That Anna would welcome him back with open arms? Let him into her life, her daughter's life simply for the asking? She'd obviously reconciled lying to him with her conscience. Had it even bothered her that Jake would never know his own daughter? He couldn't believe it had been an easy decision for the loving, generous girl he'd known.

But if it hadn't been easy, then why was she continuing the charade? He could have understood it better if Carl were still alive, but he'd been dead five years. Anna had no valid reason for keeping the truth from him any longer.

"Must be a mighty bitter persimmon you swallowed," Wes said from the doorway. Light spilled from behind his father, casting a dim gloom into the kitchen.

Too absorbed in his own misery, Jake hadn't heard him drive up or enter the house. "Where have *you* been?" he asked in a surly growl. Damned if the old man didn't look happy. Jake couldn't remember the last time he'd seen that particular expression on his old man's face. Maybe when his mom had been alive, certainly not since.

His father's bushy gray eyebrows shot up. He leaned against the doorjamb and considered Jake. "I've got a bottle of Jack Daniel's somewhere. How 'bout I get it and you can tell me what burr's got under your saddle."

Jake shrugged bad-temperedly. "Bring it out, but don't expect a heart-to-heart. That's not my style, and it sure as hell hasn't ever been yours."

The smile faded from the old man's eyes and his expression shut down. *Way to go, Jake,* he told himself. Feeling like a jerk, especially since his father wasn't given to overtures of that sort, Jake tried to temper his response. "Sorry. I had a lousy day."

Without responding, Wes reached into the cabinet above the washer and pulled out a half-empty bottle of whiskey. A few moments later he set a couple of glasses down on the scarred tabletop and poured two fingers of bourbon into each one. "I keep this around for medicinal purposes," he said with the ghost of a smile, lifting the glass to his lips.

"I'm not sick," Jake said, and tossed some down. The whiskey burned a slow, welcome trail down his throat, then settled in his stomach with a warming glow.

"Close enough," Wes said, taking a seat. "You're hurting."

Oh, yeah, he was hurting. And mad as hell on top of it. He finished off his drink, watched Wes refill the empty glass.

Swirling the amber liquid around, Jake stared at it grimly. Wes had been bound to suspect something about Anna's pregnancy. He'd been here all along, watching Leigh grow up. And Jake knew his father must have had a pretty fair idea how things had been between Anna Leigh and his son. Yet he'd never said a word to him.

Of course, Jake's hasty marriage had alienated his father, as well as Anna. And Jake had been stubborn enough to resent like hell the truth in Wes's dry comment when Jake had broken the news to him. "Thought you were past thinking with your zipper," Wes had said. "Appears I was wrong." And that had been the last time they talked for two solid years.

Still, Wes didn't *know*, any more than Jake did, who had fathered Leigh. Jake felt damn certain that if he'd known, he would have told his son. Besides, Anna wouldn't have confided in Wes. Why would she when she'd had Carl to turn to?

No, any ideas Wes had would just be more speculation. Jake didn't need speculation, he needed the truth. And that had to come from Anna, willingly. If he pushed her, forced her to prove paternity, she'd never forgive him. That would only make matters worse between them. Besides, he couldn't do that to Leigh. Putting her through paternity testing would hardly win him points with his daughter. No, the news about her paternity would have to be broken to her very carefully. He was helpless, until and unless Anna decided to come clean. Caught between the bronc and the fence, with no pickup men in sight. Closing his eyes, he cursed and reached for his glass.

"Your mother left me once," Wes said, breaking the silence.

Jake's eyes popped back open, his head jerked up to stare at Wes. His father had worshipped the ground Cora Rollins walked on. She'd known it, too, even if Wes had never come right out and said it. It had been obvious, even to Jake, in the way he treated her.

"Mom left you? When?" he asked, stunned.

"Before you were born."

"Why?"

Wes lifted a shoulder and sipped his drink thoughtfully. "Doesn't matter. I screwed up and she left. She was right to leave."

"She came back," Jake said.

Wes nodded. "But not right away. It took her a long time to forgive me. A damned long time to trust me again."

"You were married. She loved you." He couldn't reconcile the idea that his father had ever screwed up badly enough for his mother to leave him. Wes had always done the right thing. Always. All Jake's life, anyway.

"Point is, it didn't happen overnight. Not the forgiving and not the trusting." He took another drink and fixed his gaze on Jake. "Women need time, son."

Jake snorted and muttered a curse. "She's had time. Sixteen years of it."

"You've only been back a week. What did you expect?"

"I don't know." He took another drink and said, "I'll tell you one thing I didn't expect, though. I didn't think she'd look even better now than she did as a girl. And I sure as hell didn't think she'd still get to me. Not like this. Not this much."

Wes chuckled and shook his head. "You're in trouble, son."

"Yeah, I know."

His father rose and clasped a gnarled hand on Jake's shoulder. "Give her time, Jake."

As he reached the door Jake said, "Thanks." Wes halted and their gazes met. "Thanks, Dad."

Wes nodded and went out.

Time. Well, hell, Jake thought, draining his glass. It was worth a shot. And while he waited he meant to find a way to get the upper hand. He was through letting Anna call all the shots.

THREE DAYS LATER, Jake waited outside Anna's round pen, watching her put a couple of kids through their paces. Twin boys around eight years old, he thought. He liked watching Anna work. Liked seeing her interact with the kids. You could tell she enjoyed the lesson, enjoyed the children. She'd always liked kids. He remembered they'd talked about having a houseful of them, someday. But that day had never come.

Over the past few days he'd thought a lot, though he wasn't any nearer to a solution to his problem.

Maybe his old man was right and he should just back off and give Anna some time, but that didn't sit right with him. He'd already missed fifteen years of his daughter's life. He didn't want to miss any more.

Still, Anna was bound to wonder about Jake's motives. Bound to know by his earlier comment that he suspected the truth. How to approach her, that was the key. She reminded him of a skittish green filly, one who needed careful handling. And he could do that. Get to know her again, gain her trust—then who knew what might happen?

To his surprise, things were going better with his dad than he'd expected. He and the old man seemed to have come to a shaky truce, mostly by not talking about anything either of them figured was a touchy subject.

Well, the friendly respite would be put to the test when Jake told him of his plans for buying a place and raising quarter horses. Jake's refusal to have anything to do with the cattle business had always been a major bone of contention between them. Jake had hated the cattle business, something his father had never been able to understand. Could they deal with that now, put it in the past? He didn't know, but he sure as hell hoped they could.

Jake had never been given to a lot of introspection, but in the past few months he'd looked more closely at himself than he had in the preceding thirty-five years of his life. He hadn't liked what he'd seen.

The dissatisfaction had been building, with his so-called friends, his life in general. And the women—

oh, man, the women. They'd begun to all seem the same, to run together until he couldn't summon the energy to even go out anymore. None of it seemed to mean anything. None of it mattered. An empty life, that's what he had, and when he finally admitted that, he decided to change it.

That's why seeing Leigh and realizing she might be his daughter had hit him so hard. Regrets. He had a corral full of them. For marrying Cookie. For throwing away what he'd had with Anna. For alienating everyone who'd loved him to chase after a dream that had been just that—an illusion.

So he'd decided to quit avoiding his father and see if they could have some kind of relationship, even after all these years. And even more than that, he wanted to know the truth. He wanted a chance to know his daughter.

Anna turned just then, laughing at something one of the twins had said. It hit him, subtle as a horse stepping on his foot, the easiest way to get to her.

Why hadn't he thought of it before?

CHAPTER FIVE

ANNA STOOD by the arena, watching with a critical eye while Jake helped the twins load the horses into the trailer. Though he did most of the work, she could tell the twins thought they were in charge. Okay, fine, she thought. So he's good with kids. Big deal.

Leaving the situation in Jake's hands, Suzie Nelson, the twins' mother, walked over to her. Anna and Suzie had been friends for nearly twelve years, since the Nelsons had first moved to town. Though Anna considered Suzie her closest friend, she'd never discussed Jake with her. There had never been a reason to.

From the curiosity rampant on Suzie's heart-shaped, pixie face, though, it seemed likely that was about to change.

"You know I'm not very subtle," Suzie said, pushing dark bangs out of her eyes. "So, I'll just ask straight out. What's going on with you and that gorgeous hunk of man?"

Not expecting the blunt question, Anna choked on the soda she'd been drinking. Grinning, Suzie beat on her back until she recovered.

"You didn't tell me you knew him," she continued while Anna tried to catch the breath she'd lost.

"In fact, you haven't said word one about him and he's been back for almost two weeks now. Leigh told Blaire he's been over here. And now he's here again—" she waved a hand in his direction "—looking right at home."

Cursing nosy friends and talkative daughters, Anna struggled for calm. "Nothing is going on, Suzie, other than we're working on the charity rodeo together. I'm sure you've heard by now we were—"

"Childhood sweethearts," her friend interrupted. "Yeah, yeah, I heard." She glanced at Jake and shook her head. "But, honey, he's no child anymore and neither are you. Come clean, Anna. What's going on?"

"Nothing," she repeated emphatically, setting her empty can on the ground beside them. "Just the rodeo, and that's it. The rest of it is ancient history and it's going to stay that way."

Suzie raised a slim eyebrow and smirked. "Oh, right. You're totally immune to a great-looking guy you just happened to be engaged to once upon a time. Or is the engagement part just gossip?"

"No, that was true. What else did you hear?" She slid a look at Jake to reassure herself that he couldn't hear them. Luckily, he was still occupied with the kids.

"That you broke up, but Ross dragged me off before Becky could finish the story."

"You'll hear it sooner or later. The whole town knew." Remembering, she gripped the top rail. "Jake dumped me. Went off on the national circuit and married another woman."

"While he was engaged to you?"

Anna simply nodded.

"What a jerk. That must have been awful for you."

Suzie didn't know the half of it. "It was. So now you know why I'm not crazy about getting involved with him again."

"Yeah, but..." Frowning, Suzie watched Jake. "Anna, you two were awfully young."

Anna stared at her incredulously. "What does that have to do with anything?"

"People do stupid things when they're young. They make mistakes." She shrugged. "I did. I bet you did, too."

"Yes, I did. I got involved with Jake." Seeing her friend's skeptical expression, Anna continued. "He practically jilted me at the altar, Suzie! For heaven's sakes, it's not just a peccadillo like—like leaving the toilet seat up or something."

Suzie laughed. "Okay, I admit that could put a damper on things. But—" she hesitated before going on "—maybe he's changed." When Anna started to protest, Suzie held up a hand. "Think about it, okay? He's not married now and neither are you." Turning serious she added, "I know how much you loved Carl, Anna, but he's been gone for a long time now."

Anna stifled the pang that memories of Carl always brought. She missed him still, and knew she always would. Carl would have known how to deal with Jake, with the secrets she'd kept for so long. She could almost hear him, his slow drawl, his calm good sense that made the answers to thorny problems seem so obvious. But Carl wasn't here, and she would have to find those answers on her own.

Suzie thought she should give Jake another chance. But Suzie didn't know Jake was Leigh's father, either. She didn't understand that Anna had to make sure Leigh didn't end up hurt by her mother's mistakes.

"There's nothing between Jake and me but history. And that's all there ever can be. Give it a rest."

Her friend propped her hands on her hips and nodded sagely. "History? That's not history in his eyes when he looks at you. I talked to him while you were working with the kids and he never took his eyes off you."

In spite of herself, Anna flushed. "Your romantic nature is showing. It doesn't mean a thing."

"He's interested," Suzie insisted. "*Real* interested. I can tell."

Anna shook her head, but gave up convincing her friend. He's interested, all right, she thought. But in Leigh, not her. He'd made it clear what he thought of Anna when he'd dumped her for another woman. If she couldn't hold his attention when she was young and pretty, why should she be able to now— older, plainer, and even more ordinary and unexciting than before?

Eventually Suzie, her kids and their horses loaded up and moved on. Anna gazed at Jake resentfully. The kids were hanging out of the truck windows waving madly—at him, she was sure, not her. *Just because he's good-looking and doesn't mistreat animals and children is no reason to fall for him again,* she reminded herself. Jake Rollins still had his faults. Major faults. The kind that broke hearts and destroyed lives.

"Good little riders, aren't they?" he commented as he reached her, gesturing at the receding truck and trailer rig. "Have you been teaching them long?"

"About six months." She gave him an impatient glance. "Look, I'm busy. I've got to feed the horses and take care of some tack and about fifty other things. Are you going to tell me why you came over?" He'd arrived in the middle of her lesson and had been hanging around ever since. Making himself useful, which perversely, irritated her.

"I'll give you a hand," he said, beginning to walk with her to the barn. "I'll even muck out stalls if you want me to."

"I can do it myself." She knew she sounded petulant, but she didn't care.

"Darlin'," he said with a mischievous grin lifting the corners of his mouth, "didn't anyone ever tell you not to look a gift horse in the mouth? Especially not one who's willing to do some of the dirty work."

Much as she hated to admit it, he had a point. Reaching the barn, she gestured at the loft. "Fine. Don't think I won't take you up on that offer of cleaning stalls, either. But I need a bale of hay thrown down first."

"Okay. Can do." As he reached for the ladder, he asked, "Where's all your help?"

"Leigh is at a friend's and José and Luis, my ranch hand and his son, are getting ready to go to a wedding."

"Is that all the help you have? A couple of men and a teenage girl?"

Stung by the criticism she heard behind the question, she fired back, "For your information, I'm doing just fine."

"You're working yourself to the bone, is what you're doing."

"Yeah, well, life happens to be hard work for some people, Jake. *My* life's not all fun and games."

His jaw tightened and she felt briefly ashamed at the jab. Especially since he'd spoken no more than the truth. She was busting her buns and barely staying above water. If she could have afforded more help she'd have hired it. But she couldn't admit that to Jake.

"Look, I didn't mean— All I meant was, it's bound to be hard doing everything on your own. Especially with raising a kid, too. You don't even have your parents to fall back on. I heard your mother moved away."

Was that the image he held of her? A poor, pitiful widow, floundering without a man? She looked him in the eye. "I'm a single mother. That doesn't mean I'm helpless."

"I never said you were. You have a good thing going here, Anna. It took a lot of guts to go for it after—" He stopped in midsentence.

"After Carl died. You can say it, Jake. He's been gone for almost five years now."

He pushed his hat back, looked down at the ground before meeting her eyes. "Anna, I know it's too little too late, but...I'm sorry about Carl."

"Not sorry enough to come for his funeral." She

hadn't meant to say it. Didn't know why she had, but the words had tumbled out. To put distance between them?

Her words clearly bothered him. "I didn't know or I would have been here. My father tried to get hold of me to tell me but I was—" he hesitated, looking uncomfortable "—hard to find."

A blaze of sudden fury shook her. "Of course, you didn't know. Why would you? You never bothered to keep up with what happened here. Not to Carl, not to your father." *Not to me,* she thought, surprised at the stab of despair the knowledge still brought with it.

"There are a lot of things I regret, Anna. That's one of them."

She didn't answer. She didn't want to think about Carl, didn't want to feel the grief that surfaced when she thought of his death. And she didn't want to think about Jake, either. About what they'd had together. What Jake had so easily thrown away. And all for a woman he hadn't even managed to stay married to a year.

"I'll be in the tack room," she said and left him.

A short time later, while she polished the bits, he joined her. Picking up a soft cloth, he spread it with saddle soap and started on one of the saddles sitting on the big stand in a corner of the room.

They worked in silence for a few minutes. An uncannily comfortable one that reminded her of countless other times when they'd worked side by side, the smell of horseflesh, saddle soap and hay surrounding them. The first time Jake had kissed her had been in her family's barn, she remembered.

She'd been angling to get him to kiss her for weeks and finally, on a cold February day, she'd succeeded.

She flushed and shook her head, trying to get rid of the unwelcome memories. "Bad idea," she muttered, wishing that particular memory hadn't come to mind.

"Did you say something?"

"No, nothing." Great, now he had her talking to herself out loud.

"We need to set the date for the rodeo. I talked to a stock contractor, name of Buford Jones. Ever met him?"

"No, but I've heard of him," Anna said. "He has a good reputation."

"I know. I mentioned a couple of tentative dates to him—the first and second weekend of June. He was fine with either, but we need to decide. Today, if possible."

"All right. How about the first weekend?"

"Sounds good to me. I'll let Buford know. I've set up a meeting with him for week after next. Wanted to make sure you could be there."

She looked up from the bridle in her hands. "That's why you came over? Haven't you ever heard of a telephone?"

"Yeah." He caught her gaze. His slow, sure smile almost made her forget what they were talking about. "But if I'd called I wouldn't have gotten to see you. And I wanted to see you," he added, his voice and the color of his eyes both deepening.

Stupid, she told herself, damning the jolt of pleasure his words gave her. *He's working you.* Scowling, she lowered her gaze. "What time and where?"

"Two weeks from Friday. Around five, in Amarillo. I know you said mornings were better for you, but he won't be in town until afternoon. Can you arrange your classes so you can make it?"

"A meeting? Why can't we arrange this over the phone? Why does it have to be in person?" She walked over to hang up the clean bridle on the four-pronged tack hook dangling from the ceiling. Grabbing another, she started rubbing the cloth over the bit with unnecessary force.

"Because none of us has conference calling," he said, "and this seemed like the easiest way. Besides, meeting face-to-face is important and you have a way with people. What's the big deal, Anna? It's just Amarillo, a forty-minute drive away."

The big deal? It was a forty-minute drive away with Jake, that's what the big deal was.

"Surely you can stand to drive to Amarillo and back with me. Or maybe," he said, as if reading her thoughts, "you're afraid you'll enjoy yourself too much."

Anna snorted. He needed a good swift kick in his ego. "Tell me, Jake, have you been seeing anyone about these delusions?"

He laughed out loud and stroked his finger in the air. "Second one."

Anna couldn't help smiling at his good-natured response. "All right," she said, conceding to the inevitable, "I'll arrange it so I can get away."

"Good deal. I'm looking forward to it." He smiled again, flashing a dimple.

Dimples should be illegal for men over a certain age, Anna thought, hoping she wasn't making a big mistake.

"LINDA PRINCE called you earlier," his father told Jake that evening. The newspaper he was reading crackled as he shook it out. "Said for you to get back with her."

He didn't say anything else, though Jake knew he had to be curious. Linda, an agent with an Amarillo company, had grown up in Happy and handled a lot of real estate deals in the area. Which Wes was bound to know.

"Thanks." Might as well tell him now, he thought. They had to discuss it sometime. "I'm looking for some land around here. Thinking about settling down."

Wes stared at him for a moment and Jake could have sworn he saw a gleam of pleasure in his eyes. Then his father looked down at his newspaper and grunted.

"I'm going to breed and raise cutting horses. Train them, too," Jake continued, waiting for the inevitable criticism. His father had been no more impressed with the horse business than Jake had been with the cattle business. Their past was littered with battle after battle over Jake's breeding horses, riding broncs, or doing anything other than giving up his childish dreams, settling down and helping Wes run his ranch.

"If you're looking for a place near Happy, you might have a long wait. Not much for sale around here since Silas Merriwhether bought up everything for his cattle operation. One of the biggest in the state, you know.''

"Yeah, that's what Linda said. She's been pushing me to look at the Mercer place, but it's thirty miles south of here.'' And Jake had a definite stake in staying near Happy.

"No water to speak of, either. Mercer's been leasing water rights from his neighbors for years. Bet that little Realtor gal didn't mention that," he added dryly.

Jake frowned. "No, she didn't. Thanks.''

"Buying land's not something to rush into,'' Wes said.

"I'm looking around, that's all." Jake curbed his irritation. "Not rushing into anything."

Wes laid his paper aside and looked at Jake skeptically. "So you're planning on sticking around.''

"Yeah. You got any objections to that?"

"None of my business.''

"That's not what I asked." Jake took an irritated spin around the room. "Shit, we still can't talk. I don't know why I ever thought we could.''

Unperturbed, Wes said, "You still rile mighty quick."

"And you still can't—'' He broke off, shaking his head. What was the use? His father would never say what Jake wanted to hear. And he was a grown man, for God's sake. Why was he still looking for the old man's approval, especially when he knew he'd never get it?

Wes continued as if Jake hadn't spoken. "Reckon you'll stay here until you find a place. You can use the empty stalls in the barn if you need 'em.'' He looked Jake over shrewdly. "Bet you've got your eye on some prime horseflesh."

A peace overture, Jake thought. And it was as close as he was likely to get to the old man admitting he wanted him to stay. "I've got my eye on as pretty a filly as I've ever seen."

"That a fact?"

He nodded. "Yeah. One of Anna's horses. Now I've just got to convince her she wants to sell her to me."

"Reckon that's not the only thing you're trying to convince Anna of, is it?"

"You don't miss much, do you?"

"Son, that one's as plain as fresh-plowed ground."

Unsure whether he was irritated or relieved by his father's reaction, Jake went to the kitchen to call Linda.

CHAPTER SIX

LEIGH FOUND Luis working in the barn. He looked up when he heard her and smiled, the smile that her friends swore made him look like Ricky Martin, but to Leigh he just looked like Luis. Dark, straight hair, dark eyes, and underneath his sometimes macho attitude, a sweet guy. At least, he always had been to her.

"Hey, *chica*. What's up?"

She reached his side and grabbed a pail, dumping feed into it as they talked. "Luis, you've got to help me. You know that rodeo in Oklahoma I was telling you about?"

"*Sí*. What about it?"

"I need to convince Mom to take me. And I don't think she's going to go for it."

"No *dinero?*" he asked sympathetically.

"The money's part of it. But she made me promise to give it a rest after the last one. And I wanted to go to it so bad, I said I would." She frowned. "But I didn't know about the Oklahoma one when I said that."

"Maybe you could get a job. That way she wouldn't be out the entry fees."

"Maybe. I wish..." Her voice trailed off. "I wish Dad was still here. He understood how I felt about racing. Mom— Well, sometimes I don't think she remembers what it's like to want to do something so bad.''

Luis put a hand on her shoulder and squeezed sympathetically. "You miss him."

"Yeah." She sighed. It still hurt, though the ache was dull now instead of so sharp. "Lots. You're lucky to have your dad."

Luis laughed. "Not when I've done something he doesn't like."

"At least he's there to yell at you."

"I don't remember your *papá* yelling much."

"No, he didn't. All he had to do was look at me a certain way and I knew I'd screwed up and disappointed him." And she'd have done anything to avoid getting that look. Luckily, he hadn't given it to her much.

Luis took the lid off a bucket and grimaced. "No oats. And I'm already late for basketball practice."

"You can take off. I'll borrow a bag or two from the Rollinses. And if you ask real nice, I'll finish up for you."

His face lit up. "*Gracias.* I owe you one, *chica.*"

"You owe me more than one," she said and grinned. "But who's counting?"

Luis picked up his coat and shrugged into it. "Why don't you ask Mr. Rollins for a job?"

Confused, she asked, "He's already got help, doesn't he?"

"Not old Mr. Rollins. Jake. With his horse breeding operation."

Why hadn't she thought of that? "That's a great idea, Luis! I'll go borrow the oats and ask him then.'' She glanced at her watch. "I wonder if I have enough time? Blaire's coming over in about an hour.''

"Blaire, huh?'' He grinned and winked at her. "Maybe I'll miss practice today.''

Leigh punched him lightly on the arm. "Coach would kill you. And since when have you had the hots for Blaire? I didn't even think you liked her.''

"She's pretty,'' he said simply. "*Muy bonita.* But not as pretty as you,'' he said, and tugged her hair.

"Yeah, right. You just want me to finish your chores.''

He left with a laugh and a wave. Luis and Blaire? she thought. Who would have guessed?

LATER THAT DAY, Anna finished forking hay and strode to the barn entryway, squinting at the surrounding fields yet another time. Still nothing. Where in the world was Leigh? She knew Anna depended on her help after school. It wasn't like her to take off without so much as a note.

She walked back inside to the tack room and wanted to scream when she saw Luis had left the bag of feed exactly where he'd opened it—again. Not only that, but excess feed littered the floor, which meant she'd have to clean that up, too. Oh, her aching back, Anna thought, feeling a warning twinge.

It didn't matter that she was perfectly capable of doing it, she hated dumping the fifty-pound bags of feed into metal cans. But since she didn't want to be overrun with rats and mice that no amount of cats could combat, she dumped the feed, muttering under her breath all the while.

For the most part José's son was a good kid. But he was young, just a year or so older than Leigh, and often forgetful. He'd undoubtedly been running late for basketball practice. Anna had to admit, the star athlete stood a better chance of getting out of Happy on a basketball scholarship than he did helping his father out at her place. But knowing all that didn't make her any happier to be left—literally—holding the bag.

Leigh and Luis were good friends. Such good friends that both Anna and Luis's parents, the Villareals, had once worried they'd become serious about each other long before they were ready. But so far the two acted more like brother and sister than sweethearts.

Anna liked Luis and he'd been a good friend to her daughter. He worked hard, studied hard and—other than his habit of leaving the feed bags open without dumping them into the cans—he was a great kid. Still, she didn't want Leigh falling in love as young as she had. She had the scars to prove what a disaster that could be.

Of course, Leigh was only fifteen. Anna still had several more years to worry.

A shout from outside alerted her that her truant daughter had arrived. Anna stomped out of the barn, but the scolding on her tongue died with the sight of the man beside Leigh, sitting on his big blood bay like he'd been born on a horse—which he practically had. Of all the people Leigh could have brought home with her, she thought with a surge of exasperation, why did it have to be Jake? Swallowing her angry words, she crossed her arms over her chest, braced her legs, and tapped her well-worn boot on the ground. "Well?"

"Mom, I'm sorry I'm late." Leigh swung out of the saddle, looking young, vibrant, happy. Suddenly Anna felt a thousand years old and as cranky as the Wicked Witch of the West. "We were out of oats and Luis had to go to practice, so I said I'd take care of it. I swear," Leigh continued, "I just went over to borrow a couple of bags." She led her horse, Peanuts, into the barn and tied him to a post to groom him.

"I was schooling my new mare," Jake put in, "and Leigh showed up just when I needed a hand. How about if I help with the chores? It's the least I can do. She really bailed me out."

Having to crane her neck to look at him was giving her a crick, which she suspected he knew. Anna saw his lips twitch and knew her anger wasn't lost on him either. *Bailed him out,* she thought. *Right.* "No. Thank you." Her chin raised farther and she gave him a cold glance. "Leigh and I can handle it ourselves."

"Anna."

She heard the chuckle in his voice and wanted to smack him. "Thanks anyway, Jake. You'd better get back to tending your own horses."

Jake shrugged, gave her a Machiavellian smile and turned to Leigh. "Thanks again, Leigh."

"I had a great time," she said, looking up from brushing the horse. "I really like your new mare.

She's a sweetheart. And you'll think about what we talked about?''

"Sure will. But remember, you need to talk to your mom first."

He tipped his hat and started to go, leaving Anna wondering what in the world that was about. Just then Blaire and Suzie Nelson arrived.

The next thing Anna knew Leigh had abandoned Peanuts and the girls were falling all over themselves to capture Jake's attention. If she'd been in a more charitable mood she'd admit he handled them well. He didn't appear to notice the starry-eyed look on Blaire's face, and Leigh's expression wasn't much different. Damn the man! He could charm a snake out of its skin.

"Blaire's really good with horses, too," Leigh said as her friend nodded enthusiastically. "Maybe we could both help you with the new mare next week."

"Leigh, I'm sure Jake is busy," Anna said quickly. "He doesn't need—"

"Actually, I do need some help. But you two clear it with your parents before we discuss it in detail," he added, including Suzie in his smile.

Suzie, Anna noticed sourly, looked damned near as bedazzled as her daughter. Did no one see through the man but her?

"We'll talk about it later," Anna said. "Don't let us keep you," she added pointedly to Jake, ignoring the surprised look Suzie shot at her.

He grinned, secure in the knowledge, no doubt, that Anna would have a hard time coming up with a reasonable excuse for denying the girls such an opportunity. She watched him leave, silently gritting her teeth over how her daughter had played into his hands. Again.

She didn't hesitate but cut right to the heart of it. "Leigh, I don't think it's a good idea for you to spend so much time at the Rollins ranch."

Leigh turned to her, looking puzzled. "But, Mom, I haven't been. Today was the first time in nearly a week—well, except for a couple of days ago—anyway, I haven't been over there that much."

"Just how many times *have* you been there lately, young lady?" Anna hadn't realized Leigh had been making almost daily visits to the Rollins ranch. Wonderful, just wonderful.

"I don't know," Leigh said and shrugged. "A few. Jake doesn't mind. And he said Mr. Rollins doesn't either. He said—and Mr. Rollins did, too," she added brightly. "They said to come over any time. And anyway, Mom, I asked him if he could give me a job. He doesn't have any regular help yet. You're not going to say no, are you? I mean, why would you?"

She set her jaw and tried to speak calmly. "I'd rather you didn't."

"But why?"

Why? Because the conniving man was invading their lives, stirring up trouble. Making her question decisions she'd made over a decade ago. Because she didn't want Leigh anywhere near Jake Rollins if she could help it. Because it scared her spitless to think that Leigh might be falling under his spell. A very potent spell, Anna had reason to know.

But she could speak none of those reasons. Finally she resorted to the phrase she'd always sworn she wouldn't use. "Because I said so, that's why."

"See, you can't even think of a good reason!" Leigh burst out. "You're just being mean!"

"You already have more work than you can handle here. You know I depend on you, Leigh."

"But, Mom, Jake would pay me and then—"

Anna interrupted, her hands curling into fists of impatience. She strove to keep her voice calm and level, but she didn't quite make it. "I wouldn't feel comfortable with you taking a job there," she said, consciously unclenching her jaw. "I don't want you to haunt the Rollins place, job or no. And this is not the time to discuss it," she added, tardily aware of Suzie and Blaire standing by silently.

Leigh rolled her eyes and switched adults. "Mrs. Nelson, you don't mind if we help Jake, do you?"

Biting her lip, Suzie glanced at Anna. "Why don't you let your mother and I discuss it, Leigh?" she asked diplomatically. "You and Blaire go on in the house and I'll help your Mom out here."

"Meow," Leigh muttered sotto voice to Blaire as they left. "I can't believe she doesn't want me to have a job. I don't know what *her* problem is."

"Mothers are like that sometimes," Blaire said philosophically.

Anna puffed out her breath and shook her head. Turning to Suzie she said, "Thanks for backing me up."

Suzie shoved her unruly hair out of her face and gazed at her a moment before speaking. "Of course I backed you up. We mothers have to stick together. But, Anna, I've got to say, I'm as mystified as the girls are about this. Why do you have a problem with Leigh and Blaire learning something about Jake's training methods? You know how skilled he is and how they love horses. It's a great opportunity for them.''

Oh, she knew his skills, all right. Too well. She pressed a clenched fist to her stomach. "It's not that." If it only were that simple. But Jake's agenda was perfectly clear to Anna, even if no one else saw it. "I don't want Leigh taking a job. I need her here."

"Well, I understand that, but surely an occasional day at the Rollins ranch wouldn't hurt."

"Jake's not a good influence. I don't think they need to be around him that often."

"Not a good influence?" Suzie stared at her in surprise. "Are we talking about the same man? The word's been out for weeks now. He's known for his work with charities and youth organizations. And he's pledged a bundle for the new library, too. What's so bad about that?"

Anna spoke through gritted teeth. "Suzie, I think I know him a lot better than you do. Please don't recite me chapter and verse about how wonderful Jake Rollins is. I know better."

Suzie pursed her lips and scrutinized her. "Just what's going on with the two of you?"

Anna frowned at her. "Nothing. Absolutely nothing. I told you that days ago. And nothing's *going* to go on, either."

"Uh-huh." Suzie's skepticism showed clearly. "Why?" she asked after a moment.

Exasperated, Anna turned from her and picked up

the brush. "Why do you think? Remember the story? The guy dumped me. Left me high and dry."

"Honey, don't think I don't sympathize about that. I really do. But it's been years now and you were happily married in the meantime. And I don't think that's all there is to it."

"Oh for heaven's—" Anna broke off, slapping the brush against her palm. "What makes you say that?"

"I've known you too long. You're not acting like yourself. Come on, Anna. Spill it." She glanced at her watch. "Ross and the twins won't be back for a couple of hours. I've got plenty of time. So talk to me."

Anna hesitated. She'd kept her secret for sixteen years. No one but Carl, and she'd recently found out, her parents, had ever known the truth. She'd never discussed it with her mother, and with her mother in California with her own problems, now didn't seem the time to start. Anna hadn't needed to talk about it…until Jake had come back.

But this was Suzie, her best friend. As close to her as a sister. A woman who had shared her grief and her joys for the past twelve years. Whatever her failings, and she did have some, Suzie didn't gossip. She would never discuss anything potentially harmful to Anna or to Leigh. Why, she felt about Leigh like Anna did Blaire. As a daughter.

And Anna badly needed a confidant, because she had flat run out of answers. Talking to another woman, one who knew her and cared about her, might do her a great deal of good.

Her decision made, she set the brush down and

put Peanuts in his stall before walking to the doorway to check and make sure the girls had gone inside. "Let's sit down," she said, motioning to the tack room.

Suzie followed her and pulled up a folding metal chair. "So I was right. There is more to it."

A lot more, Anna thought. She took a seat beside Suzie, drew in a deep breath and let it out slowly before beginning. "You know the basic story. Jake went on the rodeo circuit all those years ago and that's when we broke up." Suzie nodded but didn't speak. "When Jake left me...he didn't just leave *me*. He left Leigh, too."

Suzie stared at her blankly before her mouth fell open. "You mean he left you *pregnant?*"

Anna nodded, feeling like a hundred-pound bag of feed had been lifted from her chest. Why hadn't she realized how badly she needed to talk to someone?

"That bastard!" Suzie sprang to her feet and paced the length of the cramped room. "He left you when he found out you were pregnant? And I thought he was a nice guy! I can't believe he had the nerve to come back after—"

"Hold on," Anna interrupted. Suzie halted in midstride and looked at her. "He didn't know I was pregnant. I didn't tell him. I meant to, but then he told me he'd gotten married and—" she shrugged "—well, I wasn't about to tell him after that."

"Oh, Lord, Anna." She passed a hand over her brow. "What did you..." Her voice trailed off and then she said, "You married Carl. Did Carl know?"

Anna stared at her incredulously. "Of course he

knew! Do you think I'd marry him with that lie between us? What kind of person do you think I am?''

Suzie sat beside her again and patted her hand. ''I'm sorry, honey, I didn't mean it that way. This is just a surprise to me. You and Carl were so—'' she spread her hands ''—I don't know. So together by the time I met you that I never imagined something like this. Carl adored you and Leigh.''

''Yes, he did. Carl was a very special person. He loved me, and when Leigh was born, he loved her, too. But that doesn't change the fact that the reason we married—and so quickly—was because I was pregnant. With Jake's child.''

Suzie seemed at a loss for words.

''So there it is,'' Anna continued despondently. ''Jake is Leigh's natural father. And I know he suspects it. If you could have heard some of the things he's said…oh, he suspects it all right.''

''Is that why he's here?''

Anna nodded. ''Among other things. But I believe that's one of his major reasons for coming back. He's taking every opportunity to insinuate himself into my daughter's life.''

''Maybe.'' Suzie slid her a speculative look. ''But I don't think that's all he wants. I've seen him watch you. He wants you back.''

''Ha! I doubt it. He's only trying to get to Leigh. And by God—'' she smacked her fist into her palm ''—I'm not having it. He's not going to ruin my daughter's life, too.''

''But, Anna,'' she leaned forward, speaking earnestly, ''how can you be so sure he'll ruin it? What if he enriches it? Is it fair not to allow Leigh the chance to know her biological father? Or her grand-father? What about Wes?''

Anna closed her heart to the wave of guilt that plagued her whenever she thought of Wes. ''I—I'm sorry about Wes, and I feel terrible about it, but I had no choice.'' Suzie didn't speak, but simply gazed at her. ''What would you have done?'' Anna demanded. ''Think about it, Suzie. What choices would you have made in that situation?''

Suzie worried her lip before answering. ''I don't know. But to never tell Jake he had a child... It's hard for me to imagine having to make that kind of decision.''

''I didn't make it lightly. Once I'd made it, and married Carl...'' Softly, she finished the sentence. ''I owed my loyalty to my husband. And I didn't want to hurt him more than I already had. He married me knowing I loved another man. And never once reproached me for it.''

''Anna, I remember the two of you before he died. I know you loved Carl.''

''Yes, I did. But that came later.'' She had been determined that Carl wouldn't regret marrying her. Still, she hadn't expected to come to love him so deeply. Or to lose him, either.

''But Carl's gone now, Anna. And Leigh—''

''I can't tell her, Suzie. The truth will destroy her world. Leigh has no idea. None. She's never had an inkling that Carl wasn't her natural father. How am I supposed to tell her something like that? Tell her I've lied to her for her entire life? That her father isn't her father? Can you imagine the shock that would be?''

Suzie shook her head. "I have a feeling you're going to have to find a way to tell her."

"I won't do it. I won't do that to my daughter."

"You may not have that choice. If things go on in the direction they're headed."

Anna put her head in her hands. "I hope you're wrong."

"It might not be so terrible, you know. Jake might stick around this time. And he might be good for Leigh, and for you. Remember," Suzie continued, "to be fair, you never told him the truth. You can't know what he'd have done."

"I can't afford to be fair!" Sick at heart, Anna looked up at her and shook her head. "It doesn't matter. I won't risk it, Suzie. I can't risk what hearing the truth will do to Leigh."

"I think Leigh's stronger than you believe she is, but it's your decision. And I can't say you made the wrong one in the past. It's obviously the only one you felt you could make. At the time." Anna stared at her as she added, "But things change, and we have to adapt."

Suzie fell silent for a bit. "So what are you going to do about Jake?" she asked eventually, when Anna remained quiet.

"I don't know. But the worst thing is..." Anna shut her eyes and groaned.

"What?"

"I still have...feelings for him."

Suzie smiled and said shrewdly, "You mean you've got the hots for him."

Anna scowled. "Dammit, all right. Yes."

"Who wouldn't?" Suzie drawled, getting a reluctant laugh from Anna. "Maybe you owe it to yourself as much as to Leigh to give Jake another chance," Suzie continued. "I know you're protecting Leigh. But be honest. You're protecting yourself, too. Especially your pride."

"Maybe. All right, yes. But if I don't protect myself, how can I possibly watch out for Leigh? You don't understand, Suzie. You still have your husband. You and Ross are a team. You turn to each other, trust each other. I'm trying to raise a child completely on my own."

"I know, Anna. And you're doing a great job with Leigh." She covered her hand and squeezed. "Don't think I'm not on your side, because I am. But I've been worried about you for a long time now. All you ever do is work and take care of Leigh. You haven't had a date in months. You haven't even tried to get on with that part of your life."

"How am I supposed to date?" Anna protested. "I don't have time to date. I have a business to run, a daughter to raise."

Suzie smirked. "My point, exactly."

"Besides that, there are no men around here who aren't either upwards of seventy-five years old or married. Well, very few anyway."

"There are men in Amarillo. I know how many dates you've turned down."

"Blind dates!"

"Nevertheless." Suzie crossed her arms over her chest and fell silent.

Suzie was right, Anna realized. She hadn't tried very hard to find someone else. But then Suzie had never lost the man she loved. Anna had. Twice.

"It hurts too much," she finally whispered. "Too damned much."

Leaning forward, Suzie said, "Would you trade your time with Carl? Even knowing that you'd lose him?"

Give up Carl? And all the joy and love she'd found with him? "No. Of course not. I may not have loved him when I married him, but I grew to love him very much. No, I wouldn't trade a minute of it."

"Knowing how it ended, would you trade your time with Jake?" Suzie persisted.

Anna shook her head. "How could I? I wouldn't have Leigh. She was worth it."

"Then how do you know that giving Jake another chance wouldn't be worth it?"

"I don't." Her hand clenched on her thigh. "But I don't know if I can survive it a third time. I just— don't think I'm strong enough, Suzie."

CHAPTER SEVEN

DINNER HAD BEEN a success, Anna thought, one evening about ten days later. The Country Barn Steakhouse in Amarillo had excellent food and she liked Buford Jones very much. She and Jake and the stock contractor had had a productive, enjoyable dinner meeting and now, thank God, it was time to go home.

Shivering, Anna wrapped her coat tighter around her as she and Jake walked through the restaurant parking lot, braving a chill wind. A cold, clear Friday evening in late March, the stars in the night sky would be bright and plentiful once they left the city lights behind. For reasons not entirely clear to her, she hadn't seen much of Jake over the past week. Until he'd picked her up late that afternoon to bring her to the meeting.

And that was the way she wanted it, Anna reminded herself, guiltily aware that she'd been looking forward to the afternoon with far more pleasure than she should have. Surely she hadn't been so foolish as to look forward to spending some time with Jake.

Not that it mattered if she had. Jake had been all business, she thought, with a pang of what felt suspiciously like disappointment. The entire forty-

minute drive to Amarillo he'd talked of nothing but
the upcoming rodeo and their plans for it. Not a
single flirtatious comment or suggestive remark,
nothing even remotely like a move. Maybe he'd finally taken her at her word and realized she wasn't
interested in taking up where they'd left off. And a
good thing, too.

So why did she find that thought depressing?

Determinedly, Anna shoved that train of thought
out of her mind. The rodeo was really shaping up.
The basics had been set in motion. They now had a
stock contractor, the date was set for the first weekend in June, the saddle maker had agreed to start
work on the prize-winning saddle, and Jake had already firmed up several sponsors, with more in mind
to approach.

Best of all, though, she'd made it through dinner
able to assure herself that she felt little more for Jake
than curiosity and mild attraction. She put her conversation with Suzie firmly out of her mind. She
didn't have the hots for Jake, she assured herself.
But there was nothing wrong with admitting she
found him…distracting. Any woman would. And
she had been involved with him—a thousand years
ago.

Yet sometimes she could swear it had only been
yesterday. He walked the same, his long-legged,
sexy stride making it hard to keep up with him, even
with her height. And his voice—oh, that voice
sounded every bit as resonant and beguiling as it
had years ago. More, come to think of it.

"So, what do you want to do?" Jake asked her
once they'd climbed inside the truck. He started the

engine and blew on his hands. "Damn, it's cold tonight."

Startled by the sound of his voice, the one she'd just been fantasizing about, she turned her head to look at him. "Do? Go home, of course."

"Why? It's early still. Let's have some fun."

She stared at him, unable to ignore the glitter in his eyes. Was it just a reflection from the dash lights, or did he have some devilry in mind? "Fun? We didn't come here for fun, we came for a business meeting."

He gave her a grin. "Relax, Anna. What do you think I'm suggesting? Nude mud wrestling?"

Taken aback, she laughed. A moment later, though, she narrowed her eyes at him. He was definitely up to something. "Okay, if not that, then what are you suggesting?"

"Nothing terrible, I swear." He raised a hand as if to pledge. "I thought we could go dancing. There's a place called the Midnight something... Cowboy, I think it is."

"Rodeo," she said. "Midnight Rodeo."

"Yeah, that's it." He flicked on the heater. The air blasted out, hot and strong. He stretched his arm across the back of the seat and gave her an easy smile. "So, how about it?"

Lord, she hadn't gone dancing in years. She'd been to the country-and-western club he'd mentioned a time or two before with a group of women friends, but she hadn't danced. *Of course you haven't been dancing, you idiot. You haven't been on a date in six months or more. Just like Suzie said, you never do anything but work.*

But she couldn't break that streak with Jake. Could she?

Well, why not? she asked herself. What was the big deal about a little dancing?

He looked at her like he expected her to turn him down. Like it amused him that she would refuse. "You're on, cowboy. Let's go." She jerked on her seat belt, fastening it in place. "The club is at the corner of Georgia and Forty-fifth. You can't miss it, there's a neon sign in the parking lot that's half as big as Amarillo."

A SHORT WHILE LATER they pulled into an enormous parking lot where a rainbow of neon lights flashed brilliantly against the night sky. A sea of chrome-edged pickup trucks spanned the lot endlessly.

Jake parked the truck, slid out and slammed the door behind him. Anna felt a niggle of...not fear, but apprehension. Maybe it wasn't such a good idea to go dancing with Jake.

Her door swung open and Jake stood in the doorway smiling at her. Too late now. *Get over it, Anna,* she told herself. *It's not that big a deal.*

She stuffed her purse underneath the seat and let him lead her inside. Jake bypassed the slot machines, pool tables and bar to swing her into a two-step immediately.

Startled, she nearly tripped, but he held her up, laughing, and kept moving. Jake had always moved well, but somewhere along the line he'd really learned to dance. Once she relaxed and followed his lead, Anna caught the rhythm and began to enjoy herself. So much that she hated to stop when the band took a break. Besides, dancing to such loud music required no talk and Anna was still leery of the subjects Jake might bring up.

He went to get drinks while Anna looked for a seat. Spying a tiny unclaimed table in the ring of seating encircling the dance floor, she pounced on it, then practically had to go to war with someone from another table to hold on to the extra chair.

"Down, girl," Jake said, returning and handing her the soft drink she'd asked for.

She laughed. "I thought you'd want a chair. They seem to be at a premium here."

"We could have shared," he said, his mouth curving upward. "I wouldn't have minded."

Anna drew in a sharp breath and fought to keep her smile. Better not to respond to that, she thought, as a flash of unwelcome heat shimmered through her body at the image his words provoked. She changed the subject quickly, before he could add any more. "Have you found a place yet?" she asked him, then picked up her soft drink and drank some thirstily. Jake had grinned when she'd turned down a beer in favor of a soda, but she'd decided her inhibitions were plenty loose without throwing alcohol into the mix. No, she needed to keep a clear head tonight.

"A place of my own?" he repeated. "No. It may be a while before I do. Seems there's not much for sale around here."

"You could look farther away. I hear the Mercer place is for—"

"Nope. No water, according to my father. Besides, I'd like a place near Happy."

She wanted to ask him why it was so important

for him to settle close to Happy, but she didn't dare. He might tell her, and she had a feeling she wouldn't like the answer. "So what are you going to do?"

"Wait." He grinned and took a drink of his beer. "Unless you've got some land you'd be willing to part with?"

"Sorry. I sold off what I didn't need after Carl died." Remembering, she ran a finger around the rim of her glass. She'd hated to part with land that had been in Carl's family for generations, yet it had been too much for her to handle alone. With Carl gone she couldn't manage both the farming and the riding school. So she'd chosen what she was most familiar with. Carl had been the farmer, not her. She'd kept enough land to grow her own hay and pasture the horses and sold the remainder.

"Have you asked your father? He's the one I sold to."

"Ask my old man if I could buy his land to breed horses on? Are you crazy?"

Anna stifled a laugh at his horrified expression. "Maybe he's…I don't know, mellowed." Wes's disapproval of Jake's youthful dreams of raising horses had been loud and clear, Anna remembered. The two had had many bitter fights over it. And once Jake's mother had died there'd been no one to make peace between them. Sometimes she wondered if that wasn't part of what had driven him away.

"Wes Rollins, mellow? I don't think so." He looked pensive for a moment and added, "Still, he did say I could use the barn if I started acquiring some horses before I found land. Which was more than I'd expected from him. That's why I was able to pick up that new mare.''

"He's missed you," Anna said, restraining herself from touching his arm. She wanted to offer comfort, as she would have in the past. Bad idea, she told herself.

"He wouldn't admit it, even if he did." Tilting the bottle up, he swigged some more beer. "Do you know he never showed up, not to one lousy rodeo, not to one single event I ever rode in." His mouth tightened, thinned. "I won five national championships and he never saw a damned one of them.''

Pain surfaced in his eyes, causing her a pang of empathy, unwanted, but impossible to ignore. "He was hurt. Angry. And he's a proud man, Jake." *Like his son,* she thought.

Jake shrugged. "Yeah. Whatever.''

This time she gave in to the urge to touch him, resting her fingers lightly on his arm. "I think he really is happy you're here, even if he isn't able to say it. He's been alone a long time.''

His mood shifted, as swiftly as it had when they were younger. He smiled. "I'm not so sure he's been all that alone. At least not recently.''

"What do you mean?" The music started again. She drained her drink as Jake stood.

Chuckling, he pulled her onto the dance floor with him. "I think he and Mary Gallick have gotten pretty friendly lately.''

"Really?" Though the idea surprised her, it made sense when she thought about it. "He's been coming to all the library fund meetings. And come to think of it, he's always watching her. In fact, he never takes his eyes off her. Maybe you're right.''

"Guess we'll find out, sooner or later," Jake said, and dropped the subject as his arms encircled her. Despite her best efforts, her breathing quickened. Her back tingled where his palm rested warm against her. Her hand, the one he held firmly clasped in his, tingled, too. He didn't handle her suggestively, he simply guided her steps, yet his touch kindled a longing deep inside her.

A longing she didn't intend to succumb to.

Sometime later, while seated at the table taking another break, the song started. The singer crooned a country ballad about taking chances. Anna looked up to see Jake in front of her, holding out a hand.

She should say no, should claim to be tired, anything except dance a slow song with him. Because she was nowhere near as indifferent to him as she'd like to be. And she had the feeling that Jake knew it, too.

But tonight she felt carefree, reckless. Young. And she wanted, just this once, to indulge. To pretend she was eighteen again, and nothing bad had ever happened.

So she stood, let him lead her onto the crowded dance floor, let him take her in his arms and bend his head down to hers. Let him pull her close until their bodies brushed against each other and her senses swam.

To be held in a man's strong arms again felt wonderful, to let the beat of the music seep into her soul, to close her eyes and rest her cheek against a solid shoulder, to inhale and breathe in the spicy scent of his aftershave, the intensely male scent of him. Better than anything she'd experienced in a long, long time.

Worse yet, it felt right. And it shouldn't have. She didn't want to get involved with Jake again, couldn't afford to let herself be swept off her feet and then unceremoniously dumped the instant something better came along. She'd be crazy to give him the chance. He wanted to know the truth about Leigh, not get together with her again.

Didn't he?

"Anna?"

His deep, seductive voice sent a shiver of longing up her spine. She turned her head to gaze into his eyes and knew he was going to kiss her. And she wanted him to, wondered what would happen when he did. Everywhere their bodies touched shimmered with awareness. Beneath her palms she felt the play of muscles in his back, felt the iron hard strength of his thighs rubbing against hers.

"What?" She barely breathed the word but she knew he'd heard her.

His gaze dropped to her mouth, raised to her eyes, dropped to her mouth again.

Think with your brain, Anna, not your hormones. But when he lowered his head to hers, and his mouth hovered a breath away from hers, she knew her brain didn't stand a chance.

She'd been so good for so long. Proper, respectable, dependable. And untouched. She couldn't remember the last time a man had held her in his arms. Couldn't remember the last time a man had kissed her. And she could remember all too well the last

time she'd made love. There had been no one since
Carl.

Was it so bad to yearn for a little excitement, a
little tenderness? To want to be held, kissed, and
yes, loved again? No, of course not, she thought, but
the problem was that she shouldn't be wanting any
of those things from Jake.

Logic didn't come into it. She still wanted him.

He touched his mouth to hers, and time spun out.
His lips moved over hers, oh, so slowly. As slow
and tender as the mournful wail of the guitar in the
music throbbing in the background, Jake reac-
quainted himself with her mouth. Anna closed her
eyes and sank into the kiss, letting the sensations
wash over her. His tongue slid over her lips, slipping
inside teasing, tempting, tantalizing.

Her arms tightened around his neck as he edged
her closer still and continued to kiss her, tasting her,
learning her, making her mouth his. Not a hard kiss,
but soft, and tempting as midnight sin. This was no
kiss from the boy she remembered. No, this man had
acquired a dangerous knowledge of kissing—and
other skills she could imagine in all too vivid detail.

Jake raised his head and they stared at each other
for an endless moment. He looked as bemused as
she felt. Jake Rollins, ladies' man, befuddled by a
simple kiss?

Not possible.

CHAPTER EIGHT

JAKE FINALLY figured out the problem on the drive home. He'd lost his freaking mind. Simple as that. Kissing Anna was one thing. Letting it get to him was not in the plans. No way, no how. A kiss, for God's sake. It didn't mean anything.

Shouldn't mean anything.

You're overreacting, cowboy.

Anna was a beautiful woman. Nothing wrong with enjoying a beautiful woman.

He took a sideways glance at her. She hadn't spoken since they left the Midnight Rodeo. Since he'd kissed her on the dance floor. Probably having second thoughts, too. Her scowl certainly looked like it.

"The meeting went well, didn't it?" he ventured, both to break the silence and the tension simmering in the truck cab.

She glanced at him. "What? Oh, yes, it did. Jake, there's something we need to talk about."

"About the rodeo? Fire away."

"No. It's about—it's about Leigh."

His heart stumbled for a minute before he got hold of himself. Anna wouldn't choose now to confess, would she? Not when she'd been doing everything possible to deny the truth. He didn't dare hope. "What about Leigh?"

Out of the corner of his eye he saw her grip her hands together in her lap. "I've told her, and now I'm telling you, that I don't want her over at your place all the time."

He nearly smiled, despite his disappointment. He wondered how she'd justify her command. "Why not?"

"It's just—there's no reason for her to hang around there. People might—they might misunderstand."

Yeah, they might begin to wonder again about her parentage. But of course, Anna wouldn't admit that was her chief concern. That and his finding out the truth. He played along with her, though. "What's to misunderstand? I like Leigh. She's good with the horses and she likes to work. I'd give her a job in a heartbeat if you'd let her take it."

"She already works for me."

He could almost hear her teeth grind. "You're not doing the same things I am. You're running a riding school. I train horses."

"It doesn't look good to have her over there constantly," Anna insisted stubbornly.

"Why? She isn't alone with me. Besides the ranch hands or my father, she brings Blaire with her most of the time. Why is it a problem? C'mon, Anna, just spit it out."

"Because it's—it's just—" She huffed out a breath and started again. "Why are you so interested in my daughter anyway?"

"She's a nice kid. What's not to like?"

"It's…strange, that's all. You can't have that much interest in a teenage girl."

"I like kids. Some of the high school boys come out there, too. Your ranch hand's son, for one."

"Luis? Luis comes over, too?"

Her bowled over expression made him want to laugh. He shrugged. "Sure. And some of the others." A good many of the others, actually. "Look, Anna, are you worried I have some kind of designs on Leigh?" Let her wiggle out of that one, he thought.

"I didn't say that! Don't put words in my mouth."

He hid another smile. "That's what it sounded like to me."

"Well, it wasn't," she snapped. "Oh, forget it."

They pulled into her driveway. He switched off the truck and decided on a direct attack. "I don't have designs on Leigh."

Her eyes narrowed as she stared at him but she said nothing.

"But Leigh's mother," he added with a wicked smile, "is another matter."

Her mouth fell open and she stared at him. "I—you—just because I let you kiss me—"

"You kissed me back," he reminded her. "And you enjoyed it."

She seemed to be struggling with herself. Finally she said, "That's beside the point."

He smiled again. "I think it's very much the point." And he intended to use the chemistry still between them to get exactly what he wanted.

His daughter.

Come hell or high water, he meant to claim his daughter. And no matter how much Anna moved him, no attraction to her could be allowed to interfere with that goal.

LEIGH HEADED to the barn. The perfect time to talk to her mother, she knew from experience, was just before her Saturday classes started. Anna would be so busy getting ready for them that she might say yes just to get Leigh off her back.

"Where have you been?" Anna asked when she entered the barn. She stood in the alleyway currycombing Peanuts, Leigh's big Appaloosa gelding. "I've got a full load today and I really need your help. Makeup classes from when it snowed last week, plus the regular classes. Help me saddle him, will you? I want you to demonstrate some techniques to the students."

Leigh grabbed the hoof pick and went to work on Peanuts's hooves. Her mother left and returned a few minutes later with the saddle pad, waiting until Leigh finished before laying it on the horse's back.

Leigh took a deep breath and started in. "Mom, there's a rodeo in a couple of weeks in—"

"Hold it right there," Anna interrupted. She took hold of the girth and fastened it beneath the horse's belly. "No more rodeos for a while, Leigh. We talked about this before the last one. Remember? You said if you could go to the Houston rodeo, you wouldn't ask to go to another for two months."

"But, Mom, it's been *way* over two months!" she protested. "It's been closer to three," she added triumphantly. She slipped the bit into his mouth and looped the bridle over his ears. "And, Mom, this one is gonna be great! If you'd just listen, it's not even very far away." That was kind of fudging the truth, since it was in far eastern Oklahoma, but still, it was a neighboring state.

Her mother let out her breath with the effort of hoisting the saddle onto Peanuts's back. Leigh watched her cinch up the girth and check over everything. Finally she spoke, but they weren't the words Leigh wanted to hear.

"No, sweetheart. I can't afford the entry fee or the time off. And we've had this discussion before. When I say no, I mean it."

"If you'd let me work for Jake, I could get enough for the entry fee," Leigh said in her best wheedling tone. "I'd pay you back as soon as I made enough. Come on, Mom, please." She would have asked Blaire's Mom to take her, but Blaire couldn't go to this rodeo because of some lame reunion her family was going to that weekend.

"No. I'm sorry, but I can't do it. Not this time. There'll be another one."

"It's not fair! You have time for everything but what I want to do."

"That's not true and you know it. I have responsibilities here, Leigh. I can't shirk them to take you to every rodeo that strikes your fancy."

"You just don't want me to go. Just like you don't want me to rodeo. You could take me if you wanted to." She swung herself into the saddle, fighting tears.

Her mom put her hands on her hips and gave the exasperated sound that she made whenever she was irritated. "Drop it, Leigh. I don't have time for an argument right now. Classes start in half an hour and the students will be here any minute."

"You never have time for me. If Dad was here he'd let me go." She saw the pain in her mother's eyes, but rushed on regardless. "Dad always had time for me. But all you care about is your school. You don't care what I want at all!" She wheeled Peanuts around and trotted out of the barn, but instead of going to the arena, she headed for the fields that adjoined the Rollins's place. She heard her mom call after her and knew she'd probably get grounded for taking off, but she didn't care. Let her mother teach her dumb classes by herself. Anna cared more about the stinking riding school than she did her own daughter.

ALL IN ALL, Wes thought as he drove along checking fences, things weren't going too badly. Mary... He smiled at the thought of her. Now there was a miracle. A few days after they'd gone to dinner she asked him over and cooked for him. For reasons he couldn't figure, she seemed to enjoy being with him, even if he never could think of anything to say. And thank God, she knew when to keep her mouth shut, too, and didn't need to yap all the time to be happy. He remembered a woman he'd seen for a while after Cora died and Jake had left home. She'd about driven him crazy with her chatter. Mary talked, but she didn't chatter just to hear herself. Yep, things were definitely looking up.

As for Jake, Wes still didn't understand his desire to breed horses, but if he hadn't changed his mind after twenty years of wanting to do it, then Wes didn't figure he ever would. Besides, the cattle business wasn't exactly easy money right now. Maybe it was a good thing that Jake wanted to do something different. Still, horses weren't an easy market either. And the Rollinses had always been cattlemen.

Looked like Jake was fixing to change that.

Spotting a break in the fence line, he stopped the pickup. Before he got out of the truck, he pulled on his gloves and wrapped his ancient fleece-and-denim coat more tightly around him. Damn, every winter seemed colder than the last one. Had March always been this cold? Maybe it was just his age catching up to him.

Damned arthritis, he thought fleetingly, as a twinge invaded his knee joint. A sharp gust of bitterly cold wind hit him when he opened the door and he cursed again halfheartedly. The cold air made the arthritis worse, but aside from taking aspirin, which aggravated his gut, there wasn't a lot he could do to relieve it.

Eyeing the break, he pulled out his wire cutters and cut off a length of wire from the roll in the back of the truck. He crimped the ends, making a hook in each one and then walked over to the fence to repeat the process on the busted wire. He'd just attached the come-along, intending to stretch the wire tight, when he thought he heard something. Not a bird. No, it sounded more like a faint cry.

Glancing up and down the fence line, he didn't see anything. After another look around the pasture he went back to work, cranking the wire tighter and cussing the weather while he did.

There it was again. Now it sounded like some-body yelling. Squinting, he looked around again. A movement over by the draw caught his eye and he saw a splash of color against the dirt, a figure hud-dled on the ground, he decided as he went to inves-tigate.

As he walked closer, he recognized Leigh Connor waving at him. He knew her, of course, just like he knew everyone who lived in or around Happy. Be-sides, the Connors' land bordered his own, so nat-urally, from time to time he saw the girl. Lately he'd seen her a lot more often, because she'd been hang-ing around the barn, bringing one of her girlfriends or the Villareal boy with her. But up to now they'd never talked much. Most times they just waved to each other in passing.

Wes had never told a soul that he attended the local rodeos whenever he could because he knew Leigh might be entered in the barrel racing event. He hadn't seen Jake ride—in person, anyway—since he left home. He regretted that decision now, but there wasn't a thing he could do to change it. The water had passed under that bridge a long time ago.

So instead he watched Anna's daughter compete.

"Oh, Mr. Rollins, I'm so glad to see you. I didn't think anyone would find me," she said, and burst into tears when he hunkered down beside her. "I thought I'd freeze to death," she said between sobs.

Thank God she was dressed for the weather, in a heavy denim-and-leather jacket and gloves. Her head was bare, though, and she looked mighty cold. He thought she must have been out in the weather for some time. She was in sad shape, her pretty, young face blotched and red, her lips nearly blue. Pain filled those big blue eyes. Eyes so much like Jake's it sent a pang stabbing through his heart.

"Good thing I was checking fence, then. You get dumped? Are you hurt?" Silly question, he thought. If she hadn't been hurt she'd have been walking home instead of lying in a field in the freezing cold.

Leigh gulped and nodded, struggling not to cry. "My ankle. I must have come down on it. I tried to walk, but I could hardly stand up. So I tried hopping, but it hurt so much I had to quit."

"Hit your head?" He didn't think she had, but he wanted to make sure before he moved her.

"No, it's just my leg."

He rose. "Let's get you out of this cold." Stripping off his coat, he did his best to ignore the arctic blast of air. "Here, put this around you," he said, ignoring her faint protest. "I'll get the truck. Have you home in two shakes."

The engine hadn't been off too long, luckily, so the heater began to blast warm air as he pulled up beside Leigh. "How'd you come to part company with your horse?" he asked as he took his coat back, then picked her up. She was no bigger than a minute, he thought, and set her as gently as he could in the front seat of the truck before going around and sliding in himself.

She dashed the tears away with a gloved hand. "Peanuts shied at something. A rabbit, I guess. He took off after he threw me."

"Peanuts, huh. That big Appy gelding I see you ride sometimes?" She nodded. "Headed for home,

I imagine,'' Wes said, putting the truck in gear. ''How long you figure you've been out there?''

''I don't know. A while.'' She started crying again. ''If I broke my ankle that means I can't ride. And if I can't ride I'll just—I'll just die,'' she wailed dramatically.

At a loss with how to deal with all the waterworks, Wes kept driving and prayed she'd stop soon. ''Probably not broken,'' he said, inspired. ''Just a sprain, I reckon.''

She stopped sobbing, thank God. ''Do you think so?''

''Yep,'' he said, perjuring his soul without hesitation. ''You'd be in more pain if it was broken.'' Anna would be worried, he knew, when the horse showed up without its rider and the rider never showed up at all. ''Too bad I don't have a phone with me. To give your mother a call so she won't worry.''

''She won't care.'' Leigh swiped at her nose with her coat sleeve.

Wes seriously doubted that. ''Course she will.'' He sent Leigh a sharp glance. ''Your horse is bound to be home by now. Bet she's worried sick.''

Leigh shook her head mournfully. ''I took off instead of helping her with her classes. She'll ground me for sure. And there's a dance next weekend at school and now I won't be able to go.'' Fresh tears streamed from her eyes. ''Not that it matters since my leg is broken.''

Wisely, Wes didn't smile. He didn't know a lot about teenage girls but any fool knew better than to rile a female when she was already plenty upset. ''Why did you run off?''

"Because she's so unfair! She won't let me do *anything*. There's this great rodeo coming up and she won't take me."

"Well, maybe she has a reason."

"Sure she does. She doesn't want me to rodeo, so she's being mean about taking me."

Wes cleared his throat but didn't say anything. Leigh went on. "I don't see why she's so against it."

He had a real good idea, but he wasn't going to touch that one, not with a ten-foot cattle prod. Instead he made a sympathetic noise and listened to Leigh rant.

"You understand, don't you, Mr. Rollins? I mean, look at Jake. I bet you didn't give him a bunch of grief about rodeoing."

He couldn't let that pass. "'Fraid you'd lose that bet. Jake and I never have seen eye to eye on that. Fact is, he left home because I thought his wanting to rodeo was a lot of foolishness." And he hadn't come back for sixteen years.

That stopped her in midtirade, her mouth forming a perfect circle of consternation. "Oh! I didn't know that."

He shrugged. "No reason you would. But your mama has her reasons, I'm sure. Why don't you talk to her about them?" He didn't envy Anna that talk. If Leigh was anything like Jake had been, and he had a feeling she was, then it would be mighty hard to change her mind.

Luckily they pulled up to Anna's just then, before they could plunge any deeper into a talk he really didn't want to have. "I'll go find your mother."

He hadn't taken two steps before Anna came out of the barn leading a chestnut mare. She looked confused when she saw him standing there.

"Wes? What—"

"I've got your little girl in the truck." He jerked his head toward it. "Found her in my field when I was checking fence."

"Oh, thank God," she said, hurrying toward him with the mare in tow. "When she didn't come back, I—I was just about to go look for her. Is she all right?"

"Pretty much." He kept stride with her until they reached the truck. "Think she sprained her ankle."

Anna thrust the reins into his hands just before Leigh opened the truck door and tumbled out into her mother's arms. Since she was crying again and incoherent, Wes had no idea what either of them said. He mumbled something about stabling the horse, which neither of them heard, and left them alone.

When he returned a short time later they were still hugging. He cleared his throat and waited until the cold began to seep through his coat and remind him that Leigh should probably be inside and warming up. "Maybe I should carry her in. She's been out in this weather a while now."

"Oh, thank you, Wes," Anna said, turning to him. "You're right, of course." She stepped back to let him pick up Leigh. "Just put her in the kitchen. I think we're going to have to cut that boot to get it off."

"But, Mom, they're my new boots!"

Anna opened the kitchen door and smiled at her

daughter. "We can try to get it off without cutting it, but I don't think it will work."

After Wes set Leigh down, Anna held out her hand to him. "I don't know how to thank you. Peanuts came back quite some time ago. I was starting to really worry as the time passed and she didn't show up."

"No problem," he said, taking the hand she offered. "You want some help getting that boot off?"

"Well..." She looked at her daughter, then back to Wes. "We've already imposed on you enough."

"No such thing."

She smiled at him. "Thanks, then. I could use the help."

"What about your class?" Leigh asked her. "I don't see anyone around."

"It's so cold today, they're all in the barn. I left Sally in charge. They're just taking care of tack right now, anyway. I'll check on them as soon as we get your boot off."

It didn't take much pulling on her injured ankle to convince Leigh to let them cut the boot. And it was pretty clear, Wes thought, as the three of them looked at her bare, swollen ankle, that she'd sprained it badly—at the least.

"I'm not gonna be able to ride, am I?" she asked her mother, her mouth curved down into a mournful pout.

Anna shook her head. "Not for a while. Here." She dug into the freezer and pulled out a bag of frozen peas, handing them to Leigh. "Put this on it while I make an ice pack. We'd better go get it X-rayed. You might have broken a bone in there."

"Are you going to ground me?"

A half smile on her lips, Anna paused to ruffle her hair. "You've grounded yourself, haven't you? Let's just hope the X rays don't show that it's broken." She smacked her head with her hand. "Oh, Lord, X rays. I'll have to cancel those classes so I can take you into Amarillo." Glancing at her watch, she said, "This group is almost out of time. As soon as they leave, we'll go, Leigh."

"I can wait here if you want to go on and take her," Wes said. "Explain what happened."

"That would be great. If you're sure..." Wes nodded and she went on while grabbing a plastic bag and dumping cubes in it. "Suzie Nelson should be here soon. Ask her if she'll stay and tell the next group that the class is canceled, and why. I'm sure she won't mind, she usually stays for the twins' class anyway. There's no way I can get hold of all of the students—most of them have already left home."

"Will do."

Ignoring her protests that she could walk with help, Wes carried Leigh to her mother's truck while Anna checked on her class. "Don't go thinking it's broken until they tell you it is," he told the girl.

"Okay." Her smile was a little wobbly, but it was there. "I guess you know lots about broken bones and stuff like that, huh? From Jake, I mean."

"He got himself stomped a time or two," Wes admitted. And judging from his stiff gait in the mornings, Wes suspected he'd broken a bone or two since he'd left home, as well. Stood to reason. Saddle bronc riders tended to run to broken bones. "But he mended. So will you."

"Thanks, Mr. Rollins. I'm really glad you found me."

He smiled. "You be more careful next time you're riding in those fields, you hear?"

Wes met Anna on his way to the barn. "Be interested to see how long you can keep that little gal off her horse."

She glanced toward the truck and smiled. "It won't be easy. Especially if her ankle is only sprained and not broken."

"I remember one time Jake busted his wrist. Never said a word about it until after the rodeo the next night."

"I remember that," Anna said. "When I asked him about it afterward he said it wasn't the hand he held on with, so there was no reason not to ride. I'm sure he thought it was worth the pain, since he won the event."

"Yep. Reckon he did."

"Wes, I—I wish..." Her voice trailed off and their eyes met and held for a long, intense moment. She sighed and shook her head. Whatever she'd been about to say, she seemed to think better of. "Thank you."

"Go on. Don't you worry. I'll take care of things here."

He used the phone in the barn to ring Jake. "Get over to Anna's," he said, when Jake answered.

"Dad? What's going on?"

"Anna needs you."

"Is she all right?" he demanded.

"Yep. But she needs your help. Get on over here and I'll tell you about it."

"On my way."

Wes cracked his knuckles and grinned. Yessir, the perfect solution. No reason for Anna to miss out on the income from those lessons when Jake could take over for her.

And giving Anna a reason to be grateful to his son wouldn't hurt a thing, either.

CHAPTER NINE

"MOM, WHEN ARE they coming back?" Leigh asked some three hours later. "I'm tired of being here. I want to go home."

"Me, too," Anna agreed wearily, glancing at her daughter perched on the gurney in the emergency room cubicle. "Someone will be back after a doctor reads the X ray." She hoped. She slumped in the uncomfortable, straight-backed plastic chair beside the bed and rubbed the back of her neck.

"But it *hurts,* Mom. Why can't they do something? Why do we have to just sit here and sit here?"

Anna sighed and tried to muster patience. Leigh was scared and in pain. And they had been there a long time. Forever, it seemed like.

"Because that's what happens when you go to the emergency room. Here, look at this magazine." She handed her an ancient copy of *Time.*

"Get real, Mom." She gave her a disgusted look and rolled her eyes.

"Look, that's all I could find. There's nothing we can do but wait. We have to make the best of it."

Leigh sniffed but didn't say anything else. A few seconds later she started leafing through the magazine. Anna wasn't sure which was better—listening to Leigh's grumbling or being left alone with her thoughts.

And her guilt.

Not about the tiff with her daughter—that was a normal part of raising a child. No, Anna cringed every time she thought about Wes Rollins.

Leigh's grandfather.

Guilt. Oh, she'd suffered torrents of it over the years. But in the past she'd always managed to convince herself that whatever she had to do to protect Leigh—and Carl—was the right thing to do.

Even if it meant denying Leigh her grandfather.

Just then a white-coated doctor popped in, sparing Anna further soul-searching. She turned to her eagerly.

"Good news," the doctor said. "The X ray showed no fractures. Looks like a sprain." Smiling at Leigh, she added, "We'll wrap it and you'll need to stay off it for a couple of weeks. Have you fixed right up."

"Wonderful. Oh, that's wonderful news," Anna said with heartfelt thanks.

"A couple of weeks? Oh, no," Leigh moaned.

The doctor patted Leigh's arm. "Don't worry, the time will pass quickly. I'll send someone in to wrap it."

"Yeah, in about a year," Leigh muttered after the woman left.

"Probably not that long," Anna said, hiding a smile. "This is great news, honey. No cast."

"Yeah, but I'll be on crutches and I won't be able to cheerlead and—oh, forget it. You don't understand. This really sucks!"

Anna restrained herself from reprimanding her about her language. Leigh returned to her magazine, wiping her eyes every now and then.

Her thoughts returned to earlier in the day, when Wes had brought Leigh home just before Anna had really started to panic. A sympathetic shiver flashed down her spine as she thought about the cold. Thank God Wes had found Leigh or she might be battling pneumonia instead of only a sprained ankle.

Today's events had slapped Anna in the face with the reality of her actions. By keeping Leigh from knowing her grandfather she'd wronged them both, even though she'd felt she had no other choice. She had raised Leigh to believe Carl was her father, but was that a good enough reason to cut her off completely from Wes?

It hadn't been a purely selfish choice, but one she'd made partly because of loyalty to Carl. Any whisper of gossip about their child would only have hurt Carl more, and Anna thought she'd done enough of that when they'd first married. He'd been such a loving father, and husband, and he hadn't deserved any more heartache than he'd already had. Anna sighed, remembering how much they had wanted more children, but it had never happened.

Besides, how could she have approached Wes without the risk of having to confirm what he was bound to suspect? That Jake was in fact Leigh's father. And she didn't doubt for a solitary instant that if Wes had ever figured out the truth about Leigh, he'd have told his son.

And who knew what Jake would have done back then? Demanded his parental rights? Possibly. Ruined her marriage—a marriage that had started off shaky as all get-out anyway? Almost certainly.

No, she'd done the best thing for everyone at the time. Why doubt herself now?

Because she'd seen Wes with Leigh, that's why. And it had almost broken her heart.

She clenched her fists in frustration. Damn Jake for coming home! It had been so much easier to rationalize her behavior before she had to face him daily. Before she'd seen him with Leigh and wondered whether things could have been different. Before she'd seen the naked longing in his eyes when they rested on his daughter. Before she'd felt that renewed surge of outrageous attraction and knew he felt it, too.

Anna didn't doubt Jake felt the sizzle between them, as much as she did. Her uncertainty lay in figuring out whether he truly felt something more or was merely using the potent chemistry to suit his own purposes.

And as if Jake's return wasn't enough to cope with, now she had to think about his father, too. Before she'd seen Wes with Leigh, she hadn't realized just how much she'd made him miss. Made them both miss. Leigh only saw Anna's mother and stepfather once or twice a year, and Carl's parents had died before she turned three. Wes could have been a part of his granddaughter's life all these years. If only Anna hadn't been afraid to risk the truth coming out.

And now she felt guilty keeping the truth from Jake, too, though not nearly as much as she did from his father. After all, Jake had not only left her pregnant—he'd gone off and married another woman. But if he'd known she was pregnant, what would he have changed? Would he have divorced the woman sooner and married her?

Probably, she admitted. Which was why she hadn't told him. That would have been a great start to a marriage.

Yet her marriage to Carl had worked, even though she'd gone into it loving another man.

Bottom line was, she'd chosen her course years before. She glanced at Leigh, who'd dropped the magazine and had tumbled into the exhausted sleep of a child. A wave of love swept her as she gazed at her daughter. Reaching out, she tucked a strand of baby-fine blond hair behind Leigh's ear, swallowing hard around the lump in her throat.

Anna's guilt would once again have to take a back seat to protecting her daughter. To tell Leigh the truth after all these years would rock her world to its foundation. She couldn't risk destroying her daughter. Leigh was, as always, Anna's first concern.

INTENT ON MAKING SURE Leigh was all right, Jake hung around Anna's after he and her ranch hands had finished up work for the day. Though Wes had assured him Leigh hadn't seemed too badly hurt, Jake wanted to see her for himself.

Not to mention that he wouldn't mind seeing Anna, he thought, smiling. The smile faded as a new concern hit him. Surely they wouldn't keep Leigh overnight. Would they?

Worrying about someone else was new to him.

And he had to admit, he didn't like it much. How did Anna stand it? If something as simple as a tumble from a horse set him on edge, then what must she be going through? Suddenly Anna's opposition to Leigh's chosen career offered a whole new perspective. One he'd never even considered.

For the first time he wondered if maybe some of his old man's objections to his profession and career choice had been rooted in concern. In the past he'd put it down to his father's need to always be right. That or pure orneriness. Maybe he'd had it all wrong.

The slam of a car door alerted him to Anna's and Leigh's return and he rushed out to meet them.

Anna pulled a pair of crutches from the pickup bed on her way around to open the other door and handed them to Leigh.

"Hi, ladies," Jake said as he reached them, attempting to mask his concern with nonchalance. He studied Leigh's expression for pain. "What's the verdict? I don't see a cast. Is that a good sign?"

"Sort of," Leigh answered as she struggled out of the truck. "Hi, Jake. What are you doing here?"

"Oh, just giving your mom a hand." Anna didn't speak, but sent him a sharp look. Falling into step with Leigh, he commented, "You're pretty good with those crutches." Very good, actually. He wondered how many times she'd hurt herself and found he didn't like that notion, either.

She scowled. "Stupid things. It's just a sprain, the doctor said."

"A bad sprain. And you need to stay off it and

keep it elevated," Anna said as they reached the house.

"I know, Mom. I will. Can I call Blaire? You said I wasn't grounded."

Anna smiled wryly. "I said you'd grounded yourself, and you have. But you can call Blaire. We'll talk about our...disagreement later." At the door, she turned to Jake. "Where's Wes? Or Suzie? What do you mean, helping—"

He interrupted her before she could get further into it. "Make sure Leigh gets that ankle up. I'll fill you in later. I'll be in the barn."

Twenty minutes later he was in the tack room rubbing oil onto a saddle he'd just cleaned. He glanced up to see Anna standing in the doorway, hands on hips and a rueful smile on her face. "Gotta say one thing for you. When you help out you don't do it halfway. The barn looks better than I've seen it look in months. And the horses— Well, you're a miracle worker." She glanced at her watch questioningly. "How in the world did you manage it all?"

Jake smiled but shrugged it off. Amazing what an offer to give him some pointers on bronc riding had done for Luis's energy and enthusiasm for cleaning. "Just gave José and Luis some help. José seems to have his hands full around here."

"That's a fact," Anna agreed, walking inside and closing the door behind her. After hanging her coat on a hook, she picked up a cloth and a bit to polish. "And he works harder than anyone I know."

"No harder than you do," Jake said, aware of the hours she must put in to run a successful school on top of everything else she had on her plate. And judging by her horses, her students, and the facility, he knew she ran a good school.

She waved a hand in dismissal. "José and his wife are saving for a place of their own."

"What'll you do when they get it?"

Anna looked up and shuddered. "I try not to think about it. I guess I'll have to make do with temporary help. And José will still help me out whenever he can."

But she'd need new help, which was often hard to come by. High school kids weren't always dependable and most of the unattached men in the area worked the bigger ranches. Still, not much point worrying about something like that until it happened. "I take it you got Leigh settled. Is she all right?"

"She will be."

Anna looked tired, he thought, watching her rub the back of her neck before bending again to her task.

"It's just a sprain," she added with a heavy breath. "Thank goodness."

Jake walked over to her, reached into his back pocket and pulled out his wallet. "Here, before I forget, one of your students brought this check with him."

"Thanks." She laid the bit down and took the paper from him, glancing at it quickly before frowning. "Preston? Why did he leave me a check today? He pays by the lesson."

"Probably because he took a lesson."

She stared at him blankly for a moment. "Took a lesson? How?"

Jake didn't answer, he simply smiled at her.

"You—you taught my class?"

She looked as totally dumbstruck as she sounded. "Classes," he said, nodding. "Don't worry, I don't think I drove any of them off." Or so he hoped.

"I—I—" She stammered to a halt. "You didn't have to do that. Taking care of the horses and cleaning the barn was enough. More than enough. You didn't— I don't know how to rep—"

Uncomfortable with her gratitude, he interrupted. "Dad called and told me what happened. I had some free time, so I couldn't see any reason for you to have to cancel when I could hold the classes for you." He flashed her a grin. "You'll be happy to know you're in no danger of losing your students to me. The Nelson twins told me I wasn't nearly as good as you. Or as smart. Or as pretty."

She laughed. "You must have made them do something they didn't want to do."

"Yeah." Remembering their thunderstruck expressions, he chuckled. For some reason they'd confused him with an easy touch. "Mucking out stalls wasn't high on their list."

"No, it never is. They're great kids, but they're—"

"Hellions," he finished, drawing another laugh from her. It made him feel good to hear her laugh and to know he'd helped lighten her day.

"I won't argue that. Suzie maintains they were switched at birth with her own perfectly behaved angels." She rolled her eyes. "She's always threatening to switch them back."

"Good luck," Jake said, sharing another laugh with her.

"Well, it's nice to know I was missed. But seriously, Jake, you didn't need to—"

"Anna." He laid his fingers over her lips. "It's no big deal. Just a favor."

Their eyes met. Her mouth softened beneath his fingers, inviting him, enticing him. Her eyes darkened, deepening the green to pure jade. Desire. He read it plainly in her eyes, and as quick as lightning felt an answering tug in his groin. He didn't stop to think, didn't want to think. He wanted to taste her, needed to taste her, wanted to lose himself in the sweet forgetfulness of a kiss. His hand slid around to the back of her neck, drawing her nearer. He wondered if she'd pull away. Prayed she wouldn't. His other hand raised to her hair, to gently tug the rubber band loose and spread that mass of pale, pale silk over her shoulders.

She gasped softly, her lips parted, her tongue slipped out to moisten her lower lip, leaving it glistening…and unbelievably tempting. All the more erotic because he didn't believe she knew she was doing it.

When he touched his lips to hers she didn't struggle. Instead, she melted against him the minute their lips met. Her arms came around his neck and he pressed her closer, walking her backward until her back rested against the door to the small, cozy room.

He deepened the kiss, sweeping her mouth with his tongue while her tongue made teasing forays against his. She tasted sweet, so damn sweet, and she felt so good in his arms he didn't want to ever let go. And though he wanted to think that any woman would have felt the same, he knew it wasn't true. He knew he was holding Anna.

Her arms tightened and she moaned. A small sound, but he heard it and it notched the heat up even higher. He cupped her breast and groaned himself as her nipple beaded against his palm. Straining, she pressed her breast into his hand and he continued caressing her through the layers of cloth. His mouth sought the rapidly beating pulse at the hollow of her throat, and he breathed in her scent like a man dying for air. Sweet, spicy, feminine. Anna.

She tugged his head up and kissed him again, her mouth as wild and unruly as his. Jerking her shirt out of the waistband of her jeans, he slid his hand over bare, warm flesh, every bit as silky soft now as it had been all those years ago. His hand slipped inside her bra, his fingers rolling her nipple until she gave a strangled moan.

He wanted to make love to her, to be inside her, to feel that deep, hot glide into sex. He slid one hand over her denim-covered rear and pressed her against him, used the other to unfasten the buttons of her cotton shirt.

He heard a thud from beyond the door, but he didn't stop kissing her. When he heard it again he looked up, glancing around until he realized the sound came from a horse kicking its stall. And it would take a lot more than that to halt what was happening here. Her skin, so smooth and lovely, beckoned him and he lowered his head to her neck.

"Jake, wait."

Occupied in trailing kisses along her neck, cupping her sweet rear and drawing her even nearer, her shaky plea barely registered. "Ignore it," he said huskily, spreading her shirt open and stroking her breast through her plain white cotton bra. "It's just a horse kicking."

She repeated her plea, stronger this time. "Stop." Her voice was breathless, but very clear. And those sure as hell weren't the words he wanted to hear.

His arms still holding her—hell, supporting her—he drew back and stared at her. "Anna—"

She pushed at his chest, her breath coming fast and uneven. "Don't. I—I can't do this."

He let her go, slowly, and stepped back. He should have known it was too good to be true.

"I'm sorry," she said, her hands shaking as she fumbled to refasten her buttons. "I know I encouraged you to think that I wanted— I'm sorry."

It gave him a small consolation to know she was still affected, but it didn't make up much for the raging ache of frustration he felt just then.

"This is—this is going way too quickly for me."

And not nearly quick enough for him. "You were enthusiastic enough a minute ago."

"I know." She wouldn't look at him, but finished straightening her clothes. "Let's just say I came to my senses."

Before it was too late, he knew she was thinking. *You're rushing her, Jake,* he told himself, jamming his hands in his back pockets to keep from punching the wall. Don't rush your fences, he'd always been told. Except Anna wasn't a fence. She was a warm,

sexy woman who a few minutes ago had been kissing him mindless.

But nothing would happen now and there was no
point in being angry with her. Hell, he didn't blame
her. Much. Maybe he was going too fast. It cost him,
but he managed a grin. "Whatever you say. But
you'll be sorry in the morning."

"Part of me is sorry right now," she said, surprising him with her confession. "But, Jake, you
have to admit, we can't just take up where we left
off."

He gave that a moment's thought, but for the life
of him couldn't see her point. "Why not?"

"Because I'm not sure I want to, for one thing,"
she snapped, regaining her customary sharp tongue.

He arched an eyebrow and gave her a sardonic
smile. "That's not what it seemed like a few
minutes ago."

"I realize that. Just because I'm—I'm attracted to
you doesn't mean I have to act on it." He said nothing, waiting to see what else she'd say. "Besides,
there's still too much between us. Too much anger,
too much hurt. We haven't worked through it."

"Do you want to work through it, Anna?" Did
she want to bury the past? Or did she plan to use it
to keep him at arm's length? Where he couldn't hurt
her. Where he could never acknowledge his child.

She looked him in the eye. "Yes. I do." She
paused, then added, "I think we need to—to at least
come to terms with our past if we're ever going to
move on."

He took a seat, crossed his arms over his chest

and leaned back in the chair. "You got ideas on how we do this, then? Work through our past, I mean?"

"Well—" She took a turn around the room, before halting in front of him. Hands on hips, she stared at him for a silent, unblinking moment.

"You could start by telling me how the hell you managed to marry another woman when you were engaged to me."

CHAPTER TEN

JAKE WINCED. Anna never pulled her punches. "Ouch," he said, rubbing a hand over his heart.

"And while you're at it," she said, the glare spilling from her eyes cold enough to freeze hell, "you can tell me why the first I heard that you'd fallen in love with another woman was when you called me up out of the blue and told me you were married."

"I didn't exactly fall in love with her," he said before he thought. *Oh, good, Jake. Great response.* Frequently the truth made a lousy answer.

"Oh, excuse me, how silly of me to think you might have loved the woman you married," she said, the sarcasm dripping off her tongue. "Then tell me, Jake, why did you marry her?"

Because Cookie had orchestrated it that way, although that wasn't the whole story. Remembering how she'd spent the weeks before the finals playing him like a lassoed calf, he shuddered at his youthful stupidity. Anna wouldn't believe it, but he'd stayed faithful to her—and Cookie had taken that as a personal challenge. He admitted he'd been tempted, really tempted. Cookie had been gorgeous and very, very willing. He'd managed to resist her, though, until that one night. The night of the finals, when he'd won and the two of them had gone out celebrating.

But much as he wanted to, he couldn't blame everything on her. "Cookie was—"

"Cookie? Her name was *Cookie?*" Anna's voice rose on the last word and she stared at him in utter disbelief. "Oh, my God. I can't believe this! You left me for a woman named after a snack?"

"It was a nickname." He squirmed uncomfortably in his chair. "Hell, Anna, I can't help her name."

"No, I guess you can't. I suppose you're going to tell me you couldn't help *yourself,* either."

"I could have stopped it." Except he'd been too drunk to pay much attention. He raked a hand through his hair and rose to pace the small room. "Would it make you feel better if I told you I got what was coming to me?"

A corner of her mouth lifted. "Maybe."

"The marriage was a disaster from the get-go."

"No wonder. If you didn't love her—"

"Love her?" He shook his head, remembering the arguments, the lies, Cookie's spending habits, and most of all, her predilection for sleeping with every male between the ages of eighteen and eighty regardless of her marriage vows. "Honey, I didn't even like her. She was headline news, all of it bad."

"Why did you do it, then? Were you that desperate to get away from me?"

The tremor in her voice cut straight to his heart. He started to reach out to her, then realized she'd hardly be in a mood to be comforted by him. "Anna, it wasn't like that. It was never you. The marriage just—just happened.''

"How?'' She fisted her hands on her hips and stared at him. "I don't understand how something like that, how a *marriage,* can just happen.''

His mouth tightened into a grim line. "It's pretty simple. I got drunk, got stupid, got married. Hell, I could barely remember anything when I woke up the next day.'' But he sure as shooting remembered the cloying, suffocating feel of Cookie, wrapped around him like a bad dream. "I thought I was having a nightmare.''

"You weren't the only one,'' Anna muttered, taking a seat in one of the folding chairs. She crossed her legs at the ankles, crossed her arms and leveled a long look at him. "So what happened after that?''

He took a chair, straddled it and faced Anna, prepared to tell her the rest of it. The sleazy, ugly truth of it. "We had a difference of opinion. A major one.''

"Over what?''

His mouth twisted into a wry smile. "Cookie didn't believe in limiting herself to one man. Even if he was her husband. Or maybe especially if he was her husband. By the time we'd been married three months she'd slept with all my enemies and most of my friends.'' Not to mention every other male who drifted within her orbit.

"I called her on it.'' He shrugged, long past the hurt that had caused him. "Hell, she didn't give a flip. She'd married me on a whim and she regretted it every bit as much as I did. She thought it would be fun to be married to the reigning World Champion bronc rider. Fun.'' He laughed harshly. ''I guess she found out different. She walked out, cleaned out my pockets and my bank accounts on her way, and I never saw her again. We divorced through the mail.''

For a moment, Anna didn't speak. ''It was bad,'' she finally said.

''Oh, yeah. I'd say that's an understatement.'' Bad enough that he'd never been tempted since. At least not to get married. ''I can't blame everything on her. I was no prize, either.'' Beginning his marriage while in love with another woman hadn't exactly been a smooth move. Still, he'd been faithful to his wife.

Whether he would have remained faithful if they had stayed together... He doubted it seriously. He'd been too young, too full of himself, and most of all, he hadn't loved her. But none of that mattered now. Cookie had been a mistake, the worst he'd ever made. Long gone and unlamented. But she'd taught him a few good lessons.

Still frowning, Anna gazed at him. ''What kind of friends did you have that they'd sleep with your wife?''

''Easy come, easy go. And Cookie was hard to refuse, at least until you got to know her. Had a body that just wouldn't quit. Her b—'' Recalling who he was talking to, he halted. ''Never mind.''

''Good stop,'' she said.

He thought he caught a glimpse of a smile, but couldn't be sure. ''After we divorced I thought about calling you. But I didn't figure you'd speak to me. And if you did, I knew it sure as hell wouldn't be anything I'd want to hear. Not after what I'd done. I didn't find out until a couple of years later that you'd married Carl." And he didn't know until much later that she'd also had a child. Which was why he'd never connected Anna's child with their affair. Until he'd seen Leigh.

"Your father didn't tell you?"

Jake laughed humorlessly and shook his head. "Nope. He made it real clear he had no use for me after I told him about Las Vegas and the marriage. I didn't talk to him again for two years. Figured it would suit us both better that way." Remembering, he glanced away for a minute. "Hell, it could have been pure cowardice. I didn't want to hear what he had to say, either."

He rose to stand close to her. "Anna, I did a lousy thing, a stupid thing, all those years ago. Leaving you like I did, calling you... Just because I didn't know how to break it to you doesn't make it any less wrong. No one, least of all me, is going to deny that. But I can't change it, either. It happened. There's nothing either of us can do about it now."

She didn't look satisfied. But he couldn't help that; he'd bared his damn soul to her. He decided he'd opened up enough. Especially when Anna had some explaining of her own to do.

"What about you, Anna? Are you going to tell me how you came to marry Carl within—what?—a week after I supposedly broke your heart? I'd say your heart mends awful quick."

She flushed but answered him steadily. "You don't know a damn thing about it."

They stared at each other a long moment. She wouldn't bend, but neither would he.

"Tell me why you married Carl," he repeated.

The phone rang. Jake cursed when Anna sprang to answer it.

"What?" she said, clutching the receiver like a lifeline. "Yes, I'll be there in a minute."

A moment later she hung up and turned to him. "It's Leigh. She needs my help. I've got to go in now."

"Saved by the proverbial bell," he said, his jaw hardening. "Darlin', you've got the luck of the devil."

She tossed her hair out of her face and after fishing around in her pockets, slipped a rubber band around it. "I don't know what you're talking about."

"Oh, yes, you do." Snagging her arm before she could run off, he drew her near. Resistant at first, after a moment she allowed it. He used one hand to tilt her face up, looking deep into those jade-green eyes that sometimes hid so much of what she felt. "We're not finished with this, Anna. Nowhere near. Not with this—" He kissed her then, slow and deep, intent on giving her something to think about. Something to remember. "Not with anything," he added.

OVER THE NEXT couple of weeks, Jake learned a few things. About patience. About frustration. About wanting what was best for someone else—even if it meant you wouldn't get what you wanted any time soon.

Stopping by Anna's almost daily didn't help him

overcome his obsession with Leigh, either. It only made him angrier that he'd missed so much of her life. Angry at Anna, but more than that, angry at himself for wasting all those years. Years he might have spent with his daughter. Years he might have spent…with Anna?

Anna. Oh, man, Anna. She drew him every bit as much as the prospect of seeing his daughter. When had she become so fascinating? How had he managed to let her get to him again? He was supposed to be the one in charge here, yet Anna held every card.

Including the knowledge of his daughter's true parentage.

He strolled through the barn without seeing Anna or Leigh, ending as he usually did, in front of Sugar's stall. Sugar was as sweet a mare as he'd ever seen and he'd been toying with the idea of buying her from Anna from the minute he saw her. He had a feeling Anna wouldn't let her go cheaply, either. Especially not to him. He leaned his forearms on the top of the door and laughed as the mare nuzzled him, seeking food.

The dun mare was no dummy. She'd figured out after a couple of visits that Jake nearly always brought a treat with him.

He heard a noise and turned his head to see Leigh hobble into the barn. "You about sick of those crutches?"

She stopped and made a gagging motion with her finger. "One more week," she said, continuing toward him. "I still won't get to do all my jumps, though."

"Jumps?" he asked, thinking of horses before the answer occurred to him. "Oh, cheerleader stuff?"

"Yeah." Leaning her crutches against the stall door, she searched her pockets while rubbing the mare's nose but she came up empty. "Sorry, Sugar. No sugar today," she said and smiled when the horse blew out her breath in something like a huff. "And basketball season is nearly over. It really sucks that I had to wreck my ankle now."

"Cheer up. At least you'll be okay by the rodeo."

"That's true," Leigh said, brightening. "It's going to be totally awesome, isn't it?"

"I hope so," he said, breaking a carrot in two and handing half to Leigh. "Tell me something, Leigh. Did you and your Mom raise this mare from a foal?"

"Sugar?" She glanced at him after letting the mare have the carrot. "Yeah, we sure did. I was there when she was born and Mom let me name her. Why?"

He smiled. "Oh, no reason."

She stared at him a minute before her eyes narrowed in exact imitation of one of her mother's sharp-eyed glances. Her eyes might be the color of his, but their expression favored Anna more than him. "You want to buy her, don't you? For your horse farm."

"Me?" Carefully hiding his smile, he shook his head. "Nah. What would I want with this broken down old nag?"

Leigh fired up so fast it was comical. "She is not a nag! She's one of the best quarter—" She cut herself off and punched him in the arm as he laughed. "You—you—I can't believe I fell for that!"

"What's so funny?" Anna asked, entering the barn and looking at them suspiciously.

Whenever she came upon him with her daughter she looked just like that. Just what did she think he planned on doing? Blurt out the truth to Leigh before he was absolutely sure? Besides, it was Anna's place to tell Leigh. If and when she ever decided to come clean.

"Jake wants—" Leigh began before Jake cut her off.

"Jake wants to talk to your Mom about it," he told Leigh. "Okay?"

"Oh, sure. I've got to go do my homework, anyway." She waved before grabbing her crutches and making off surprisingly quickly. "Bye, Mom. See ya later, Jake."

"How does she do that?" he said, watching her go. "I never could make the stupid things move in sequence."

"Practice," Anna said dryly. "She's accident prone. I can't count the number of times she's used them." She stared after Leigh for a moment before glancing back at him. "What did you want to talk to me about? And isn't this the fourth time this week you've come over?"

Fifth, but who was counting? "It's about Sugar."

"My mare?" she said, glancing into the stall. "Well, what about her?"

"Would you be willing to part with her? I'd like to buy her." He grinned at the assessing expression that came over her face.

"Well, now, that depends on your offer." She looked him up and down before crossing her arms over her chest and leaning back against the stall door, one boot sole flat against it. "Whatever price you're thinking, double it." She waited a beat and added, "And I want the second foal."

"What?" The demand wiped his complacence clean out of him. "You've got an inflated opinion of that mare's worth, sweetheart."

She lifted a shoulder. "Says you. No skin off my nose. You're the one wanting to buy. I'm merely the one with the mare to sell. A mare with impeccable bloodlines, I might add." She studied her fingernails and shot him a grin, her eyes sparkling with audacity.

"Robber."

"I'm practically giving her away. Call me sentimental."

"Sentimental, my foot. Cutthroat is more like it."

Eventually they settled on a price satisfactory to both of them, but as he'd suspected he hadn't gotten her for a song.

"When do you want her?" Anna asked. "She's just coming out of heat."

"No reason to move her yet. I'll just pay you to board her until I get set up at my own place."

"Okay, whenever you're ready. Are you having any luck finding a place?"

"Nope. Every place I've seen has some kind of problem." Except his dad's place. And lately his father had been talking about scaling back his cattle operation. It remained a faint possibility that he

might be interested in selling off some of his land.
To the right buyer.

And Jake knew the perfect prospect. He wondered
what Anna would say if she knew she might have
a new neighbor soon. And that her new neighbor
just might be a man she didn't trust as far as she
could throw a twelve-hundred-pound gelding.

CHAPTER ELEVEN

A WEEK LATER, Leigh was almost back to normal. Though she still limped a little and had to brace her weak ankle during sports, Anna thought she'd be fully recovered in another ten days at most. On Saturday, Anna took her to the feed store twenty miles away, figuring if Leigh could go to cheerleader practice, ride her horse and do everything else that she wanted, then she could help with the chores again. Besides, if Anna didn't take her, Leigh would likely hotfoot it over to the Rollins place the instant she drove off.

Not particularly pleased with her mother's edict, Leigh buried her nose in a book the minute they climbed in the truck and read all the way back to Happy. Which didn't bother Anna in the least. She used the time to reflect on her responsibilities for the upcoming rodeo and all the things she had yet to do. Unfortunately, thoughts of the rodeo invariably led to thoughts of Jake.

Lately everything led her to thoughts of Jake. And Jake's influence with her daughter. It didn't seem to matter what she did, or how many spokes she tried to thrust into his wheel——Leigh and Jake grew closer by the day. Her daughter's conversations were liberally sprinkled with "Jake says" or "Mr. Rollins does it this way'' or any of a thousand references to the two men. Worse, Leigh saw no reason Anna shouldn't be thrilled with the Rollins men and, noticing her mother's restraint where Jake was concerned, continually nagged at her to ''give Jake a break.''

She'd like to give him a break, all right, but not the kind Leigh meant. The sneaky rat! Instead of pressuring her—or even reminding her—about her outrageous lapse of judgment the night of Leigh's accident, the creep had backed off and given her all the room in the world. He treated her almost like he would his granny. Almost.

But his eyes gave him away. The scorching looks he sent her were anything but filial.

Even if she hadn't caught his gaze on her too many times to count, she knew he watched her. She felt it in her bones, in her soul. Instead of irritating her as it should have, that intense gaze of his intrigued her...made her restless...made her edgy. It made her remember things she had no business remembering.

No matter how hard Anna tried, Jake occupied a disturbingly large portion of her waking moments. Worse, he played a starring role in most of her dreams. Feelings—forgotten feelings—bubbled up and threatened to overflow if she didn't do something about them. It didn't matter how often she told herself she didn't need a man and if she did, it sure as heck wouldn't be Jake. She was kidding herself. She wanted Jake, at least on a physical level.

Yet wanting him physically wasn't the major problem. No, she could deal with the physical needs, or understand them, at least. But what had her running scared was wanting him on another level, too.

An emotional level.

Oh, why had she ever let him kiss her again? Everything had started going to hell in a handbasket the minute he'd kissed her on the dance floor. Which had eventually led to that scene in her barn the night of Leigh's accident.

Don't go there, she warned herself, but she did regardless. Thank God she'd come to her senses before she'd let things progress further.

But a part of her wished, quite badly, that they hadn't stopped when they did.

As she exited the highway and approached Happy, Leigh pulled her head up out of the book she'd been reading. "Hey, Mom, there's something I want to ask you."

Mentally thanking Leigh for distracting her from her unwelcome thoughts, she answered. "Shoot. And before you ask, no you can't go with a date to the dance, you'll have to go with all your friends." She'd sworn long ago that Leigh wouldn't date until she turned sixteen. Fortunately, the majority of her friends' parents felt the same way.

"It's not about that, but I still don't see—"

"Leigh, we've discussed this before."

"But—" She huffed out a sigh but changed the subject. "Oh, okay. That wasn't what I was gonna ask anyway. Mom, what happened to the frown?"

Totally lost, Anna glanced at her. "What frown?"

"The one on the sign," Leigh said, pointing to the billboard gracing Happy's main street. "'Wel-

come to Happy, Texas, the town without,'" she
read.

"Some of the kids were talking about it the other
day at school. It used to say 'the town without a
frown.' Everybody's heard rumors, but nobody
knows for sure what happened to the frown."

Caught off guard, Anna drew in a breath. Playing
for time she asked, "Any guesses?"

"Sure. Aliens took it." They both laughed at that.
"But the main one is that it got bored and left."

Anna smiled at that one. "Sounds like the same
rumors I heard. Why do you think I'd know anything about it?"

"Mrs. Gallick said so. We were talking about it
in English class and she said I should ask you."

Stifling another laugh, Anna turned it into a weak
cough. "Mary said that?"

"Uh-huh." Finger in her book holding her place,
she turned in the seat toward her. "Did you take the
frown, Mom?"

Considering, Anna bit her lip. Might as well tell
her. It wasn't the worst thing she'd ever done, after
all. Her part in it had been fairly benign. "No, but
I was there when it, er, mysteriously disappeared."
Which she hadn't realized Mary knew. She should
have, though. Mary had always known what was
going on with the high school kids. "If I tell you,
though, it stays between you and me."

"Sure, Mom." She held up her little finger.
"Want me to pinkie swear?" she asked with a grin,
referring to her childhood practice of sealing a pact.

"I'll take your word for it," Anna told her. "It

happened at graduation, your father's senior year of high school.''

Leigh's eyes rounded as she stared at her. ''You mean *Dad?* Dad took it? No way.''

Anna laughed at the disbelief in Leigh's voice. She couldn't blame her. It was the only time she could remember Carl ever doing something wild and crazy. Other than marrying her. ''Yep. Your dad. Only he had help. Jake conned him into it.'' She never had figured out how.

''Really? So you and Dad and Jake were all friends?''

''Yes. They were a year ahead of me. Our school was pretty small at the time. Everyone knew everyone else.''

''That hasn't changed much,'' Leigh said dryly. ''Even the people you can't stand, there's no way to avoid them. So Dad and Jake took the frown? Why?''

Anna lifted a shoulder as she pulled into the drive. ''I don't really know. Jake just decided they needed to leave their mark on the town.'' They'd been drinking beer, she remembered. Well, she hadn't— she'd been driving—but Carl and Jake had both had a couple. Yet another thing that had been unlike Carl that night. He wasn't one of the wild ones, even though Jake and he were best friends and Jake was always getting into trouble.

No, Jake hadn't been the surprise, but Carl... He never did crazy things. How they had managed to succeed without killing themselves was beyond her. Anna remembered watching the two of them up on that billboard and laughing until she nearly wet her pants. All the while hoping the chief of police didn't take it into his head to check out the town limits. Fortunately, he'd been occupied on the main drag. Somebody had wrecked their father's pickup—pretty hard to do considering at the time the drag had only consisted of the half-mile strip of asphalt through the center of town.

"That doesn't sound like Dad."

"It wasn't. Usually he talked Jake out of stunts like that."

"So did Jake do that kind of stuff all the time?"

"Not really. Well, sometimes. But he never did anything really terrible." Except break her heart, she thought, but that wasn't illegal.

"He's not like that anymore, is he?"

"No," she said slowly, realizing it was true. "I guess he grew up. We all did."

Leigh put her book down and squirmed in her seat, getting comfortable. "Did you go out with Jake before you and Dad got together?"

Uh-oh. Treacherous ground. "Why the sudden interest in ancient history, Leigh?"

"Just wondering."

She sounded a little too innocent for Anna's comfort. "Jake and I went out a few times," she said carefully.

"But somebody said—"

"Look, honey, we'll have to talk about this later. I don't have time now." And she'd try like crazy to avoid the topic in the future. Thank the Lord they were home. She turned the truck off and said, "Find Luis or José and tell them I need a hand with the feed."

Through the window, Anna watched Leigh walk off. How long would it be before she heard more rumors about her mother and the man who was rapidly becoming her idol? How much longer before Jake himself forced the issue?

She pressed her eyes closed and faced facts. How much longer before she would have to tell her daughter that she'd lied to her all her life? And what would Leigh do when she found out?

Anna had a dismal feeling she wouldn't like any of the answers.

SATURDAY AFTERNOON a week later, most of the town had gathered at the old rodeo grounds to clean up, paint the corral, and repair the stands and chutes.

Leigh dipped a brush into a can of red paint and carefully swiped it over the corral rail. She had wanted to help the welder, but all the parents had screamed about their babies getting anywhere near the flame. Except the guys who took shop. *They* got to do whatever they wanted, Leigh thought resentfully.

Painting wasn't bad, though, especially since it put her next to Danny Williams, who she'd liked since the seventh grade. Too bad Lydia Morrow, his girlfriend, had decided to show up. Danny never had figured out that Lydia only liked him because he was a jock.

"Hey, Leigh," Blaire said, dripping a blob of paint onto Leigh's arm, "did you ever find out about the frown?"

"Blaire, you almost got that on my hair. Watch what you're doing."

"We have turpentine, you know. Chill, Leigh," Blaire said. "Well, did you ask your Mom like you said you would?"

"Yeah."

"And?"

"She told me I couldn't tell anyone."

Blaire stared at her and blinked. "But I'm not just anyone. I'm your best friend."

True. Surely Mom hadn't meant she couldn't talk to Blaire about it. "Well—" She looked around to make sure no one else was listening but the only people near enough to hear were Danny and his buddies. And they were all drooling and watching Lydia jiggle across the corral.

"What do they see in her?" she muttered, setting her brush aside.

"Who? Oh, Lydia. It's simple." Blaire gestured with her brush, spraying paint again liberally. She was starting to look like somebody with chicken pox. "A chest."

Leigh snorted. "She's so disgusting. And why are the guys so...so lame? It's not like none of the rest of us have a chest."

"Not like hers," Blaire said, resigned. "C'mon, Leigh, tell me what happened."

She quit torturing herself with watching Danny and grinned at her friend. "My dad and Jake took it."

Blaire's eyes widened. "You're kidding! When?"

"Ages ago. When they were in high school. Weird, huh?"

"No joke. How come your Mom knows?"

"She was there."

"Your Mom? No way. I'd have never thought she would do something like that. Now my Mom..." She rolled her eyes and her voice trailed off. They both laughed.

"Yeah, it's pretty funny," Leigh agreed.

They looked over at her mother, working beside Jake. Blaire said, "Do you think they like, *like* each other?"

"Who?" She stared at Blaire, then at her mother. "You mean Mom and Jake?"

"Well, yeah. I think he likes her. He's always real nice to her whenever I see them around each other. He looks at her a lot. And smiles. And your Mom smiles, too, only not so much when he's looking at her."

Leigh shifted uncomfortably. She hadn't thought about it that much. Well, maybe a little. Especially since she'd heard rumors that they used to be a thing. But her mom hadn't answered her questions about that. Not really, anyway. "I don't know. She's always telling me not to hang around the Rollinses too much, like she has something against them. Besides, aren't they kind of old for, well, *that?*"

"Your mom's not that old. And neither is he," Blaire added with a sigh, staring at Jake. Frowning, she looked at Leigh. "What's wrong? I thought you liked Jake?"

"I do." She glanced at him, saw him hand something to her mother. And smile. A flirty smile. Oh, wow, maybe Blaire was right. "It's just...I don't know, weird. Ya know? She's my Mom."

"Yeah, I guess," Blaire said, and dropped the subject.

But Leigh thought about it afterward for a long, long time.

NOT CERTAIN how it happened, Anna ended up working side by side with Jake late in the afternoon. They didn't talk a lot at first, beyond a few requests for a hammer or a nail. Music blared in the background, the kids having brought a couple of boom boxes with them and then tuning them to the same station. Constant noise. In stereo, yet, Anna thought. Now, toward dusk, she had a nagging headache and wished for nothing as much as blessed silence.

"What is that?" Jake asked.

"What?" She looked up to see him staring at the nearest boom box. "You mean the music?"

"Yeah." He took a nail out of his mouth and asked, "Who is that singing? Or should I say what?"

Anna tilted her head, straining to distinguish the lyrics or the voices. "Smashing Pumpkins, I think. It's pretty old, don't you listen to the radio?"

"I'm a country-and-western man, darlin'," he drawled, getting a laugh from her. "Didn't you know that?" He shot the nail home and grinned at her.

She stared a moment, caught by the dimple on his right cheek. "I thought you might have broadened your music appreciation in all these years."

"I have. I like some old rock and roll, too. Creedence Clearwater's not too bad."

"Ah, progress," she teased.

"Okay, who's that?" he asked when a new song came on.

"Jewel," she answered absently, concentrating on sinking the nail into the wooden seat without banging her thumb. Unused to carpentry, her hands had about had it for the day. "A girl from Alaska, I think."

"How come you know so much about pop music?"

She shrugged and stretched to get the kinks out of her back. "I don't, really. But it's kind of hard to avoid when you live with a teenager."

He gave her a long level look. "I wouldn't know about that," he said before turning back to his work.

Anna bit her lip and swung away, reaching blindly for another nail. Knowing he intended just the reaction she'd given didn't make her feel any better. Why did she allow him to make her feel bad? He had chosen to leave all those years ago, not her. Jake Rollins wasn't blameless here.

But neither was she. The fact remained that she was still keeping something—someone—very important from him. His daughter. His flesh and blood.

"Jake—" she began. He looked up, lifting an eyebrow in inquiry. "Do you want to get something to eat afterward?" As if a dinner invitation would make up for her continued silence? Well, it was the best she could do at the moment. She held her breath, waiting for him to blast her.

"Sure. Sounds good."

There he went again, she thought, her eyebrows drawing together in a frown. Being nice when she'd expected anything but. He was doing it on purpose, dammit. Confusing her. Softening her up.

Making her want him.

She stalked off, careful not to come near him again until much later. After giving herself several lectures.

"Ride with me?" he asked, shoving his hat back on his head and smiling at her in a way that sent her reeling back into the past.

The lectures hadn't done a bit of good.

"Is Leigh going with us?"

Anna shook her head. "No, she's already left with Blaire. She's spending the night out."

"All right. I'll bring you back here after dinner to pick up your truck."

Get a grip, she told herself. *It's no big deal.* "Okay. What do you want to eat?"

"I'm starved. How about the diner?"

As the only place in Happy that served a complete meal, Helga's Diner bulged to its limit when they arrived. Helga, a bad-tempered old woman who had delighted in tormenting her help, and often her customers, had long since passed on. But the diner remained to this day, as much a landmark as the frownless welcome sign leading into town or the railroad tracks through the center that had once made Happy a hub of commerce and activity.

Déjà vu, Anna thought again as Jake held the door for her and she stepped inside. Helga's had been one of their hangouts as kids, and it was still the local high school hangout. The only thing that had changed were the machines in a cubby off the main room. Pinball in her day, now mostly replaced with video games. She saw her daughter and several of her friends and waved. "Maybe this wasn't such a good idea,'' she said as a booth miraculously opened up.

"Why?'' He waited until she slid into the red vinyl booth to slide in opposite her. "It's just dinner.''

Her hand gestured, motioning at the other customers. "You, me. Together. Here. It's going to cause talk, just wait.'' She plucked a yellowed menu from behind the chrome napkin dispenser and opened it, even though she knew the choices by heart. "You're the local celebrity come home and I'm—''

"The prettiest woman in town,'' he finished, just as the waitress walked up.

Oh, great, Anna thought, flushing. Blabbermouth Brenda, the biggest gossip in town. And judging by the sour smile the woman favored her with, she'd definitely heard Jake's comment.

"Hi, Jake,'' she cooed, fluttering long, fake lashes and flipping a swath of improbably platinum-blond hair over her shoulder. Brenda never had paid much attention to the health codes. "Long time no see.''

"I was in here last week, Brenda,'' he said, not looking up as he scanned the menu, apparently oblivious to her attempt to capture his interest. "Remember? You waited on me then, too.''

Brenda's come-hither smile grew a bit pinched. "Oh, well, yeah, but…'' Her voice trailed off and she turned to Anna with a vengeful stare. "You ready to order?''

Anna hid a triumphant grin. Sweet revenge. Brenda had held a grudge against her since high school, when Anna beat her out for head cheerleader. "Hamburger and French fries. And a Diet Coke."

Jake ordered a cheeseburger and milk and Brenda left, thwarted once again.

"Do you still drink a half gallon of milk or more a day?" Anna asked him.

"Sometimes." He glanced at her curiously. "Why?"

"That's how the grapevine knew you'd arrived home. Your dad bought extra milk and Becky spread the word."

His expression turned to one of disgust. "Some of these people need to get a life."

"They have one," she said, laughing. "And gossip is one of its high points."

He grunted but otherwise didn't respond, reminding her of his father. She eyed him consideringly from beneath her lashes and changed the subject. "You weren't very friendly a minute ago, Jake. Why is that?"

He shot her a dirty look. "Because I don't have any interest in being Brenda's flavor of the week, that's why." Leaning back in his chair, he crossed his boots at the ankles. "I remember her from high school."

"Maybe she's changed," Anna said blandly. "People do."

"Some people," he said, taking a drink of water. "She hasn't."

True, but she wondered how he'd found out so quickly. "She's been lonely since her divorce."

"Yeah, right. Brenda is a piranha. Can we talk about something else?"

She laughed and let the subject drop. "Is that your father and Mary Gallick over there?" she asked, motioning at a table in the corner.

"Yep." He glanced at them and smiled. "I'll let you in on a secret. I think I may be getting a new stepmama."

"Really? I've seen them together lately, but do you think they're that serious?"

Jake nodded. "Oh, yeah. He's practically living at her house. Comes home to sleep and work, but that's about it. I've never seen him like this. Not even with my mother."

"Does it bother you?"

"No." He looked surprised. "Why should it? I like Mary. I think she's good for him. For both of us. He's been a lot more mellow than I remember. Could be Mary has something to do with that."

"Still," she said, thinking of Leigh and her reaction if Anna were to ever… "What about your mother?"

"Anna, she's been gone for seventeen years. It's past time for him to move on with his life. She wouldn't have wanted him to be alone forever."

Somehow, Anna thought as their food arrived, she didn't think Leigh would be quite so understanding. Not that it mattered, since she had no intention of remarrying.

After dinner Jake took her back to her truck, turned off his own and killed the lights. "What's your rush?" he asked as she put her hand on the door handle.

"No rush. I just need to get home." Before he brought up something she didn't want to discuss.

He put a hand on her arm, not restraining her, just letting her know it was there. "You said Leigh was gone for the night."

Swallowing hard, Anna nodded.

"It's time we talked."

"I don't think we need—"

"Anna, it's time."

Though he removed his hand, she still felt the pull, the force of his personality pinning her like a dead bug to a science project board. Time was running out faster than she'd believed possible. And she wasn't ready for the truth. Didn't know if she ever would be ready to tell Jake—and Leigh—the truth.

"Wh-what do you want to talk about?" she finally asked, knowing what he would ask her. Dreading the answer.

He shook his head and smiled, but his smile wasn't happy. "Why did you marry Carl, Anna?"

CHAPTER TWELVE

WHY DID you marry Carl? The question echoed in her mind, numbing it, making clear thought impossible. Even expecting it, it still destroyed her. "I— I loved him."

"Try again," Jake said, his gaze flickering over her in disgust. "That one won't fly."

"How dare you say that to me? I did love Carl."

"Bull. Maybe you loved him later, but you know damn well you were in love with me. Yet you married Carl a bare week after I called you. I want to know why."

Her heart twisted. *Forgive me, Carl. I can't tell him the truth, I can't.* "It—I—I married him on the rebound," she whispered, hot tears squeezing between her eyelids, tracking slowly down her cheeks.

"I don't think so."

Taking refuge in anger, she turned to face him. "Then you tell me, Jake, since you know everything. Why did I marry him?"

He looked her straight in the eye and his voice sounded cold, deliberate, as bitter as a grim winter wind. "You married Carl because you were pregnant. With Leigh. With my child."

"No." Her breath caught in her throat; she felt like retching and barely stopped herself from wrapping a protective arm around her stomach. "No. You're wrong."

"Goddammit, Anna!" He slammed his fist down on the center of the steering wheel. "Don't lie to me. Not anymore. I know Leigh is my daughter. My God, I see it every time I look at her. I feel it, in my soul."

"I can't help what you feel. I can see how you might think that—"

"Stop it, Anna. Tell me the truth. Is Leigh mine?"

He looked more vulnerable than she'd ever seen him, or even imagined he could be. And she couldn't let it matter. Nothing mattered now. Nothing except Leigh.

"No." The word came out strong, clear—and a lie. Protecting her daughter shouldn't have shamed her, shouldn't have swept her with a dark surge of unbearable guilt, yet it did. But she couldn't risk it, couldn't put Jake's need for the truth above her daughter's welfare.

"The truth," he repeated. "For once, just tell me the truth. I'm asking—no, I'm begging you to tell me. Tell me that Leigh is mine."

"The truth," she said, hardening her heart to the plea in his words, in his eyes, "is that Carl was her father. And you have no right, no right at all, to ask me that question."

"Don't I?" His jaw tightened, his lips thinned. His anger singed the air, wrapped slivers of grief around her heart. "I have every right. And you know it, or you wouldn't be so scared you can't see straight."

Scared? Of course she was scared! Jake was ripping her apart again, sixteen years after he'd done it the first time. She didn't answer—there was no answer.

And he didn't quit. "Was Carl her biological father?"

Dammit! Her hands curled into fists of impotent despair. Why couldn't he let it go? She didn't want to lie again, but he forced her into it. For Leigh, to keep her daughter safe, she could do anything. Furious, ashamed, she lifted her chin and glared at him, daring him to call her a liar.

"Carl was her father. In every way."

They stared at each other as the seconds ticked by. Finally he said, fury and disgust throbbing in his voice, "I never thought of you as a coward, Anna. But that's exactly what you are."

Anna didn't wait for any more. She fled the truck. But she couldn't escape her guilt.

THE LAST PERSON Anna expected to see when she reached home was her daughter. But Suzie's pickup parked in the drive meant she'd brought the girls over. Obviously, Leigh had forgotten something. Flipping on the interior light, Anna checked her face in the rearview mirror. Well, she wouldn't fool Suzie's laser eyes, but she doubted if Leigh could tell she'd been crying.

She let herself in the kitchen and found her friend leafing through a magazine and the girls nowhere in sight. "What did she forget?" she asked Suzie, laying her keys on the countertop.

Suzie glanced up and grinned. "Her dress for

church. And I swear, I told them at least four times we were going to church tomorrow.''

"She probably had something with her but decided it wouldn't do after she got to your house,'' Anna said, averting her face just a little.

"You know, I bet you're right. They'd been in Blaire's room for a while and out of the blue they decided they had to come back here.'' Peering at her sharply, Suzie said, "Okay, enough small talk. What's wrong with you?''

Her shoulders sagged. ''Is it that obvious?''

"You may cry pretty, Anna, which by the way, I find incredibly annoying, but I can still tell when you've been crying.''

Anna went to the sink and splashed cool water on her face, particularly her eyes. Grabbing a clean dish towel, she patted her face dry and turned around to show her friend. "There, is that any better?''

Suzie pursed her lips. "Good enough for Leigh. But you didn't answer my question. What's the matter? Is it Jake?''

"Why do you automatically assume it's him?'' She took the seat across from Suzie. ''And keep your voice down. I don't want Leigh to hear.''

Suzie waved a languid hand in the direction of Leigh's room. "Those two wouldn't hear a bomb detonate. Not when they're playing the radio so loudly. Anyway, I assume it's Jake because I saw you two together tonight. But you looked like you were getting along just fine when I saw you.''

"We were. Until he brought up you know what.'' Despairing, she smacked her fist down on the table. "He's tired of waiting for me to confirm his suspicions. He's going to force the issue and I don't know what to do.''

"So you put him off?'' Suzie laid her magazine down and steepled her fingers together, elbows on the table. ''And I'm guessing he didn't like it.''

Anna's laugh held no humor. "I flat out lied to him. He's furious with me.'' And she couldn't really blame him.

"Look, I don't mean to sound flippant, but have you considered just telling the man the truth? It's bound to come out sooner or later. You can't deny Jake forever, Anna. You might as well do it when you have some form of control over the situation.''

Before Anna could answer, Leigh and Blaire trooped into the kitchen, talking excitedly about the day's events. A few minutes later Suzie and the girls headed out.

"Call me, Anna,'' Suzie said pointedly.

Leigh halted at the door. "Y'all go on. Do you mind, Mrs. Nelson? I need to talk to Mom for a second.'' Then she turned to Anna and dropped her first bombshell. "Have you been crying, Mom?''

Whoever said teenage girls were totally self-absorbed obviously had never met Leigh. Anna fervently wished Leigh were more self-centered, at least at the moment. "Don't be silly. What would I have to cry about?''

Leigh tilted her head, considering her closely. "I don't know. I thought you went out with Jake. Did you two have a fight?''

"We didn't go out,'' Anna said, too emphatically. "Just dinner at the diner. No big deal. And no, we didn't have a fight. Why would we fight?''

"Stuff." She shrugged. "The rodeo or something. Anyway, I just wondered. I mean, Blaire said something today that made me think…about things." Fiddling with the car keys on the counter, she glanced away from her mother. "You like Jake, don't you?"

Flabbergasted, Anna stuttered. "I, uh, I, well, of course I like him."

"No, I mean you *like* him. Really like him." She raised her head to pin Anna with a sharp glance. "And he likes you, too."

"Leigh," she started to speak but Leigh brushed the interruption aside.

"It's okay, Mom. I just wanted to tell you that if you're, you know, hanging back, because of me…well, don't. I like Jake, too. And if it's because of Dad, well, I don't think he would mind. I mean, he and Jake were buds, right? Good buds. Maybe Dad would even be happy."

Anna wanted to sink into the floor. She knew her voice sounded strangled, but she couldn't help it. "Nothing like that is going on between Jake and me. I don't know where you dreamed up that idea."

Irritated, Leigh said, "I'm not a baby, Mom. If you don't want to tell me—"

"Leigh, I promise, nothing's going on right now. But if something does happen, something you need to know, then I'll tell you. All right?"

"Okay. I just wanted you to know that if you want to go for it with Jake, it's cool with me." She continued to look skeptical for a moment, but then she smiled.

A beautiful smile. Her father's smile.

Jake's smile, Anna thought with a knife-twist turn of her heart.

"Chill out, Mom. I wasn't trying to upset you." Leigh bent to kiss her cheek. "See ya tomorrow."

Wonderful, Anna thought after she left. Now she had her daughter's blessing to date her old flame again. If only that was all he was. She laid her arms on the table and buried her face in them. Oh, God, what should she do now?

Suzie was right. She could continue to deny Jake the facts, and risk having everything blow up in her face. Or she could tell him the truth, and lay down some ground rules when she did. Jake didn't want to hurt Leigh, she honestly believed that. But she didn't think he realized just how damaging this knowledge could be to an impressionable young girl. So she needed to tell him, make him understand.

Wouldn't it be better to tell Jake now and enlist his help in breaking the news to Leigh in the best possible way? Because she had to face facts. She would have to tell Leigh the truth. And soon.

Anna raised her head, staring unseeingly across the room. Which meant she had to tell Jake, as well. Because one thing had become very clear. He wouldn't wait forever. He intended to claim his daughter. It was up to Anna to minimize the damage.

If she could.

JAKE THOUGHT about leaving. It would be so easy to pack his bags, load up Slick, and get the hell out of Happy. But he was damned if he'd run off because of Anna's lies. No, he'd stay—and if it took him the rest of his life, he meant to drag the truth out of Anna Leigh Connor.

Too angry and restless to hang around the house, he saddled Slick and took him out for a moonlight ride. The stallion set the pace, but Jake kept him on a path he knew to be relatively free of potholes. He'd already managed to wreck his own life. Why wreck his stud's legs on top of that?

Mentally, he rehashed the conversation with Anna, wondering where he'd gone wrong. Obviously, it had been too soon to ask her for the truth. But dammit, he'd already missed fifteen years of his daughter's life. He was tired of waiting, tired of watching her, talking to her, and never being able to acknowledge her.

He wanted to know his daughter, wanted to be a part of her life. Wanted Anna to acknowledge that he was, in fact, Leigh's father. And Anna refused to tell the truth. Was it out of loyalty to Carl? Because he'd rescued her?

Or had she loved him that much?

He brushed that thought aside. She had married Carl because of the baby. And being Anna, she'd given him her loyalty. But Carl was dead now, and that reasoning no longer held true.

Before Jake had come back to town he'd questioned a lawyer. The man had said paternity testing was his best option. The mother could either agree to it or be forced, the lawyer had told him. Easy enough to do, given his and Anna's history and the number of people who had known them.

Yeah, easy to do if he didn't mind making an enemy for life out of Anna.

Besides, how could he do that to Leigh? Would she understand that he only wanted to know her, to share her, not hurt her, and not take her from her mother? Or would she hate him for disrupting her life?

And how could he do it to Anna? Because in spite of her lies, in spite of her refusal to share her daughter with him, he didn't want to hurt her. He cared about her. A lot. Too much for his own comfort. If he'd been smart, he'd have managed to make her fall for him again, without falling under her spell himself.

Too damned late for that.

Weary of questions with no answers, he turned Slick toward home, slowing the pace to cool him down.

As he and his horse neared his father's barn, he saw her, silhouetted in the doorway, light streaming from behind her. Only her outline, but he knew beyond doubt it was Anna. And he wondered just how much more she intended to put him through tonight.

He didn't speak but simply rode past her, dismounted and took off Slick's bridle, replacing it with a halter. He tied the lead rope to a post and went to work. She said nothing, watching him for a moment before walking over to help him take care of his horse. Silently they shared the familiar tasks, rubbing him down, brushing him, giving him feed and water. Finally they washed up at the sink.

Jake dried his hands on a towel and leaned back against the stainless steel sink, crossing his arms over his chest. He broke the silence with a question. "Why are you here, Anna?"

Carefully, she put down her towel and faced him. "You know why. We need to talk."

"I tried that earlier. You weren't much in the mood. For the truth, at least."

She bit her lip and looked away from him. "Could we go inside? I forgot my coat and I'm freezing."

She probably was, wearing only a flannel shirt and jeans. And he didn't like that his first reaction was the desire to take care of her. Without speaking, he started out of the barn. Grabbing his coat in passing, he tossed it to Anna. She caught it with a murmured word of thanks and followed him.

What was he supposed to think? Had she really come to tell him the truth? There would be no point in giving him more lies. He knew the truth; he only lacked her confirmation.

The house was cold and dark, almost more uninviting than the barn. "I'll get a fire going," he said, leading her to the living room. "Dad won't be back for a couple of hours." No timely interruptions tonight.

Jake took his time setting the fire, both to give himself a chance to think and to give Anna a chance to squirm. After making sure the fire had caught, he took a seat on the faded plaid sofa. Yet another relic of his childhood, he wondered if his father ever intended to replace his worn furniture. Again, he felt a surge of irritation at the old man's stubborn refusal of his help. But right now he had other things to worry about. Like lies. And truth.

"Have a seat, Anna. And then you can tell me what you're doing here."

She shook her head, electing instead to pace in front of the fireplace. Jake admitted she looked better in a faded pair of jeans and an old blue plaid flannel shirt than any woman had a right to, but it annoyed him that he could think of her looks at a time like this.

But then, it had been some time since he could look at Anna and remain unaffected. If he'd ever been able to.

When another few minutes passed without her speaking, he lost what little patience he had left. "Take your time," he said sarcastically. "I'm in no hurry. Maybe you'd like to put this off until next week. Or never, more likely."

"I know you're angry," she said, breaking her silence finally. "You have a right to be. But this isn't easy for me."

"Obviously. It's not easy for me, either."

She stopped pacing and faced him. Took in a deep breath and met his eyes.

"Leigh is your daughter."

CHAPTER THIRTEEN

JAKE CLOSED HIS EYES. His daughter. He had a daughter. Oddly, knowing what was coming hadn't made Anna's words any less of a shock. Finally, to know the truth. To hear Anna confirm what he'd believed in his heart all along.

Why didn't he feel triumphant? Vindicated? Instead he only felt frustrated.

He opened his eyes to look at her. "Why did you lie to me for so long? I could understand it if Carl were alive, but he's gone, Anna. This can't hurt him any longer."

"But it can hurt Leigh. It could devastate her." She strode across the room to stand over him like some kind of protective angel. "I didn't know what you'd do if you knew the truth. Whether you'd tell her, whether you'd— I didn't know what you intended. Was I just supposed to trust you? A man I didn't even know any more? A man who I hadn't seen in almost sixteen years?"

"Dammit, Anna, you—"

She cut him off with the slash of her hand. "I had to think of Leigh. Not you, not me, but Leigh." She paused to let that sink in. "Think about it, Jake. Can you imagine how she'll feel when she finds out the truth? When she finds out the only father she ever knew lied to her? When she realizes I lied to her, too? And have gone on lying, every single day of her life.''

''I don't know.'' He shoved his hands through his hair and sprang up to pace the floor, too unsettled to sit calmly while Anna rained questions on him that he'd never even considered. ''Hell, I don't know how I feel. How can I possibly know what she'll feel?''

''Well, I do. I'll tell you how she'll feel. Betrayed. Deceived by the two people she should have been able to depend on for anything. Her mother and the man she always thought of as her father.''

Halting, his eyes narrowed as he stared at Anna. His hold on his temper, already tenuous, snapped. ''From everything I've heard, Carl *was* her father. He saw her first step. Heard her first words. Bathed her. Put her to bed. Read her stories. Carl put her up on her first horse.'' His hands clenched into fists of impotent anger. ''If that's not being a father then I don't know what is.'' And he, her biological father, hadn't even known his daughter existed until a few months before.

''Yes. Carl did all those things. And he lied to her. Just like I did.''

Jake lifted a shoulder and shot her a caustic look. Right now he didn't have a lot of sympathy for either Carl or Anna. ''Your choice.''

''That's right. I made a choice.'' She propped her fists on her hips. ''And while I owe Leigh an explanation, I'm not going to justify myself to you. You lost all your rights when you left me high and dry.''

"Why the hell didn't you tell me you were pregnant?" he shouted. "I'm not a bloody mind reader. I didn't know."

"And if I had, what would you have done? Divorced your brand-new wife?"

"In a heartbeat."

"Jake, can't you see how impossible that would have been? You'd have married me out of duty. And we'd have come to hate each other. We wouldn't have lasted six months."

"We'll never know, will we?" he snapped. "You and Carl took that choice away."

Her jaw tightened, her eyes flashed fire. "And what about your choice? When you chose to marry another woman? If you hadn't done that I'd never have been forced to make such a decision."

Stalemate. He couldn't justify his actions, any more than she could. But Anna was right about one thing. If he hadn't married Cookie none of the rest of it would have happened.

Anna went to him, put her hand on his arm. "Yelling at each other, blaming each other isn't solving anything. The point is, we have to deal with the here and now. My choices, your choices—they don't matter anymore. But you know who does? Leigh matters. She's the most important one here."

He couldn't argue that. And he truly wanted what was best for his daughter. But that didn't make him willing to forget he had one.

"I thought about what you said," Anna continued, looking at him earnestly. "About my being a coward. And you're right, I am. But the problem is,

Jake, that I'm not afraid of what the truth can do to me. It's Leigh I'm afraid for.''

Shrugging off her hand, he said wearily, ''She makes a convenient excuse, doesn't she?''

''It's not an excuse that I want to protect her. Surely you can underst—''

Jake raised a hand to cut her off. ''I don't want to hurt her either, Anna. But I've missed fifteen years of her life. Fifteen years that you've had to watch her grow up, to play with her, to guide her, to be with her. I've missed all of it. And I don't want to miss any more. I want to know her. To be a part of her life.''

Her eyes glistened, unshed tears turning them a deeper shade of green. ''I know you do. I'm just not sure how to go about it.''

''I'm not, either. But there has to be a way.''

''How? We can't just say, 'Oh, by the way, Leigh, Jake is your biological father' without any kind of warning or—or some kind of preparation.''

''So your solution is not to tell her at all?''

''No. I didn't say that. But I—I can't tell her yet. At least until I can think how to do it.'' She put her hands to her head and whirled away from him. ''You know the truth now,'' she said, her voice thick with emotion. ''Can't that be enough, at least for a little while? If you care about Leigh at all you'll give me a chance to figure out the best way to tell her.''

Dammit! Why did it feel like every compromise was his—and his alone? He didn't want to wait another minute. He wanted to tell Leigh, tell the world that he had a daughter. Shout it from the center of town. Spend time with her. Beyond that, even angry as he was now, he wanted to spend time with Anna, too. But he also didn't want to blow his chances— with either of them.

More than anything, he wanted what was best for his daughter.

Jake laid a hand on Anna's shoulder, gently turning her to face him, his hands lingering to clasp her slender shoulders. She looked at him in mute appeal, but she didn't speak. Beneath his hands, she felt slight, fragile, but he knew that was an illusion. He felt the strength emanating from within her. Strength to raise her daughter alone and to run a full-time business while doing it. The strength to face her husband's death, and go on with her life.

He didn't want to add to her burdens, not unless she forced him to. He owed her a chance. More, he and Anna owed Leigh the least hurtful experience they could manage. "It's your call. You know her better than I do. If you think Leigh's not ready to hear the news, then we'll wait."

Her eyes welled up, tears threatening to spill. "I knew you'd understand," she whispered.

For a moment he wondered if she'd ever understand *him*. Ever really trust him again. "Did you? Or did you think I was going to force you to tell her immediately? No matter what it might do to her?"

She shook her head, swiping away tears with the back of her hand. "I know you care about Leigh, Jake. I can see it every time you're with her. You don't want to hurt her any more than I do."

"That's the last thing I want." His fingers tightened on her shoulders, forcing her to look at him. "But she's going to have to know. And as far as I'm concerned, the sooner the better. I won't wait forever, Anna."

No, he wouldn't, Anna thought. But at least he'd agreed to give her some time. Time to figure out how to tell her daughter that Jake Rollins, her mother's old flame, was also her biological father.

"You won't have to," she said.

He dropped his hands and stuck them in his pockets. "So where do we go from here?"

She stared at him, still surprised that he'd conceded her point. But she shouldn't have been, she realized. Jake had been proving that he'd changed ever since he'd come back to town. "One day at a time, I guess. I won't discourage her visits to your place anymore. And of course, you're welcome at ours any time."

He seemed surprised. "What have you said to her? Did you forbid her to visit me?"

"No, but I've objected pretty strenuously to all the time she's been spending over here." Her mouth twisted. "For all the good it did me."

He smiled at that—a wistful, vulnerable smile totally unlike his usual expressions. "At least she doesn't hate me. That's encouraging, anyway."

He didn't know how easily she could read his expression, Anna thought, and suffered a guilty pang of conscience. She realized again how lucky she'd been to have her daughter's love…and here Jake was grateful for a crumb.

"No, she doesn't hate you. In fact, tonight she gave me permission to, uh, go for it with you." As soon as she spoke she wanted to kick herself, but she couldn't take back the words. She hadn't thought before she blurted them out. She'd only wanted to make him feel better.

He laughed. "'Go for it?' Leigh thinks you have a thing for me?"

"I told you before she's a romantic." Anna shrugged. "She thinks we're interested in each other. She doesn't realize you're only being nice to me because of her."

He grasped her shoulders again and looked at her, a half smile tilting at the corner of his mouth. "Anna, that's the dumbest thing I've ever heard you say. You have to know there's more to it than that."

"Do I?" At his intent expression, her heart started to pound. She wanted, so badly, to believe there was more, but could she afford to?

He cupped her face in his hands and looked deeply into her eyes. In his she saw desire flare, and a lurking humor beneath it.

"Yeah," he said huskily. "You do." His mouth came down on hers. His lips moved firmly, possessively, making her head reel and her thoughts scatter like dust in the wind. His hands dropped, his arms wrapped around her to pull her close and settle her from chest to thigh against the hard planes of his body.

Thinking wasn't an option. Instead, she wound her arms around him and kissed him back, giving herself up to the sensations buffeting her. For a moment, only for a moment, she told herself, she would simply enjoy. To experience Jake's hunger, his desire again, to know beyond doubt that he wanted her, made her feel alive in ways she hadn't in years.

It seemed so right to be in his arms. As if she'd come home.

He groaned and caressed her rear, pressing her against him so she knew the full strength of his desire. His lips traveled to her neck, nuzzled the pulse now galloping at the hollow. Her head fell back in abandon, her skin tingling everywhere his hands or lips touched. If she hadn't known better she'd have thought herself close to fainting.

"Any more clueless comments you want to make?" he murmured against her skin. His breath was hot, his hands strong and sure, and very, very knowledgeable.

Comments? She couldn't think, much less talk. And she should, she knew, be thinking. She had no business abandoning herself to her feelings, to her newly awakened sex drive, to those emotions she thought had died with Carl. But oh, Jake's hands felt so good gliding over her, and she wanted, no needed to feel them on her bare skin almost more than she needed to breathe. He fondled her breast and she moaned, gasping when he slid his hand inside her shirt and bra to finally, finally touch her.

Seconds later they stumbled to the couch. He sat, pulling her onto his lap, and kissed her again while he toyed with her breast and his fingers gently tugged her nipple until she wanted to beg for mercy.

"Damn, Anna, you're melting." His voice sounded husky, and thick with desire. He unbuttoned one button, then two, shoving aside the shirt to take her nipple in his mouth, sucking it through the fabric of her bra.

"I'm…not," she managed to gasp out.

"Yes, you are." She felt his chuckle at the same time she heard it. "And I like you like that. It's sexy."

"Jake, wait." She pulled his face up and touched her lips to his, lingering regretfully over the kiss. "This isn't solving anything."

"Oh, darlin', I beg to differ." He snuggled her closer so she felt his hard length against her hip. "It's taking care of a lot of my problems."

"No, I meant with Leigh."

"She would definitely be in the way here."

"I'm serious, Jake."

"So am I. Dead serious." He took her face in his hands and searched her eyes, looking more solemn than she'd ever seen him. "Don't you see what's happened? I've fallen for you, Anna. All over again. Only this time I've fallen even harder."

Anna sucked in her breath, unsure what to say. In her heart hope flared like an oil well fire, but cold reality whispered doubts in the back of her mind. Because if she trusted Jake then she laid not only her heart on the line, but her daughter's as well.

And if she didn't trust him… Did second chances come along more than once in a lifetime? Could she and Jake really recapture what they'd once had? Or better yet, make something new and stronger?

"I want to make love to you, Anna. It doesn't have a damn thing to do with anything except that I want you so much it hurts. And you want me, too. I feel it when you kiss me." His lips took hers, softly, lingeringly. "I see it when I touch you." His finger skimmed over her nipple, and he smiled, watching it tighten into a hard crest. "Don't deny us this chance."

"It's not that simple. I—"

The kitchen door slammed, jarring both of them. Their eyes met. "Your father," Anna said, scrambling to refasten her buttons.

Muttering a curse under his breath, Jake brushed her fingers aside to do it himself. "Relax. He's not stupid. Your truck is outside. He'll take his time before coming in here."

They heard a cabinet open and close, and a scraping sound that Anna imagined was a chair being pulled out. Finishing with her buttons, Jake grinned and then kissed her nose. "You're blushing. It's cute."

"I am not. I simply don't want him to think— Well, I don't want him to think…" Her voice trailed off and she stood.

"Exactly what he's thinking?" Jake finished.

"Hush, here he comes."

But Wes didn't linger. He walked through the living room, nodded at both of them and said, "Evening, Anna. Early day tomorrow," before disappearing through the doorway leading to the hallway and the bedrooms.

"What did I tell you? So," Jake said, rising and taking her hand in his. "Where were we?"

"I'd better go." Right now. Before she said to hell with being sensible and went with her feelings. But oh, why was her hand tingling? For heaven's sake, he was only holding it.

He brought her hand to his lips and kissed it. The tingling intensified and her stomach trembled with a quick flutter.

"But you don't want to leave, do you, Anna?"

"No," she tried not to gasp as he turned her hand over and kissed her palm. "But it would probably be the best thing."

"The best thing for who?"

"Both of us." She pulled her hand out of his and crossed her arms over her chest. "This will— If we make love it will complicate everything."

"Everything is already complicated."

"Exactly."

"You're scared. That's the problem."

Automatically, she started to deny it, but she decided she owed him the truth. "Yes. I'm scared."

"You think I'm going to break your heart again."

That pretty much summed it up. She nodded, not trusting herself to speak.

"There's nothing I can say, Anna. All the promises in the world won't change how you feel. I can tell you I've changed, I can show you I have, but I can't promise not to ever hurt you again. I can promise I'll try my damnedest never to hurt you, but I can't swear I won't."

"I know," she whispered.

"But there's one thing I can promise you. I love you, Anna. And I'm not giving up on you and me. But this isn't about me, it's about you. I can tell you I love you a thousand times and if you don't believe it in your heart, nothing I say, nothing I do will matter a damn."

Her pulse picked up speed. "You didn't say that before."

"Didn't say what?"

"You didn't say you loved me."

"Sure I did."

She shook her head, hiding her growing smile. "No, you said you'd fallen for me. It's not the same."

A frustrated expression crossed his face. He propped his fists on his hips and glared at her. "Is there a point to this? I tell you I love you and you lecture me about semantics?"

"Jake. Oh, Jake." She held out her hand and let her smile bloom. "Come home with me."

CHAPTER FOURTEEN

SHE HADN'T been nervous until now. On the brief drive over from the Rollins place Anna hadn't thought at all. Not surprising since Jake's hands had been all over her and her free hand had been all over him as well.

But standing by the dresser in her bedroom, the room she'd once shared with Carl, she wasn't sure what she was feeling. Unable to decipher the enigmatic expression on Jake's face, she couldn't be sure of his thoughts, either. "It's silly, but I—I feel awkward."

He smiled then, that easy, sexy smile she found so devastating. "You don't look awkward. You look beautiful."

"Yes, and such a sexy outfit I'm wearing, too," she said, dragging a hand down the faded flannel shirt she wore.

"Anna, do you really think I care what you're wearing? You've just made my dreams come true. You could be wearing a feed bag and I'd still think you were beautiful."

He'd always been good with words, she thought, but she wanted to believe he meant what he said. He took a step toward her and still nervous, she turned to face the mirror, wrapping her arms around herself. She felt his fingers at the nape of her neck, carefully lifting her hair and draping it over one shoulder. His hands rested lightly on her shoulders and she could feel his body's warmth behind her. Her gaze raised to meet his in the mirror. In his eyes she read a man's desire, and the knowledge steadied her.

The soft light thrown by the bedside lamp gave their reflections a hazy, dreamy quality. Except for his fingers on her shoulders he didn't touch her. And then he bent his head and laid his lips on the curve of her neck. She sighed and raised her arm, her palm to his cheek. He turned his head and kissed her palm before returning to sample her neck again. His arms came around her and his hands, those big work-roughened hands with so much talent, settled on her stomach just beneath her breasts.

"Still nervous?" he asked softly.

Biting her lip she looked at him in the mirror. "It's that obvious?"

He smiled and began to unfasten her buttons, un-hurriedly slipping each one from the buttonhole. "Did you know I used to dream of spending an entire night with you?"

Mesmerized by the slow progress of his hands, she shook her head. He peeled the fabric back and slid the shirt down her arms until it slipped off to pool at their feet. His palms felt deliciously rough against her skin as they smoothed up her arms, and his hands looked dark and strong against the pale-ness of her own skin and the stark whiteness of her bra.

He flipped open the front clasp of the plain bra

and said, his voice a husky murmur that tingled along her spine like a caress, "And I used to dream about undressing you like this. Really slow, removing the layers so I could see every curve, touch every curve." His fingers moved inside the open bra, over her bare breasts. "I wanted to see and touch every inch of your skin. You have beautiful skin, Anna."

Her breathing quickened, her pulse raced as he slid her bra off and cupped her breasts. Unable to tear her eyes away, she watched as his hands caressed her, handling her breasts as if they were something precious. Her breath hitched as he nipped her earlobe, very gently, then skimmed his lips down her neck in heated kisses.

He twined her other arm around his neck as well. She sank her fingers into the hair at his nape and sighed as he stroked her again, his hands running over her breasts and stomach, sliding over the denim covering her hips.

"Lately," he said, stroking her languidly, "I've been having a hard time looking at you without imagining getting you out of all these clothes you wear." He popped open the button on her jeans and slowly tugged the zipper down. "Without imagining what it would be like to make love to you, all night long."

"Jake." She started to turn in his arms, but he stopped her, dragging down her jeans and kneeling behind her, helping her step out of them one leg at a time. He planted kisses from the backs of her knees all the way to the nape of her neck until he stood behind her once again, fully dressed, while she leaned back against him wearing only a pair of high-cut hot-pink bikini panties.

"You still like bright colors," he said, tracing a finger over her panties and sliding it teasingly underneath the elastic band.

"You—you're wearing too many clothes," she managed, tightening her arms around his neck.

"Patience. Don't worry, I won't be for long." His hands slid down her torso, slipped inside her panties to caress the burgeoning ache.

Her head fell back on his shoulder. She dragged his head down to meet her lips in a hot, demanding kiss. "Take me to bed, Jake."

"Not yet." He peeled her panties down until she could wiggle out of them. "See how beautiful you are." His big hand closed over the thatch of blond curls at the apex of her thighs and her eyes fluttered half-closed at the delicious assault on her senses. His finger probed, parted her and slipped inside.

Anna gasped, her back arching in pleasure. He played her body like a love song, evoking chords of sensation as his fingers slid inside and withdrew and he teased and stroked her until her climax swept her up and shattered her in a storm of emotion.

His mouth covered hers and he swallowed her cry while her body throbbed and shuddered with the aftermath of her release. Finally, half faint with pleasure, she sagged in his arms and he swung her up, carried her to the bed, and hastily lay her down. Seconds later, she heard his boots hit the floor with a thud. She watched him unfasten his shirt, fighting for breath as he slipped it off, revealing smooth, beautiful muscles rippling under golden skin. When his fingers fell to his pants she sat up and said, "Let me help."

"I'm not sure that's a real good idea right now. If you get my drift."

Seeing the clear evidence of his arousal, straining for release, she smiled. "Too bad. You'll just have to endure it." Leaning forward, she kissed his navel and her fingers worked at the button of his jeans, releasing it before lowering the zipper. She took him in her hands and met his eyes at his harsh gasp. Slowly, she stroked him, determined to bring him to the same fever pitch to which he'd brought her. From the intermittent sound of his groans, and the way his fingers sank into her hair with each stroke of her hands, she thought she was succeeding very well.

He reached for her hands, holding them together between both of his. "Hold that thought," he told her, and stepped back. Pulling several foil packets from his hip pocket, he tossed them on the night-stand, and rapidly shucked his jeans, briefs and socks. Then he came down beside her, pulling her on top of him, bare skin to bare skin.

Sighing, she leaned down and kissed him deeply, their tongues gliding against each other, their hearts beating erratically. His hands caressed her hips, stroking her, pressing her against him. His pelvis rocked upward, reminding her of what awaited her. She wanted him inside her. Now. Sooner than now.

"I can't wait any longer," he murmured in her ear, reading her mind.

She rolled off him and he grabbed a packet from beside him and ripped it open. Anna took it from

him and their eyes met as she held it in her hand.
"My turn," she said at the quizzical lift of his eyebrow. Jake smiled and lay back, watching her from
beneath heavy-lidded eyes. Slowly, she unrolled it
over his hard length, wringing another groan from
him as she did.

Suddenly she found herself flat on her back beneath him. "This won't wait any longer. I have to
be inside you," he said, his voice a husky promise.

"That's exactly where I want you." He took her
face in his hands and kissed her.

He entered her slowly, but she couldn't help a
small sound of discomfort as she adjusted to him.

"Anna, do you—"

"No, don't stop. I want you, Jake. Now."

He groaned and half laughed. "That's good. Real
good," he murmured and rocked his hips forward.
"Because I want you. So much." Pushing inexora-
bly, firmly, he continued until he was deep inside
her body. He withdrew, entered her again in faster
and faster thrusts until her hips were bucking up
against him and her arms wrapped around him in a
stranglehold. Slipping his hands beneath her hips,
he angled her to take him more deeply, driving into
her over and over until she exploded in a torrential
downpour of emotions and sensations. With a final
hard thrust he came, too, gasping her name before
he shuddered and lay still.

NEARLY ASLEEP, Jake lay on his back with Anna
snuggled up against him, draped half across his
chest. Making love with her had been even better
than he'd imagined it would be. And he still

couldn't quite believe it had finally happened. He hadn't meant to blurt out that he loved her earlier. For one thing, he hadn't been sure she'd believe him. But his mouth had functioned independently of his mind, which had been a good thing in the long run.

Replete, they hadn't even managed to turn off the bedside light. Though he hadn't had nearly his fill of looking at Anna, morning would come early. Besides, he figured they'd be awake later in the night as well.

He rolled over to turn off the lamp and knocked over a picture sitting on the bedside table. When he righted it he came face-to-face with the ghost of Anna's past. Anna and Carl. Not a family snapshot—Leigh was nowhere in it—but a picture of Anna and Carl alone. Obviously important to her, or else why would it sit on her bedside table? Where she could see it every night as she went to sleep. Wake up to it every morning.

He couldn't tell when it had been taken, except it had to have been some years after they married, since Carl, at least, looked a good bit older than Jake remembered. Carl had his arm wrapped tight around her, hugging her to him, and Anna's face was turned up to his in an expression of pure joy. Carl's held a sort of wonder as he looked back at her.

But the thing that really got to him, the thing that stuck in his craw with a shaft of pure, blistering jealousy was that the two people in the picture didn't look like a couple who had married for a child's sake.

The couple in the picture looked at each other like they were in love.

He felt a cool, feminine hand on his shoulder. "That was taken right after we opened the school," Anna said quietly. "Carl died about a year later."

"You look happy," he said, keeping his tone carefully neutral.

"We were." Her tone was soft, regretful, and it tore at his heart. "Carl loved farming, but he knew how important the riding school was to me. We— we had a hard time saving enough to start it. I couldn't have done it without him. He—we made a lot of sacrifices to make it a reality."

Well, wasn't that just dandy, Jake wanted to snarl. Saint Carl to the rescue—again. He closed his eyes, fighting a futile, searing jealousy. Knowing it reflected badly on him. He should have been glad Anna had had someone to turn to when she'd desperately needed it. Glad that Carl had loved her and her child and provided a safe and happy home for them.

But Carl's obvious feelings for Anna didn't bother him so much. After all, he'd always suspected Carl of being halfway in love with Anna. And he might not like it, but he could handle that she'd turned to his best friend. He could even handle that she'd married him.

But he hadn't realized until that moment, until he saw the picture of the two of them together—and without Leigh—how Anna had felt about Carl. Dammit, marrying him was enough to deal with.

Had she had to fall in love with him, too?

Silent, he snapped off the light and lay down. If

there had ever been anything more useless, more just plain stupid, than being jealous of a dead man, he didn't know of it.

"What's wrong?"

"Nothing." Nothing he could talk about, anyway. "What makes you think something's wrong?"

Pulling the sheet around her, Anna sat up and clicked the light back on. "I can feel tension vibrating out of you, Jake. Talk to me."

He knew her well enough to know she wouldn't quit until he talked. And maybe he wanted to after all. Maybe he wanted to hear what she had to say. "That picture—it made me realize something."

"It's just a snapshot, Jake."

One she kept beside her bed. A constant reminder of another man. "You loved him. You were *in love* with him."

She sucked in her breath and was silent a moment. "Yes, I did love him. I was in love with him. Do you have a problem with that?"

Hell, yes, he had a problem with it. He didn't want to think of Anna with Carl. Making love with Carl, loving Carl. He didn't want to think about her with anyone but himself.

When he didn't speak, she continued. "Did you want me to tell you I didn't love Carl?"

Yes. Irrational or not, that's exactly what he wanted. "It was…just a surprise, that's all. I hadn't realized, exactly—"

She interrupted. "You should have. He was your best friend. He was a good man. Don't you think he deserved a loving wife?"

His jaw tightened. Put that way, it made him

sound like some kind of monster. Of course Carl had deserved *a loving wife*. Dammit, he knew it wasn't right, but he couldn't help his feelings. "I didn't say he didn't." But why did it have to be Anna? The love of Jake's life. The woman he'd thrown away in the stupidity of his youth.

"When I married Carl I didn't love him. Obviously, he knew that. But he never gave up on me, never reproached me. When I think of what I must have put him through, especially that first year, I'm ashamed." She took Jake's hand in hers. "But people change, Jake. I couldn't grieve for you forever. And one day I just...fell in love again. With Carl."

"You don't have to justify anything to me. I'm the one who left you. I don't begrudge you what you had with him." But he was sure as hell jealous of it. And wishing he was a better man didn't change that.

"Jake, I loved Carl. A part of me will always love him. But...he's gone. And I need to move forward. Both of us need to move forward. Because there are things about your past I have a hard time with, too. We're just going to have to deal with them, and your problems with my past. We knew it wouldn't be easy."

No, it wouldn't be easy. And the past wasn't the only problem they had to deal with. They hadn't scratched the surface of their problem with telling Leigh the truth.

"I can tell you one thing," she added, placing her hand over his heart.

His chest hurt when he looked at her. Who would have imagined that he would go and fall crazy in love with her again? He covered her hand with his and squeezed gently. "What?"

She leaned down and kissed him, slowly, deeply. "I love you. We've finally found each other again. Let's not waste our second chance. Not many people get one."

She was right. He needed to let the past rest easy. "You sure grew up smart," he said, wrapping his arms around her and kissing her again.

She laughed and returned his kiss. "You know what the best thing about all this is?"

"Great sex?" he hazarded, trailing his lips down her neck to her breast and teasing her nipple with his tongue.

She sighed and stretched, giving a purr of satisfaction. "That, too. But I was thinking that to me the best thing is, I'm happy again. Really, truly, deliriously happy. I can't remember the last time I felt like this."

He intended to keep her that way. And to make certain that when she dreamed of someone, she dreamed of him, not her dead husband. He pulled back, framed her face in his hands, his thumbs resting at the pulse now fluttering in her neck, and looked into her eyes. "I love you, Anna."

"I know," she whispered, and kissed him. "I love you."

They made long slow love and then held each other, until Anna fell asleep in his arms. But sleep eluded Jake. Because he knew that no matter how hard he tried, he might never be able to deal with the fact that Anna had once loved Carl Connor every bit as much as she loved him.

CHAPTER FIFTEEN

ANNA HUNG UP the phone and cursed—silently, since she didn't know Leigh's whereabouts. Less than two months before the rodeo and the country-and-western singer they'd booked for the event had just canceled. She'd suspected that things had been going way too smoothly, and she'd been right. At least the band for the dance hadn't dropped out on them. Still, they needed a celebrity, or at least a semicelebrity, for the rodeo. They'd just have to find someone else, that's all. Surely everyone couldn't be booked up.

Right.

She wandered into the living room, trying desperately to think of who they could convince to play. For free, yet. Blank. Nothing. Her mind was a big, fat, useless blank. Maybe Jake would have some ideas.

"Hey, Mom, where are you?" she heard Leigh shout from the kitchen. "Guess what happened today?"

"In here," she called, wondering why Leigh sounded so deliriously happy.

Leigh burst into the room, whirling around in excitement. "Danny Williams and Lydia Morrow broke up."

"And Danny would be…"

"C'mon, Mom." Leigh turned astonished eyes to her. "You know who he is. The really hot guy in my class. I've only liked him for, like, forever."

"Oh, that Danny Williams," Anna said, and grinned. "How could I have forgotten."

"Yeah, and one of his friends said Danny broke up with Lydia because he liked someone else."

"And that would be you?"

Leigh deflated a little. "Well, I don't know. He wouldn't tell me. But it could be," she said, perking up.

Life was certainly exhausting when you were fifteen, Anna thought. She wouldn't go through those ups and downs again for anything. Of course, she'd had some serious ups and downs of her own lately.

"So, what's up with you, Mom?" Leigh said, throwing herself into the easy chair. "Is that a new blouse? It's really pretty."

Anna glanced down at the turquoise Western-style blouse she'd tucked into a pair of jeans and finished off with a wide black-and-silver belt. "Not new. I just haven't worn it much." But she hoped to see Jake later and had suddenly found herself riffling through her closet for something, anything, to wear that hadn't seen a thousand washings. She'd found the blouse crammed into a far corner of the closet.

"Can I borrow it?"

Anna laughed. "No way. Last time you wore one of my blouses you spilled pizza sauce down the front."

"Oh, yeah. I forgot about that." Leigh leaned

down and flipped through some of the papers spread over the coffee table. "So, are you paying bills? Is that why you look kinda crabby?"

"I do not look crabby," she said automatically. When Leigh snorted she added, "Okay, maybe a little. That's rodeo business there, not my bills. The singer just fell through." She paced over to the fireplace, noticing it hadn't been cleaned in ages. Another chore she had no time for. "I don't know who we're going to get."

"Ask Jake." Leigh shot her mother a calculating look from under her lashes. "Unless you think you won't see him. Of course, he's only been over every night for over a week. And," she added with a smirk, "you're wearing that new blouse."

Caught. Anna had sworn she'd tell Leigh if anything important happened between her and Jake, but she hadn't known how to broach the subject. This seemed like an appropriate moment. Drawing in a deep breath, she began, "About Jake. About Jake and me. We've, uh—that is—we've been seeing each other." There, she'd finally said it.

Leigh widened her eyes. "No kidding?"

Anna laughed. "Okay, okay. I guess that's obvious."

"Nah, Mom. Not at all." Leigh danced over to give her a hug. "Don't worry, Mom. I'm cool with it. I told you I would be."

Great. She was cool with it now, but somehow Anna doubted she'd be so cool when she discovered Jake was her biological father.

The doorbell rang. Leigh ran to get it, throwing a

knowing smile over her shoulder as she opened the door. "Hey, Jake. Long time no see."

"I was here yesterday. Does that mean you're sick of me, squirt?" Jake asked as he entered, hat in hand.

"No, that means she's being a smart aleck," Anna said before Leigh could answer. He was looking at Anna with a half smile that she could interpret very easily. Hopefully, Leigh couldn't.

He wore an old pair of jeans, tight and faded at the stress points and a snowy-white T-shirt underneath an unbuttoned soft blue cotton shirt the exact shade of his eyes. Her mouth practically watered when she looked at him. She wondered if he knew how the color made his eyes look even more gorgeous. She doubted it. Jake never had been vain about his looks.

To divert her own thoughts as much as her daughter's, she spoke. "I'm glad you came over. We've got a problem with the rodeo. With the entertainment."

"Yeah?" He laid his hat on the table and glanced at her with concern in his eyes. "What's wrong? Something we can fix, I hope."

"We have no singer," Anna said mournfully. "And I don't know who we can get. Especially for free."

"It would be totally awesome if you could get somebody famous," Leigh said. At her mother's irritated glance she muttered, "Well, it would be."

"Who would you like, Leigh?" Jake asked her.

"Oh, gosh. Garth Brooks, George Strait. Ooh, I know, Clint Black. Somebody cool, anyway."

"I don't know any of them. How about Nate Hartstrong?"

"You know Nate Hartstrong? Really?" Leigh looked thunderstruck at the thought.

"Yeah." He smiled and tweaked her ponytail. "Not real well, but well enough to ask him. He's a nice guy. I bet he'll do it if he's not booked up."

"Oh, wow! How totally awesome!" She threw her arms around him in an excited hug, before dashing out of the room. "Wait until Blaire hears this!"

Anna had never seen a man's heart in his eyes before. But she saw Jake's as he watched his daughter race out of the room. Love. Longing. Then his expression shut down and he turned back to her and plastered a smile on his face. A smile that didn't quite dispel the sadness still lurking in his eyes.

"I hope I can deliver after that. It sure will be embarrassing to come up dry."

Anna walked over to him and kissed him lightly on the mouth. "I'm sure you can. I have faith in you."

He tilted his head and smiled at her, and this time it chased the shadows away. "Do you? Have faith in me?"

Looping her arms around his waist, she stuck her hands in his back pockets and kissed him again. "Absolutely. I wouldn't be with you if I didn't."

He sighed and cradled her head against his chest, rubbing a hand down her back. "Not that I mind, but Leigh could be back any minute."

Anna laughed and pulled back to look at him. "She's on the phone, Jake. That's good for at least half an hour. Besides, she knows about us now. Not about you, but she knows we've been seeing each other."

Clasping her arms, he leaned his forehead against hers and closed his eyes. "That's good." After a pause he asked, "When are you going to tell her, Anna?"

"I don't know. I wish I did."

He drew back and gazed at her and the hope in his eyes stabbed at her heart. "She likes me. Don't you think so?"

"Yes, she likes you a lot."

"Maybe it won't be so bad. Maybe she'll...just accept it."

Anna knew how desperately he wanted to believe that. And so did she. But she couldn't shake the feeling that Leigh wouldn't handle the news well. "Soon," she whispered, and kissed him lingeringly. "I promise I'll tell her soon."

Anna knew she couldn't postpone it much longer. For Jake's sake, and hers, and Leigh's. She had to tell Leigh the truth about her father.

But how?

"NEED TO TALK TO YOU," Wes told Jake early one morning a few days later. Mornings were about the only time the two of them ever saw each other anymore, unless Wes needed a hand with the cattle—and he didn't ask for that often.

"Sure. What's up? And if you're cooking, I'll take two eggs, scrambled."

Wes grunted and added a couple of eggs to the mix. He didn't say any more until he'd spooned the cooked eggs onto a plate, added a couple of slices of toast and bacon, and set it in front of Jake. He put his own plate down, took a piece of toast and calmly and methodically began to butter it. "I'm getting married."

With his fork halfway to his mouth, Jake stopped and stared at his father. "Married?"

"Yep." He nodded and took a bite of egg, chewed it slowly and swallowed before speaking again. "Over Easter break."

Jake's mouth opened and closed, but no sound emerged. "To Mary, I take it?" he managed after a moment of stunned silence.

"Of course it's Mary." Wes threw him an irritated glance. "Who else have I been seeing?"

"At Easter break. That's only two weeks away."

"Only time she has time off for a honeymoon. 'Less we wait for summer. And we don't aim to wait."

Jake couldn't figure out why he was so surprised, but he was. It seemed like a sudden decision, especially for a man like Wes, who'd never been in a hurry in his life, as far as Jake knew. "Where's the fire?"

Wes shot him a sharp look from under bushy gray brows, scraped some egg onto his toast and carried it to his mouth. After a moment he said, "Hellfire, son, you may have all the time in the world but I don't. 'Sides, Mary's a teacher. Needs to set an example to the kids. Can't be having a man hanging around her house at all hours of the day and night."

Again, Jake simply stared at him.

"You got a problem with me marrying Mary?" Wes asked, frowning.

"No, of course not. I guess you just caught me by surprise." He held out his hand. "Congratulations. You're a lucky man."

"Yep." Wes shook hands and smiled. "So Mary keeps telling me."

"I think she'll keep you in line, all right," Jake said, and laughed. "So where are you going for your honeymoon?"

"Mexico. Cancún, I think it's called."

Jake blinked, trying to imagine his father at a vacation resort in Mexico. He simply couldn't do it. "You always said there's nothing to do at the beach except sweat and you did enough of that right here."

"Changed my mind," he said, nodding. "Besides, you know how women are. As long as Mary doesn't expect me to be climbing any damn pyramids—and she's a durn sight smarter than that—I said I'd take her wherever she wanted to go. And she's got a hankering to see this Cancún place."

Jake shook his head in wonder. "I just can't see you in Mexico, sitting on the sand drinking margaritas. Mary, maybe, but not you."

Wes drew himself up and pinned his son with an ironic glance. "Son, I may be a long sight older than you, but I'm not dead yet. I don't plan on spending all my time on the blessed beach."

Jake grinned. "I see your point."

"Anyway, the wedding's at the Methodist church, two weeks from Saturday. Ten in the morning."

"Do I get to call Mary Mama?"

"Only if you want her to slap you upside the head," Wes said and they both laughed.

"Where are you going to live?" Jake asked, wondering if he would need to move out.

"Here. I can't handle the ranch from Mary's place. Not as easy, anyway."

"You'll be wanting me out of here, then. I'll see what I can find." Maybe he could rent a place in town, or even Mary's house, if she was moving out to the ranch. Too bad, because things were sure convenient with him living here.

"No need for that. Mary and I want you here as long as you need to be."

"Thanks," he said, touched. "Any time you want me out, though, just say the word."

"There's something else," Wes said after a moment of companionable silence while they both finished their meals. "I'll be needing a best man. Reckon you've still got some hard feelings for your old man, but I'd appreciate it if you'd consider it."

Jake had already started toward the sink with his dishes, but at that he turned around. "I don't have to consider it. I'd be honored."

"You would?" Wes looked shocked, then pleased. "Well, that's fine, then."

Jake set his dishes down and turned back to his father. "And, Dad, those hard feelings? What do you say we try to leave them in the past? Where they belong."

"I'd like that, son," he said, his voice gruff with emotion. "I'd like that a lot."

Of course only an idiot would think they were going to get along perfectly now, but they could do better than they had in the past. At least this time it looked as if they both intended to try.

THE DAY OF the wedding dawned warm and clear. Waiting at the church, Jake realized he had never seen his old man nervous before. In fact, he hadn't realized Wes *was* nervous until the third time he asked Jake if he'd remembered to bring the ring. Jake smiled and patted his suit pocket. He didn't often wear a suit, but then his father didn't get married every day either. "Relax. Everything's under control."

Wes grunted. "Huh. Don't forget to tell George—"

"Dad," Jake interrupted. "Your foreman knows what to do. You're not leaving for a month, for God's sake. It's only a few days. And I'll be around, too. Don't worry."

"Not worried, just making sure everything's set," Wes muttered. "That reminds me, something I wanted to talk to you about."

"Now?" He looked at his watch. "You're getting married in forty-five minutes."

Wes shot him a wrathful look. "Hell, son, do you think I'm an idiot? I know that." He glanced around the small dressing room of the church. "Step outside with me. Can't talk proper in a church. Never could."

Mystified, Jake followed. His father came straight to the point. "Been thinking for a while now about cutting back."

"Cutting back? Oh, yeah, you were saying something about it a while ago."

Wes nodded. "Cattle business has been taking some hard knocks lately. What with the drought and all. Competition's fierce. Merriwhether hasn't helped that," he added, frowning, referring to the biggest land owner and wealthiest cattle baron in the area.

"You're going to retire?"

"Not exactly. But with Mary and me getting hitched, well, I'm thinking about scaling down. Thing is, I could use another investment if I do that."

Jake stared at him, wondering what the hell any of this had to do with him. His father was asking his advice about investments? Now there's a weird idea, Jake thought.

And it seemed like an odd time to choose to talk about it, as well.

"Know you've been having trouble finding land," Wes continued. "What's wrong with right here? My place, I mean. I've got some acreage I can let you have."

Jake's mouth nearly dropped open. Acreage? Use Rollins land to breed quarter horses? And Wes had suggested it? He had to be dreaming. He'd been shocked enough when his father had given him the use of the barn while he needed it. And he'd hoped, though he hadn't counted on it, that Wes might let him buy some land. Eventually. But this...

Wanting to make sure they were on the same wavelength and he hadn't hallucinated the entire conversation, Jake said, "I'm raising horses, not cattle. You've been a cattleman all your life."

"Hell, I know that," Wes said, obviously exasperated. "Can't a person ever change his mind? Try something new once in a while?"

"Let me get this straight. You want to go into business with me? In the horse business?"

"Damnation, Jake." He slapped his thigh and glared at him. "Didn't I just say that?"

"I'm just—I'm just surprised." Shocked as hell was more accurate. "When I left home— Well, you remember how it was." Battle after battle over Jake riding the circuit, Jake breeding horses, in fact, over Jake doing anything other than giving up his foolish dreams, settling down and helping his father run his cattle business.

"Maybe I was..." He stopped, stuffed his hands in his pockets, obviously searching for words. "I might've been too hard on you."

For most people such an admission might not sound like much, but for a man with Wes's stubborn pride, it was an apology carved in stone. "I was set on leaving," Jake admitted. "I'd have gone anyway, no matter what you did. The arguments—they just made it easier."

Clearly uneasy with the conversation, Wes shrugged. "But we were talking about now. It's a simple proposition. An investment, that's all. I'm not aiming to tell you how to run a business I don't know anything about."

He knew a lot about the cattle business, though, and had a lot of contacts. His advice would be solid. As the idea took hold, Jake grinned. "You think we could manage this without killing each other?"

His father's rare smile answered him. "Don't know. We could try."

Jake held out his hand. "Well, hell. Let's go for it, then."

They shook hands and then his father slapped him on the shoulder. ''Better get back in. 'Bout time for the wedding. Got that ring?''

Jake laughed. ''Yeah, Dad. I've got the ring.''

CHAPTER SIXTEEN

ANNA HAD ALWAYS been a sucker for weddings and Mary and Wes's celebration proved to be no exception. While the ceremony was limited to family and a few friends, Leigh and Anna included, most of the town would be at the reception. Accustomed to her mother's behavior at weddings, Leigh nearly refused to sit with her. Anna remembered to bring tissue this time, though, and discreetly dabbed at her eyes during the pledging of the vows.

The reception took place at Mary's and the wedding party arrived to a small house packed with guests. Fortunately, the weather had turned out warm and gorgeous so people could spill out over the lawn instead of being confined to the house. Children, dressed in their Sunday school clothes, ran in and out of the house, banging doors and shrieking with glee while groups of people stood by eating, drinking and gossiping.

In the living room, Anna watched Mary and Wes visit with their guests and sighed deeply. "Aren't they sweet?" she asked Jake. "I don't think I've ever seen your father smile so much. And Mary looks ecstatic." When he didn't answer she glanced up to catch him staring at her instead of at his father and his bride. "What is it? Do I have icing on my face or something?"

Jake smiled and touched her cheek with his fingers, then licked one finger with a smile. "A little. Tasty, too. But that wasn't why I was staring."

She lifted an eyebrow in amused inquiry. "Why then?"

"Because you're so beautiful it makes my chest hurt."

Taken aback, Anna laughed. "Flattery will get you everywhere. At least I'm dressed up this time, and wearing makeup."

"You don't need it. I told you that before. But I like that dress."

She wore a tea-length dress with a fitted bodice with tiny buttons, a belted waist, and a scarf layered skirt in multicolored shades of blue. Since it was brand-new it pleased her immensely to have Jake's evident appreciation confirm her choice.

"Don't look now, but here comes Brenda Hoemyer," she said, referring to the waitress from the diner. "She looks like she means business and I have this feeling she's not interested in me."

"I can fix that," he said, slipping his arm around her and pulling her close.

"What are you doing?" she asked, startled. "Jake, everyone's—"

He cut her off by kissing her mouth. After a long moment, he drew back and grinned down at her. "There, that should give Brenda plenty to talk about."

"Not to mention everyone else in town," she said, stepping out of his arms. "And Leigh." But she wasn't angry. After all, Leigh knew they were dating. It was just everything else that her daughter wasn't aware of yet.

"I got rid of her, didn't I? She's disappeared, thank God. And Leigh is having a blast flirting with Luis and ignoring that blond-haired kid. See the one glaring at her and looking sulky?"

Anna glanced at the boy he motioned toward. "Danny Williams. Her current heartthrob. And I think he's supposed to look cool, not sulky."

"Looks sulky to me. She's sure making him suffer right now. Poor kid, I know just how he feels."

Anna shot him a skeptical look. "I did not make you suffer."

"Oh, darlin', I'm suffering right now. But you could put an end to that."

"Is that a fact? And how would I do that?"

He bent to murmur in her ear. "Come home with me after the reception is over. I want to be with you."

Her heart stumbled. She couldn't think of anything she wanted more. "But what about—"

"José said he'd take care of things at your place. And I know you don't have any classes today."

No, she hadn't seen any sense in trying to schedule classes around Easter weekend and a wedding that most of the town would be attending. As for Leigh, since she didn't have to work she planned to go out with her friends and spend the night with Blaire.

Seeing the heat simmering in Jake's eyes, warmth climbed in her cheeks. It didn't take a mind reader to know what he was thinking. "I might be persuaded."

He smiled and took her hand. "In the meantime, I'm sure Mary and my father would appreciate it if we checked on the food."

"The table's so packed right now it's near to breaking," she protested.

"There's something missing. Come with me." He led her to the kitchen, and out through another doorway into the hall. Seconds later he pulled her into an empty room, closed the door and backed her up against it.

"Jake, this is cra—" She broke off with a groan when his hands found her breasts. "Crazy," she finished, just before she grabbed his head and pulled his mouth down to meet hers.

They kissed hungrily, greedily, while he pulled her bodice down and freed her breasts. He bent and pressed a kiss to the top of each breast, then circled the nipple with his tongue. Anna flattened her palms against the door, leaned her head back and drew in great gulps of air. It didn't help. She still couldn't breathe, and when he took her nipple inside his mouth and sucked hard, she bit her lip to keep from screaming.

He kissed her mouth again and she felt his hands lifting her skirt and sliding underneath. Deft and sure, his hands smoothed over her rear, then he slipped one between her legs to stroke her once, twice. He drew in a quick, sharp breath. "Are you wearing what I think you're wearing?"

"Mmm." Floating, she thought. That was the only word for it. "A garter belt. Jake, we have to go back." But she didn't want him to stop. He stroked her again, slow and lingering.

"Definitely." His voice sounded husky. Promising. "Because in about two seconds I'm going to forget where we are and have you right against that door."

Anna was tempted, very tempted, to let him do just that.

He released her skirt, letting it fall down her thighs, and stepped back. "This thing had better not last too much longer." His smile widened as he gazed at her. "Darlin', if I ever saw the personification of temptation, it's you right now."

Anna glanced down, realized her breasts were still exposed and started tugging her bodice into place. "You're not so bad yourself," she said, attempting nonchalance and failing. "But we'd better get back. We don't want to miss their exit."

"Don't do that," he told her.

"What?" She fished her lipstick out of her pocket and applied it.

"Run your tongue over your lips like that. I'm already dying here."

She smiled wickedly. "Brace up, cowboy. And wipe the lipstick off your mouth."

The suggestion he murmured in her ear primed her imagination and brought another blush to her cheeks. She resolved to stop in the kitchen for a cool drink of water before she faced the crowd again.

LEIGH WANDERED over to the food table, glancing out of the corner of her eye at Danny Williams. Carelessly, she picked up a piece of cake and nibbled at it, waiting to see what Danny intended to do. Probably nothing, she thought, but she could always hope.

Just her luck, Brenda Hoemyer and Becky Swenson stopped to talk and cut off Leigh's view of Danny. She was about to move when she heard her mother's name mentioned and curiosity had her staying put.

"Look at that Anna Connor," Brenda whispered loudly. "Hanging all over the man. The least she could do is give him some space."

Leigh glanced around and saw her mother and Jake. She didn't think her mom was hanging on him. They were looking kind of goofy at each other, though, but they did that all the time lately.

Mrs. Hoemyer must not have noticed that Anna's daughter was standing close enough to spit on, Leigh thought, and angled her head to hear better. She never had liked Brenda Hoemyer, and she suspected her mom didn't either, even though she'd never come right out and said so. Maybe she'd find out why now.

"He doesn't look like he wants any space to me," Becky said as they both stared at the couple. "In fact, he looks pretty dang happy about it."

"That's all you know. I'm not surprised she's taken up with Jake again. After all, she threw herself at him enough when we were in high school."

Becky laughed. "That's not the way I remember it. He was always stuck on her. Admit it."

"Oh, yeah, he was stuck on her. Right up to the day he left her high and dry." Brenda smirked and added, "And pregnant with his baby."

Baby? What baby? Leigh thought, setting her plate down with suddenly shaky hands. Her mother had been pregnant...in high school?

"You don't know the baby was Jake's."

"Of course I do, and so do you," Brenda scoffed. "Everyone knew she had Jake's baby. Anybody with two eyes in his head knew it."

Becky parked a fist on her hip. "Brenda, you're so pathetic. You're jealous as a cat because Jake Rollins never gave you the time of day. And he hasn't since he's come back to town, either."

Leigh couldn't hear a thing over the roaring in her ears. She ran out of the room, blindly brushing past people until she reached the outdoors. Her stomach churned as she kept walking, away from the gossip, away from everyone. But she couldn't get away from the voices echoing in her mind.

Everyone knew she had Jake's baby. Everyone knew...Everyone knew... Leigh shook her head fiercely, trying to silence the hateful tones of Brenda's voice.

Was it true? Had her mother had a child? If she had, what had happened to the baby? And had her father known?

If it was true, why hadn't her mother ever told her? They were close, especially since her dad died. How could her mother not tell her that she had a brother or sister out there somewhere? How could she have lied to her about something so important?

She'd lied about Jake, too. She'd said they were never serious, that they'd only gone out a few times. Having a baby together sounded serious to Leigh.

She sank to her knees in the grass, wrapped her arms around herself and rocked.

Did she really have a brother or sister she didn't even know?

"WHAT ARE you thinking?" Jake asked Anna later that evening, smoothing his hand over her bare back. They were lying in his bed after making love and he couldn't decide if he had the energy to move. He didn't think he did.

"I'm thinking about how strange it is to be in your bed at your father's house."

"It didn't seem to bother you a few minutes ago," he said, tracing his fingers along her hip.

"It doesn't bother me, exactly. I'm all grown-up now," she said, rising on her elbow to kiss him. "But I used to be terrified to even come over to your house. I always thought your father didn't like me. I think he thinks I led you astray."

Jake chuckled. "My father knew damn well who led who astray. Remember that time he caught me trying to sneak you in here?"

"Please." She put a hand over her heart. "The most mortifying experience of my life."

"Yeah, well, he didn't blister your ears with how stupid and irresponsible you were being." He could smile at the memory now, but at the time it had been anything but amusing. "Told me to keep my zipper zipped, and if I couldn't manage that, to at least be sure to be careful. Obviously, I messed up on that somewhere."

"The canyon. The night before you left."

''That's when you...that's when you think you got pregnant?''

''I think it must have been then. Do you remember?''

''Of course I remember, Anna. I remember every time with you.'' There hadn't been that many, but even if there had he'd have remembered. You didn't simply forget a woman like Anna. He'd never managed to, anyway.

She sighed and rolled over onto her back. Jake placed his hand on her stomach and voiced a thought he'd sworn to keep to himself. ''I wish I'd been here when you were pregnant. Wish I'd seen you with your stomach all round and full of baby.'' He leaned over and dropped a kiss on her belly, imagining it swollen with his child.

Anna laughed, but he thought he heard a quaver in her voice. ''I felt like a two-ton truck. Not a pretty sight.''

''You were beautiful. I'm sure of it.''

She tangled her fingers in his hair. ''You're such a flatterer. I love that about you.''

He smiled and turned to kiss her palm as she stroked his cheek. ''Have you thought about— We haven't talked much about the future. About our future.''

''No. We haven't.''

She looked solemn. And to his mind, a little apprehensive. Well, given their history, who wouldn't be? ''You're still scared, aren't you?''

''No. No, really, I'm not, Jake. But I haven't been sure exactly where we were heading. I've just been taking it one day at a time." She paused and added, "Maybe I am afraid."

"About me?"

She shook her head. "Not about you. Afraid the happiness won't last."

"It will." He kissed her mouth slowly, deeply. Drew back and touched her stomach gently. "We're not that old. We could do it."

"Do what?"

"Have more kids. You'd have to marry me first, though."

"Jake. Oh, Jake." Her eyes filled with tears.

"Don't cry. I just thought—"

"I wasn't sure you wanted to."

He brought her hand to his mouth and kissed her knuckles. "Oh, I want to. More than I've ever wanted anything."

"Jake…there's still Leigh to think of."

Leigh. His daughter. He still wasn't used to thinking it. "When are you going to tell her, Anna?"

"I don't know how. I don't know how to explain it to her. Every time I start to tell her I…my words dry up."

"Just tell her."

She rested her head against his arm and he felt the moisture from her tears. "I've taught her—Carl and I taught her—to be honest. To tell the truth. And she learned by example as much as anything. You know how Carl was. He was so…good."

Honest. Upright. Dependable. Carl had been all those things. Everything Jake hadn't been.

She sat up, looking down at him intently. "He was a good man. And I have to tell her that good man, that man she loves as her father, lied to her. Not a little lie, but a great big, life-shattering lie.''

Jake started to speak, but she laid her fingers over his lips. "No, let me finish. And then there's me. How do I explain my choices? That all I thought about was how much I loved you and I didn't think about the consequences at all.''

"We were engaged, Anna. It's not as if you didn't expect to marry me. I'm the one who screwed up, not you.''

"Somehow I don't think that will matter a damn to Leigh.''

He crumpled the sheet in his fist. "It would have been easier if I'd never come back. If I'd never realized Leigh could be my daughter.''

"But you did come back. And I'm very, very glad you did." She kissed him deeply. "Let's not think about our problems now.''

He pulled her on top of him, sighing with pleasure at the feel of all that silken skin next to his. "For now, we won't. We'll talk about something else.''

"Talk?" she asked, and her voice held laughter.

"Figure of speech," he said, and rolled over to tuck her beneath him. He kissed her neck, nipped it, and his body tightened at her sumptuous sigh.

"I love you, Jake.''

Jake steeped himself in the warmth of her body, the scent of her skin until he could almost forget that everything might still blow up in their faces. And there wasn't a damn thing he could do to change it.

Not if he wanted his daughter to know the truth.

CHAPTER SEVENTEEN

"WHAT'S BEEN wrong with you lately?" Blaire asked Leigh as they saddled their horses for an early morning ride.

"Nothing," Leigh snapped, and swung herself into the saddle. Two weeks of wondering, worrying, driving herself nutso, and Leigh still hadn't asked her mother about the conversation she'd overheard at Mrs. Gallick's wedding. She hadn't talked to anyone about it. Not to Blaire, not to Luis, not to anyone.

"You sure are cranky." Blaire shoved dark hair out of her face, tightened the cinch and then got on her mare. "At first I thought it was PMS but you've been like this for weeks now."

Leigh shot her a dirty look. "I'm not cranky. And it hasn't been that long." She took off for one of their favorite rides, but today not even riding could help. Because her mood had been the pits for the past two weeks. Ever since she'd heard Brenda Hoemyer's gossipy voice spreading rumors about her mother.

She wanted to know if that woman had been telling the truth. But how was she supposed to ask her mother if she'd had another baby? A baby she'd obviously given away.

What if she had a sister or brother running around out there? She had a right to know that, she thought resentfully. Why hadn't her mother ever told her?

They cantered for some time until they drew near a small stand of trees that marked a tank. After dismounting, they tied their horses' reins to one of the stumpy mesquite trees. Leigh threw herself down in the grass to stare up at the sky. She could remember coming here with Blaire when they were little bitty kids. After her dad had died, Leigh had come out here alone to cry. She couldn't cry at home, since every time she did it had made her mother cry, too. And if there was anything worse than crying herself, it was seeing her mom cry.

She loved her mom, but sometimes she missed her dad so much she couldn't stand it. If he were alive, she knew she could have talked to him and he'd have made her feel better, just by being there.

But her dad was gone.

Blaire lay on her back beside Leigh, her hands linked behind her head. Thank goodness she'd shut up, Leigh thought. Maybe that's why Leigh decided to finally tell her the problem and ask her what she thought. She didn't tell her friend so very often, but she thought Blaire was pretty smart. Blaire had more sense than any of Leigh's other friends—well, except Luis. But Luis wasn't here right now, and Blaire was.

"What would you do if you heard something about your mom?"

"Heard something?" Sounding puzzled, Blaire glanced over at her. "Like what?"

Plucking a piece of grass, Leigh rolled over on

her side to look at her friend. "Something not good. Like, you know, like gossip."

Blaire's eyes narrowed as she stared at Leigh. Then she jumped up and put her hands on her hips. "Did somebody say something bad about my mom? And you were afraid to tell me? Is that why you've been such a—"

Leigh cut her off before she got any more worked up. "Not your mom. Mine."

"Oh." Deflated, she sat back down, crossing her legs tailor fashion. "Well, what was it?"

"It— I'm not sure," she hedged, sitting up. "I mean, it didn't exactly make sense."

"What did they say? And who said it?"

Leigh couldn't bring herself to tell her yet. So she answered the second question. "Mrs. Hoemyer was talking to Mrs. Swenson about my mother. About something that happened a long time ago, when she was in high school."

"Mrs. Hoemyer! She is so mean. Did I tell you that she tried to kick a bunch of us out of the diner the other day? My Mom says—"

"Blaire, I'm talking here." Sometimes Blaire totally forgot who had started the conversation, Leigh thought irritably. "What would you do? Would you ask your mother about it?"

"Well, sure. Why not?"

"Even if it's something she won't want to talk about? Something she's kept secret for a long time?"

"A secret? What kind of secret?"

"A big one. Like, major."

"Look, I don't get it." Blaire scooted over beside

her and peered at her intently. "Why don't you just talk to her?"

"It's not the kind of thing you can just haul off and ask your mother." She chunked a rock into the tank and watched the ripples spread.

"Did you hear you were adopted or something? You know, Beth Lindstrom didn't find out she was adopted until a couple of years ago. She freaked, too, but she's okay now. But if that's it, it's not a bad thing about your mother. Except I don't know why she wouldn't have told you."

"That's not it. Exactly."

Blaire huffed out a frustrated sigh. "What is it, then?"

This really wasn't something she wanted spread all over school. But Blaire could keep her mouth shut, Leigh knew from experience. Especially if she told her it was important. "If I tell you, you can't tell anyone. Not your mom, and especially not anyone at school."

"Of course I won't." She looked hurt that Leigh had even mentioned it.

"I mean it, Blaire. You have to swear you'll never tell anyone."

"What, you want me to write my promise in blood? Leigh, you know I won't talk. Not if it's important. Now spill."

She sucked her breath in, then blurted it out. "I think my mother had a baby. Before me."

Blaire's eyes rounded and her mouth opened in an O of surprise. "No way."

Leigh nodded. "Yeah, I'm almost sure she did. And if she did, she must have given it up. For adoption or something. I could have a brother or sister I've never even met.''

"But you're not positive?''

"No. But Mrs. Hoemyer sure was. And Becky Swenson didn't deny it, either.''

"A baby. Your mom had a baby? So who was the guy? Your dad?''

Biting her lip, Leigh met Blaire's gaze. "Mrs. Hoemyer said…she said it was Jake.''

"Oh, wow. How totally weird.''

"Tell me about it. She lied to me.''

"Well, yeah, maybe. But gosh, Leigh, wouldn't you lie, too? I would.''

She hunched a shoulder. "She should have told me if I have a brother or sister. I have a right to know. And she lied about Jake, too. She said they only dated a few times.''

"But you like Jake. You think he's cool.''

"Yeah, so?'' Frustrated, upset, she stared at her friend. "You don't understand. It's making my stomach hurt. I don't know what to do! I tried to forget about it and I just can't. I haven't thought about anything else ever since I heard.'' Not even Danny Williams could keep her mind off her problems.

Blaire rose, put out a hand and hauled her to her feet. "You better ask her. Your mom's cool. She'll tell you the truth.''

Maybe Blaire was right. It couldn't be much worse than the past couple of weeks had been.

"Wouldn't it be awesome if your mom had a mysterious, secret past? And with Jake Rollins, of all people.''

Leigh turned to stare at her friend. "No. And you wouldn't think so either, if it was your mother."

"Yeah, I guess you're right. I just can't see my mother with a secret past."

No, Blaire's mother didn't seem the type to have a secret past. But what about her own?

ANNA WAS standing over the stove stirring a pot of spaghetti sauce when Leigh came in.

"Mom, can I talk to you?"

"Sure." She looked up and smiled at her daughter. "Where's Blaire? I thought she was staying for dinner."

"No, she went home a long time ago."

After catching a good look at Leigh's unnaturally solemn expression, Anna asked, "Is something wrong?"

"I need to—I need to ask you something."

Anna's heart rate sped up. Leigh looked so serious. And upset. Surely she couldn't have found out...could she? She'd been awfully quiet lately, Anna realized. Not like herself at all. Which Anna might have noticed earlier if she hadn't been so wrapped up in her own emotions.

"Okay. You know you can ask me anything, honey. Let's sit down." She took a seat at the kitchen table. Instead of sitting, Leigh paced the room, coming to a halt a few feet away before speaking.

"I heard something a couple of weeks ago. At Mrs. Gallick's wedding. About—about you. And I wanted to know if it was true."

Oh, God, she knows. How am I going to explain it? "What did you hear, Leigh?"

"Do I have a brother or a sister out there somewhere?"

Anna stared at her blankly. A brother or sister? What exactly had she heard? "No. You're my only child. Why would you think that?"

"Because someone—Mrs. Hoemyer said...she said you'd had a baby. Jake's baby. And she seemed really sure of it, and so was Becky Swenson. That you'd had a baby, I mean. And since I knew it wasn't me—"

Anna's face must have given her away, because Leigh broke off to stare at her with dawning horror. "No," she whispered, shaking her head.

"Leigh, let me explain." Anna stretched a hand out in supplication.

"You mean...I'm the baby she was talking about?"

Why, why, why hadn't she told Leigh before now? Why had she waited until it was too late? "Yes. Let me—"

But Leigh rushed on desperately. "But she said—she said everyone knew you'd had Jake's baby. So it was just gossip, right? Because Jake isn't my father. He can't be."

"I've been wanting to talk to you, trying to think how I could explain to you...what happened."

"What do you mean, what happened? You got pregnant and Dad married you. Right?" Her voice was shrill, accusatory. When Anna didn't speak, she repeated louder, "Right?"

Anna rose and walked over to her. She gathered

Leigh's limp hands in hers and squeezed them before speaking. "It's true that I was pregnant when your father—when Carl and I married. That's why he asked me to marry him." Leigh looked so desperately young, achingly young. The picture of bewilderment and gathering anger. "But the—the baby wasn't his."

"No." She shook her head and jerked her hands away, staring at her mother in panic. "No. I don't want to hear this."

"I know. I understand that. But I have to tell you."

"I'm not listening!"

"Leigh," she said, taking a deep breath. *Just tell her.* "Jake is your biological father."

"Stop it! Just stop it!" She put her hands over her ears, then dropped them and shouted at Anna. "No! He's not! I don't believe you."

"Honey, please," she said helplessly, attempting to reach out but Leigh shied away in horror.

She literally crumpled, the anger draining out of her and despair taking its place. "And Dad knew? He knew you were pregnant with someone else's baby? And he still married you? Why would he do that? How could he do that?"

What could she tell her but the truth? "He loved me. He wanted to marry me. And I didn't know who else to turn to."

"You could have married my *father*," she said, spitting out the last word like a curse.

Anna clasped her hands together, desperate to make her understand—even a little. "I would have. But he—he'd left town. To compete on the circuit.

We were engaged, but he didn't know I was pregnant. Before I could tell him, we—we broke up." She wouldn't tell her now about Jake's marriage. Things were going badly enough. "Jake didn't know about you until he saw you in Houston at that rodeo."

Leigh's expression could have been carved from stone, so lacking in emotion that Anna hardly recognized her daughter. "You lied to me. You and Dad—no, I guess I can't call him that anymore, can I?"

Anna's heart twisted. "Carl was your father. In every way except biologically. He loved you every bit as much as if he'd been your natural father. Nothing that's happened will ever change that."

Leigh laughed. The most heartbreaking sound Anna had ever heard. "Everything's changed."

"Leigh, I love you. I know this is hard—"

"I hate you. I hate you for doing this to me." She didn't shout it, she stated it, which somehow made it worse. "And I hate him, too. Don't think I'm going to accept him, because I won't. Never. He's not my father. And I wish—I wish you weren't my mother."

Anna heard the door slam behind her but blinded by tears, she saw nothing. Seconds later the sound of an engine turning had her dashing to the door. "Oh, my God, she's taking the truck!" She wrenched the door open in time to see Leigh at the wheel of the pickup, peeling out of the driveway in a cloud of gravel dust.

Helpless, she stared at the receding vehicle, then ran inside to phone José, intending to borrow his

truck to go after Leigh. After five rings and no answer, she hung up. With shaking hands, she called
Jake. Relief swamped her when he answered on the
second ring.

"Jake, oh, thank God you're there." She clutched
the receiver in a death grip, trying to still her galloping heart.

"Anna? What's wrong?"

"It's Leigh. I—she knows."

"And you're not calling with good news."

"No." She almost choked on the word. "No.
She's taken the truck. Can you come right now? I
need you, Jake. Hurry."

"On my way," he said grimly and hung up.

She waited, cursing herself for being ten times an
idiot. And prayed they would find Leigh safe.

THOUGH IT SEEMED like hours, only minutes passed
before Jake drove up. She was waiting for him,
opening the truck door before he even stopped.

She didn't waste time greeting him. "Head to
town. Maybe she went to Blaire's."

"What happened?" he asked, turning the truck
around. "Why did you decide to tell her now?"

"I didn't. But she'd heard a rumor—scrambled,
of course—so I had to tell her. Oh, God! If I'd told
her before, this wouldn't—"

"Don't second-guess yourself. You couldn't have
known this would happen."

"I should have. Nothing could have been more
likely."

As they drove she scanned the side of the road,
but it was impossible to see much given the time of

night and the clouds covering the moon. "I've lived
here all my life. I know how people talk. Why didn't
I tell her?" Angrily, she dashed the back of her hand
across her eyes. "What if she has a wreck?" she
whispered, finally giving voice to her overwhelming
fear.

"Anna, she grew up on a ranch. She's been driving for years, hasn't she?"

He sounded so calm. So reasonable. But he hadn't
seen Leigh. Hadn't seen the heartbreak and despair
in her eyes before she walked out the door. Hadn't
heard the fury in her voice. "That doesn't matter.
She's upset. Angry. Not thinking. Anything could
happen. For God's sake, she's only a child!"

Jake reached over to cover her hands as she
gripped them together in her lap. "Calm down. Getting hysterical won't help anyone. We'll find her,
Anna. She'll be all right. We'll find her," he repeated, and this time Anna heard the fear in his
voice, though he tried to mask it.

And then in the silence came a long squeal of
tires, a mind-numbing shriek of rubber sliding on
asphalt, and then a sickening crash of angry metal.

In that instant, she knew. "It's Leigh."

"You can't—" Jake broke off as they crested a
hill and the cloud cover over the moon parted at the
same moment to reveal a mud-colored red truck, lying upside down with one wheel spinning drunk-
enly.

As Jake braked, Anna wrenched open the door
and jumped out, seconds later running toward the

wreck and praying for a miracle. A scene from her nightmares, one she had relived endlessly.

Leigh had rolled the pickup.

Just like Carl.

CHAPTER EIGHTEEN

Two steps behind Anna, Jake heard her frantically calling Leigh's name.

"No. Oh, God, no. Leigh!" She ran toward the truck crying out her child's name over and over, and threw herself down on her knees beside the open window. "Oh, God. She's not here." She turned to him, terror in her gaze. "Jake, she's not inside. I can't see her in there."

"She must have been thrown clear." His words sounded calm, but he didn't know how. His heart was literally in his throat. The clouds parted again to permit a small stream of moonlight to cast its glow. Scanning the area, he caught a glimpse of color a few feet away in the grass. "Anna, over here."

They reached her at the same time. She was unconscious, pale, and she looked so young and fragile it ripped his heart out. "Don't move her," Jake cautioned, seeing Anna clasp her hand. He'd had enough experience with injuries during his rodeo career to know they shouldn't move her unless absolutely necessary.

"Her pulse is strong," he said, a moment later, pressing his fingers to her neck. "She may have a concussion. Talk to her. See if you can get her to

come to. I'll get the cell phone and call the sheriff.''
He hoped like hell there was an EMT closer than
Amarillo. Forty minutes—how could they wait forty
minutes for help?

Paler than death, Anna said nothing, she simply
stared at Leigh and convulsively clutched her hand.

"Anna?" He stood, put a hand on Anna's shoulder. "Talk to her, honey."

Turning a tear-drenched face up to his, she whispered, "Just like Carl. She looks just like Carl did
lying in the hosp—"

"Don't say it." He cut her off, knowing neither
of them could bear to think of Carl. "Keep talking
to her, I'll be right back."

Even when he'd seen every vestige of color drain
from Anna's face, he hadn't realized what that sight
must have done to her. But now he remembered his
father's words, when he'd asked how Carl had died.
Rolled his pickup. Died about three days later, Wes
had said.

Reaching his truck, he yanked open the door and
grabbed the cell phone, sprinting back to the accident site as he punched in numbers. A few moments
later he was able to tell Anna, "Help's coming."
And they'd better be damn quick. "Is she—has she
regained consciousness?"

"Not yet— Wait! Her eyelids are fluttering. Oh,
thank God, I think she's coming around."

He squatted beside her, pressed a hand to Leigh's
shoulder to keep her prone. *Please God, let her be
all right. I'll do anything, just let her be all right.*

Her lashes fluttered against her cheeks. Slowly,
her eyes opened and she gazed at Jake, then her

mother with a puzzled, blurry-eyed expression. "Mom? Jake? What..." She groaned and shut her eyes. "What happened? Did I—" Another groan. "Did I fall?"

"Don't try to move, Leigh. An ambulance is coming," he told her, motioning to Anna to talk to her.

"You'll be fine," Anna said, her voice cracking on the last word. "Just fine, honey. Help is on the way."

Leigh's eyes opened again, and this time they were lucid and despairing. "I remember now." She looked straight at Jake. "You're not my father. You'll never be my father." And then her eyes closed once again.

He felt as if he'd taken a knife to the heart but he couldn't allow himself to react. Leigh's welfare came first. "Anna, don't let her go to sleep. We have to keep her awake until the paramedics get here."

Anna sent him a quick, grief-stricken glance before returning all her attention to Leigh. Jake waited for the ambulance, useless, unwanted, watching over a daughter who would never accept him.

AT THE HOSPITAL hours later, Anna walked out of Leigh's room and straight into Jake's arms. Laying her head on his chest, she burst into tears. His first thought was that the doctors had been wrong and something terrible had happened.

"Anna, honey, what is it? They told me she'd be all right. Has something—"

"No, she'll be fine," Anna said through her sobs.

"I'm sorry. It's a concussion, but they don't believe it's serious. The nurse is with her now."

"Thank God," he said fervently. "I thought she'd gotten worse."

Anna stepped back and wiped her eyes, gathering a shaky composure about her. "She doesn't want me in there, but so far I've ignored her. Oh, Jake, she looks so young. So...wounded." Her fist clenched against her breasts. "I can hardly bear it."

"The important thing is, she's going to be all right."

"I know. That's the only thing that's kept me sane. The nurse told me to take a break. She's watching her." Her hands raised to rub her temples, then jam fingers through her disheveled hair. "Jake, when she was lying there in the grass, so still, unconscious... Oh, God, I kept thinking of Carl in that hospital bed. I thought I'd lose my mind."

"I know. I realized you must be thinking about it. But she's okay. It's not like Carl's accident, Anna. You have to put that out of your mind."

"I can't. I can't stop remembering." And she buried her face in her hands and wept.

He led her to a set of chairs, and helped her into one. She was so weak, so shaken, he feared she'd fall over any second if she didn't sit. With his arm around her, supporting her, he waited until her sobs quieted and eventually stopped. He got up then and came back with some tissue, watching her wipe her eyes and blow her nose.

She gave him a wobbly smile. "Thanks."

Taking both her hands in his, he kissed them and said, "Talk to me. If it will help, talk to me."

She didn't speak immediately, but took several moments to compose herself. Though she looked exhausted, her skin nearly as pale as her hair, at least her eyes had lost that terrible haunted look she'd worn when they'd first arrived.

In a voice so low he had to strain to hear it, she began to speak. "It was late. Carl had been driving all night to get home. A business trip. He didn't go often. Partly because he didn't like leaving us alone. He hated to leave me with all the work, but sometimes he couldn't avoid it."

Jake didn't comment, but squeezed her hands comfortingly. He didn't know what to say and figured that right now the best thing he could do for her was listen.

"I waited up for him. I always did. I…missed him, even though he hadn't been gone long. We'd been married almost eleven years and I didn't sleep well when he wasn't there. So I waited." Her gaze rested on his and it was as bleak a look as any he'd ever seen. "The call came in around two. The police—the chief called me himself—but he didn't tell me much over the phone. Just that Carl had been involved in an accident and was on his way to the hospital in Amarillo. But I knew it was bad. I could feel it." She touched a hand to her chest. "Here, I knew it."

"I'm so sorry, Anna. And I'm sorry you're having to relive it."

"He was only a few miles from home when it happened. A few more miles and he'd have been home safe." She shook her head, closed her eyes, then opened them again to stare blindly in front of her.

She isn't here, Jake thought. She's five years in the past.

"I passed his truck on the way to the hospital. It looked like mine did tonight. Upside down. Only worse. One side was demolished. He rolled it when he was hit."

"Dad said a drunk driver hit him."

She nodded and her eyes held a faraway look, immeasurably sad. "Broadside. Came up over the rise and just ran right into him. The police said...the skid marks and everything made them think Carl tried to turn out of his way, but...it didn't work."

Her breath drew in shakily. "When I reached the hospital he was in a coma. I talked to him, begged him not to die. When that didn't work, I swore at him. I made bargains with God, but that didn't help either. I promised—anything. If only he could live. I held him, I even sang to him." She smiled ruefully. "He loved to hear me sing, even though I never could carry a tune in a bucket."

"Anna—" He touched her cheek, rubbed a tear away with his thumb. She was breaking his heart and there was nothing, not a blessed thing he could do to help her.

"When I lost him I thought I'd die, too. Except I had Leigh. So I had to go on. I had no choice."

He couldn't stand anymore. He pulled her into his arms and whispered, "Hush. Hush, sweetheart. Leigh is all right. She's going to be fine."

She clung to him, her fingers digging into his shoulders, her breath coming in gasps. "Jake, when

I saw that truck, when I saw Leigh lying there...so still. My heart stopped. I couldn't—I couldn't bear it if anything happened to her."

"Nothing's going to happen to her." His arms tightened around her. "We'll make sure of it."

"Mrs. Connor?"

They pulled apart to look at the nurse standing in the doorway. "Your daughter is asking for you."

Anna's face lit up. "Thank you. I'll be right there."

Jake rubbed her tears away with his thumbs. "See, she's asking for you. Go be with her."

At the doorway she turned and looked back at him. "I know you want—I'm afraid to ask—"

"She doesn't want to see me right now, Anna." Not now, and maybe not ever. "It's okay, I understand. She wants her mother." But just because he understood, it didn't stop the pain. He felt like his heart had been sliced into tiny slivers and stomped on by the meanest bronc this side of Kansas.

And now that Leigh was safe, and they knew she would be all right...would she ever accept him in her life? In Anna's life?

WHEN JAKE FINALLY dragged his tail back to the ranch, Wes was waiting for him with a sandwich. Surprised, he heard his stomach rumble. Food had been the last thing on his mind, until he actually smelled it and realized he was starved. He'd spent the night at the hospital, drinking bad coffee and waiting for Anna's periodic reports, until finally this morning Leigh had been discharged.

"How is she?" Wes asked, pulling out a chair

with his foot and practically shoving Jake into it. "Sit down before you fall down."

"She's all right." Physically, anyway. Wearily, he rubbed his eyes and tried to pull himself together. "They discharged her this morning." He raised his head to look at his father. "A concussion. That's why they kept her last night, just to be sure she was okay." He'd called from the hospital and given Wes and Mary the bare details, but he hadn't spoken to either since. He glanced around. "Where's Mary?"

"School. I said I'd call when I heard something. You get any sleep?" Wes set Jake's plate in front of him and took a seat himself.

"Not really. A few minutes here and there." He stared at the thick sandwich and his appetite deserted him. His hand curled into a fist on the table. "It's my fault. All of it is my fault. If it wasn't for me Leigh wouldn't have been at that hospital last night."

"You said she took Anna's truck and wrecked it."

"Yeah. You want to know why?"

"Reckon I've got a good idea."

"I'll bet. She was upset—no, she was destroyed. Because Anna told her I'm her biological father." He fell silent a moment and added, "You knew, didn't you?"

Wes nodded. "Figured it out."

"You never said anything to me. Not once over the years."

"Hell, Jake, how could I?" He looked frustrated, and guilty. "I didn't know anything for sure—least not until you came back to town. Anna sure as shooting never breathed a word to me. Besides, I figured it was her business.''

''I'm not trying to blame you.'' No, he was the one at fault, not his father.

''You took your time telling me once you heard the truth.''

Did he hear hurt in his father's voice? ''Anna wouldn't admit it until a few weeks ago. We wanted to tell Leigh before we told anyone else.'' He laughed humorlessly. ''Now I wish Anna hadn't told her at all.'' He looked at his father, so solid, so stoic. ''My daughter hates me. How am I supposed to have a chance with her, a chance to start again with Anna, when Leigh hates my guts?''

''What did you expect, son? That little gal had a powerful shock.''

''I guess I thought— Maybe it was stupid, but I thought she liked me. I know she did, until she heard the truth. I believed—wanted to believe—she'd come around.''

''Still could. Give her some time to adjust.''

Give her time, Jake thought, looking at Wes. ''Seems to me I remember another conversation where you said the same thing. About Anna.''

''Yep. And Anna came around, didn't she?''

''Yeah.'' He put his head in his hands and stared at his plate. ''I'm not sure Leigh will.''

''Time will tell. And some things you just can't rush, son.''

Don't rush her. He could be patient. For his daughter. As long as he had hope she might eventually come around.

He just wouldn't let himself think about what he'd do if she didn't.

CHAPTER NINETEEN

A COUPLE OF WEEKS after the accident, Leigh showed up in the barn one afternoon before riding classes started, which surprised the heck out of Anna. Since she had learned the truth, Leigh had done as little as possible in the way of chores. While it angered Anna, and forced her to work even longer hours, she tried to cut Leigh some slack. She'd had a shock, Anna reminded herself, and she needed time to adjust.

Never mind that Leigh's sullen, combative attitude was driving her crazy.

Still, she was here now. Anna glanced at her, noticing she wore her oldest jeans, almost a guarantee that she intended to help. "I'm glad you're here. I could really use some help. Jake will be here in a few minutes and—"

"Then I won't be," Leigh interrupted, tossing her hair back over her shoulder and leaning into Peanuts's side to pick up his hoof.

Exasperated, Anna stared at her a moment. "Don't be ridiculous, Leigh."

Leigh shot her a dirty look before returning her attention to Peanuts. "Why does he keep hanging around? I don't want to see him."

Anna bit back a caustic comment. "But I do. And he's coming to see me, not you."

Leigh glanced at her again, obviously puzzled, as if it hadn't occurred to her that Jake might have reasons besides seeing her to come over. She shrugged it aside, though. "Good. Because I'm not talking to him."

"Don't you think you're being awfully childish?" Of course, she was a child. Or an adolescent, which made things even harder, in Anna's opinion. Every time Anna had tried to talk to Leigh since the accident, every time she'd attempted to explain anything, Leigh had cut her off. Either by maintaining a stony silence and obviously not listening to a word she said, or by leaving the room.

She knew she needed to clamp down on Leigh's disrespectful attitude, but whenever she started to remonstrate with her she could only remember how Leigh had looked, pale and still beside the wrecked pickup. And then she'd swallow her words and thank God her daughter was alive. How could she discipline her in the face of nearly losing her?

She heard voices in the distance, Jake telling Luis he'd find Anna himself. Halting a few feet away, she saw his gaze linger on Leigh. Then he turned to her and smiled, wistfully, she thought.

"Hi. Need another hand?"

"Thank—"

"Not from you," Leigh interrupted.

"Thank you. I can always use more help," Anna finished. "Leigh, that was very rude."

Leigh shrugged but didn't speak.

Jake sighed and shook his head at Anna, picking

up a currycomb and starting on Sugar's other side. "I heard good news this morning," he said a few moments later, after another glance at his daughter.

Totally ignoring the two adults, Leigh picked out Peanuts's hooves as if it required her undivided attention. Anna wanted to shake her, but restrained the impulse. *Understanding,* she told herself for the thousandth time. *She needs understanding and patience.*

And a good spanking, Anna thought irritably. Still, she hadn't spanked her as a young child, so she wouldn't start now.

"Good news would be nice for a change," she said, injecting as much brightness as she could manage into her voice. It sounded phony as the dickens and fooled no one, she suspected. "About the rodeo or something else?"

"The rodeo."

"Great. After the near disaster with the concessions, I'll take anything."

"I thought you said the 4H was going to handle that? Easy, baby, hold still," he said to the restless mare.

"They are. Now. No, don't ask. Just tell me the good news."

He shot her a wicked grin over Sugar's back. "Nate Hartstrong agreed to sing at the opening ceremony."

"Jake, that's wonderful!"

"Yeah, it's great, isn't it? He can't stay for the dance, but since we already have a band booked for that, it shouldn't matter. And he's offered to sing gratis, since he's got a concert in Amarillo that evening." Pausing in his task, he looked over at Leigh hopefully. "What do you think, Leigh? Does that sound good to you?"

She put down Peanuts's hoof and shrugged, her lip curling scornfully. "Who cares? It'll be lame anyway. The whole rodeo's for a bunch of losers." With a disdainful glance at Jake, she said deliberately, "You're just a has-been. Nobody cares if you're there or not."

"Leigh!" Anna said, mortification overcoming her patience. "That's enough, young lady!"

But Leigh wasn't finished, her words raining down like pellets of hurtful hail. To Anna she said, "You think this dumb rodeo's going to be so great. Well, I don't. I think it sucks. And you—" she speared Jake with a hateful glance "—you're a loser, too, or you wouldn't have come back to Happy. Why don't you just go back where you came from?" Defiantly, she faced them both, daring her mother to discipline her with every fiber of her slight body.

Anna was in the mood to oblige her. Jake didn't say a word, his expression had shut down and showed nothing. But she didn't need X-ray vision to know he was hurt. She hurt for him, so she could imagine what he felt like. "I want you to apologize. To Jake and to me."

"Anna, forget it," Jake said in a low voice. "She's upset."

"So am I." She put down her brush and came around the horse to stand beside him. "I'm embarrassed to have my child act so rudely. It's time she remembered the manners I know I taught her." To

Leigh she said, "When Jake comes over he's my guest. I expect you to treat him with the same respect you would any of my friends."

Leigh's expression grew even more contemptuous. "Yeah, well he's not just your *friend,* is he?" She tossed the hoof pick down and glared at her mother.

Hands on hips, Anna set her jaw and glared right back. "No, he's not. He happens to be your father. If for no other reason than that, he's worthy of your respect."

"Don't you call him that! And I won't apologize. Go ahead and ground me. What's the difference? You've already ruined my life!" she wailed, her voice rising dramatically with her last line. She ran out before Anna could say another word.

Anna and Jake stared at each other helplessly, at a loss for words.

"She's coming around nicely, isn't she?" Jake said finally, his voice laced with irony.

Anna choked out a laugh, knowing he meant to lighten the mood. "Oh, Jake, I'm sorry. She doesn't mean it."

"Yes she does." He looked at her bleakly. "She hates my guts."

Anna placed a consoling hand on his arm and rubbed it. "No, she doesn't. Really, she doesn't. She's furious with me and she's taking it out on you."

"Yeah. Whatever." He stared after Leigh, his blue eyes clouded. "Look, I've got to get back. Left a lot of chores. I just wanted to give you the news about the entertainment. As usual, I picked a bad time. But then, it seems like any time I'm around is a bad time for Leigh.''

"Wait." She slipped her arms around his neck. "Try not to take it so much to heart," she said, and kissed him.

"Hard not to." He stared down at her, seemed about to say something, then shook his head. Once more, he leaned down and kissed her, roughly this time. "Later," he said huskily.

"Yes. Later." Anna watched him go with a sinking feeling. She couldn't allow her daughter to run her life, yet she couldn't ignore her feelings, either. But giving up Jake again... No! She wouldn't consider that. Surely with time Leigh would understand.

Or maybe she wouldn't. And then what would Anna do?

Because she couldn't give up her daughter, either.

JAKE ATTACKED his chores with savage intensity, accomplishing most of them in half the time it usually took him. But no amount of labor could keep his mind off the earlier scene with Leigh.

Why did she hate him so much? He'd tried to put himself in her place, but he'd never been a teenage girl so it was a little difficult to do. And his parents had certainly never hit him with news like Leigh had been forced to hear.

He'd expected her to be upset when she found out the truth. But he hadn't expected this consuming hatred she seemed to harbor for him. And today... He closed his eyes and pinched the bridge of his nose. It wasn't what she'd said so much as the way she'd said it. With her eyes and voice cold and cal-culated to hurt.

Wearily, he climbed the ladder to the loft and be-gan forking down hay. A has-been, she'd called him. Maybe that label had pricked a little. But to be hon-est, that's what he was. A broken-down bronc rider who yearned for better things. Who wanted to be with the woman he loved. And the daughter he'd never known. A has-been who wanted a home, a family and a business he'd been dreaming of since adolescence.

He leaned on the pitchfork, staring unseeingly at the hay. He'd thought he could have it all. Not, it seemed, if Leigh had anything to say about it.

He heard Anna's voice call his name from below. His heart leaped, and he couldn't stop the sudden feeling of hopefulness. That's what Anna did. She made him believe, gave him hope through the bad times.

Some days, though, even Anna couldn't change reality.

"Up here," he called, looking down over the edge.

Hands on hips, she gazed up at him. A smile curved her lips. Plump, pretty lips just waiting to be kissed. Her hair hung loose to her shoulders, gleam-ing pale gold in the late afternoon sun. She'd changed from earlier and wore an old, faded pair of jeans, a short-sleeved white T-shirt and red cowboy boots. And she looked great, Jake thought. Like a ripe strawberry just waiting to be devoured.

"Wanna come up here?" he asked, with a suggestive lift to his eyebrow. "I could sure use some help."

She laughed but grasped the side rails of the ladder and began to climb. A few seconds later, he grabbed her around the waist and fastened his mouth to hers.

And fire exploded between them. He hadn't meant to latch on to her so desperately—or maybe he had. She felt so good in his arms, such a loving balm for the pain that clutched his heart after Leigh's rejection. Anna's arms, soft and fragrant, wrapped around him and she kissed him back with the same fever he felt.

"Jake, what—" His hand closed over her breast and she moaned. "What are you doing?"

"I want you, Anna." Wanted her, needed her, had to have her. "Now. Here."

"I want you, too." She gasped as he jerked her shirt out of her jeans and slid his hands up underneath to cup her breasts. "But what if—" Her hands slid under his shirt, even as she protested. "What if someone—" They both groaned when she slid one hand down to his fly and gently rubbed him.

"No one's here but the two of us. Let me make love to you, Anna."

In answer she stepped back and unbuttoned her jeans, sliding the zipper down while she watched him. "What are you waiting for?" she asked, her voice husky.

"Not a thing, darlin'. Not a thing." Moments later, he spread his shirt on the hay and lay back, pulling her with him. As she slowly sank down on him, he tensed, attempting to hold back so she could grow accustomed to him. But he wanted her too much and she felt so damn good, he couldn't wait. His hands grasped her at her hips, helping her set the rhythm and he let passion take over.

Her eyes were open and locked onto his, her expression dazed as they rocked together. Deliberately, he played with her breasts, reveling in the soft sounds she made, pulling her down so he could suckle first one then the other, driving her closer and closer to the edge.

He slid a hand between them, pushing her harder, faster, thinking that she felt like paradise surrounding him with her sweet heat. He brought her mouth down to his, to possess it like he had her body. And she gave everything back ten-fold. Her hands clenched convulsively on his chest and he felt her orgasm start to take her. He watched her eyes darken and go blind, her head fall back in abandon.

Her back arched and he thrust up, exploding at the same time she did, his vision graying as the world became reduced to this. Only this. Only Anna.

He held her, he didn't know how long. Simply held her, collapsed warm and pliant on his chest, until their breathing evened and slowed.

And then he opened his eyes and reality hit anew.

His daughter hated him. And he and Anna didn't have a chance as long as Leigh remained set against them.

ANNA LAY IN the curve of Jake's arm, her head on his chest. ''You want to tell me what that was about?'' She raised her head to look at him, unsurprised to find him frowning.

"We'd better get dressed," was all he said.

Anna waited until she had tugged on her boots to speak again. "Jake." He turned to look at her and the lost expression in his eyes made her want to hug him, hold him close. The way she would Leigh when she hurt. "Talk to me."

He sat with his forearms propped on bent knees, staring down at the hay scattered in the loft before he looked at her. She could read nothing in his face, but she knew he was hurting. She could feel it.

"Leigh hates me."

"No, she doesn't. She's confused right now, that's all."

He shook his head, brushing her words away impatiently. "Anna, don't you get it? It's hopeless. You and me—it's not going to work."

Now she understood. "Ah. So that was good-bye."

"I didn't say that."

"You didn't have to—in words. I felt it, every time you touched me, kissed me."

He reached out to pull her to him. Framed her face in his hands and kissed her. "Anna, I love you."

She held his wrists, rubbed her cheek against his and sighed. "I know. I love you, too."

"And I love Leigh. I want more than anything for the three of us to be a family. But it's not going to happen. Not ever." Anna made a wordless protest, but he ignored it. "At first I thought I had a chance. That she'd get past her hurt and accept me. Today I realized she never would. I don't have a hope in hell with her."

"Jake, she'll come around. She's young and—and spoiled. It's been the two of us for so long—"

"That's not the problem and you know it. Don't try to spare me. *I'm* the problem."

"It's because it's safer for her to be angry with you. I told you before, she's furious with me, not you. You're just bearing the brunt of it." He shook his head but Anna continued. "Is this only about Leigh? Or is there something else?"

"Isn't that enough?" He gazed at her a moment. "Are you worried? Do you think I'm dumping you again?"

Her lips twitched. "No. That didn't occur to me. Are you?"

He shook his head. "No way."

"I think there are easier ways to accomplish a breakup—if that's what you want—than a pitched battle with your daughter."

He raised a hand, smoothed it over her hair. "You don't have any doubts about us, do you? About you and me?"

"No," she said simply.

"I wondered—after what I did, no one could blame you if you did."

She laid a hand against his cheek. "You were young. So was I. We both made mistakes and we paid for them. We've gotten past that. This time we'll do better."

"Do you trust me, Anna?" He took her hand, kissed it, held it close to his heart.

"Yes, I do. Why do you say it like it's such a miracle? Shouldn't I trust you?"

"Because it is a miracle." He smiled and kissed her fingers. "I don't deserve you."

"Too bad. You've got me."

"For now." He looked at her solemnly. "But if it comes down to a choice, I know who you have to choose."

"Jake, don't borrow trouble."

Releasing her hand, he stood up and looked down at her. "Yeah, we've got enough, don't we? I'm coming between you and Leigh. And I can't stand that, Anna. That's the last thing I ever wanted to do."

"We knew it would be hard at first." She rose, too, laying her hand on his arm. "We just have to understand and keep trying. She'll come around, Jake."

"Will she? God, Anna, I don't want to hurt her. And just by existing, I do."

"She'll learn to deal with it," Anna insisted.

"And if she doesn't? What then?"

Helplessly, Anna shook her head. She couldn't give him up. Give *them* up. Not yet. Not until she'd done everything in her power to convince Leigh to accept her father. And failed. She hadn't reached that point yet. "I don't know. Don't ask me questions I can't answer. Please, Jake, don't force the point now. Just give her some more time."

His eyes held such stark desperation it hurt her to look at him. "I'll have to leave, Anna. You know it. I know it. If Leigh won't accept me, I'll have to leave."

Anna didn't answer. Because the only answer she had was to agree with him. And that didn't bear thinking of.

CHAPTER TWENTY

LEIGH LAY BACK in the grass underneath the big live oak in the middle of their pasture. Her father had told her it had been planted in honor of his grandfather's birth and it was the only live oak for miles around. She remembered having picnics underneath it when she was little and spending long hours playing with her dolls in just this spot. But her favorite spot didn't feel the same anymore. Nothing did.

Her life was the pits and it was all her mother and Jake's fault.

Only a few days until the rodeo. She ought to be getting Promise ready to race, but she wasn't sure she would even show up. It would serve her mom and Jake right if she didn't go. But if she didn't, then she could kiss any chance of winning prize money goodbye.

She closed her eyes and felt tears start to leak from the corners. Crying didn't do any good, but lately, she cried all the time anyway. Just not in front of *them*.

"Hey, *chica*."

Leigh opened her eyes to see a pair of black boots and jeans and a guy's long, long legs. Luis, she thought, glad of the company. After she wrecked the truck she'd told him what had happened. But they hadn't talked much after that, mostly because Leigh hadn't felt like talking to anyone.

He squatted beside her and tickled her cheek with a blade of grass. "Ready for the big race?"

"No." And she might never be. She swallowed the lump in her throat and spoke. "What about you? Are you really going to enter the saddle bronc event?"

"*Sí.*" He grinned. "Jake says I'm a natural."

"Don't talk about him." She heard enough about Jake from her other best friend. Blaire thought she should just get over being so upset. But Blaire didn't understand it wasn't that easy.

"Okay. I won't talk about him." He shifted to sit cross-legged. "But maybe you should."

Suddenly angry, she sat up. "Are you going to be like Blaire? Tell me to grow up?" That still stung. She hadn't spoken to Blaire for two days after she'd said that. And even though Blaire had apologized, Leigh knew she didn't really understand.

"No. I think—" he hesitated and shrugged "—I'd be mad, too."

"I am mad. And I hate them. I hate them for doing this to me. My dad—" She swallowed hard. "I can't believe he lied to me. Or that Mom did." And Jake. She had really liked him. *Before.* "Why did they have to ruin everything?" She started to cry, big gulping sobs. She wished Luis would just go away and leave her alone, but he didn't.

Instead, he put his arm around her and hugged her. She kept crying, even harder, leaning into his shoulder and barely hearing the soft sound of his voice telling her to cry it out and whispering words of comfort in Spanish.

After a long time she managed to stop. She pushed away from Luis, wiping her eyes with the palms of her hands. "Thanks." She felt a little embarrassed. Luis had seen her cry before, but not like this.

He smiled at her. "*De nada.* But you have to use your own shirt to wipe your nose."

She laughed shakily and pulled up her T-shirt hem to blot at her eyes. "Thanks for understanding. For not telling me I should just get over it."

"No, but—" He worried his lip and gazed out at the field, then looked her in the eye. "Leigh, what are you going to do if your mother and Jake get married?"

Her stomach twisting with fear, Leigh stared at her friend. Marriage? She hadn't thought of that. Jake came over to see her, not her mother. But... She felt even sicker as she thought about it. Her mother had said just the other day that Jake had come to see her, not Leigh. He wanted to be Leigh's father, but that didn't mean he would marry her mother to do it. Did it?

No, she wouldn't think about that. "They're not getting married. Ever."

Luis just looked at her, his big brown eyes so sad.

She grabbed his arm in a death grip. "Why do you think that? What made you say that?"

"Heard my parents talking about it."

Leigh sucked in her breath. The Villareals talked to her mom all the time. If they thought it was true... She couldn't finish the thought.

"Maybe they're wrong," Luis said, patting her hand awkwardly.

"They haven't said anything to me. They wouldn't. They couldn't."

But what if they did?

As soon as she and Luis got back to the barn and stabled the horses, Leigh tracked her mother down.

She found her in the living room, doing paperwork at the coffee table. She tried hard not to feel guilty at seeing her mom working so hard. Clearing her throat, she waited for Anna to look at her.

"Something wrong?" her mother said, glancing up.

"I want to talk to you."

Anna stared at her for a minute and then put her pencil down and folded her hands together. "That's a change."

Leigh ignored the comment and plunged ahead recklessly. "The other day you said that Jake came to see you, not me."

"That's right."

"Why?"

Her mother looked confused. "What do you mean, why? You know we've been seeing each other."

"I thought—I thought he just used you as an excuse. So he could see me."

"Well, that's flattering," she said, and laughed. "Leigh, Jake wants to know you, but he does have other things on his mind."

"Like you."

"Yes. Like me. This can't be a surprise to you, honey. I told you weeks ago."

"But that was before..." Her voice trailed off. Before she'd known the truth. Her stomach hurt. Luis was right. Oh, she hated her life. Turning, she faced the mantel, and saw a picture of her father and her with one of the horses. Whirling around, tears clogging her throat, she said, "You don't even care that Dad's dead, do you? You never even loved him. You only married him because of me. You're happy he's gone so you can be with *him*."

Anna sucked in her breath and looked like Leigh had hit her. "You're wrong. I did love him. I loved him very much. And if he were alive, the only thing Jake and I would have in common would be you. Because I'd never have left Carl."

"Yeah, right. You say that now." Every single one of them was a liar.

"If Carl were alive I would still have told you the truth about your parentage. Because I was wrong to keep it from you before. And I was wrong to keep it from Jake."

"Then why did you?" Leigh shouted, spinning away to pace the length of the room before she came back to stand in front of her mother.

Anna bit her lip. "Because I didn't know what else to do. Your fath— Carl and I decided that it was best at the time. And as the years passed..." She hesitated and continued, "There didn't seem to be any point in telling you."

"Until *he* came back."

"That's right. But don't blame everything on Jake. He wanted to know his child. That's not a bad thing. We can't fault him for wanting that. I—I took that opportunity away from him, Leigh, and all he's asking for is a chance.''

"A chance? What if I don't want to know him? Don't I count? I don't, do I? Nothing I want matters.''

"Honey, if you'll just—''

"You're going to marry him, aren't you?'' There, it was out. The big question. Now let her lie her way out of this one, Leigh thought.

"I—we've talked about marriage. But nothing has been decided yet.''

Tears sprang to her eyes. "I bet you think if you get married I'll have to call him my father. Well, you're wrong! I won't do it. I won't!''

Frowning, Anna spoke slowly. "Leigh, I don't think you understand the situation. It's my fault, I should have explained this to you before now. Sit down, sweetheart, and let me talk to you.''

Furious, hurting, Leigh only shook her head.

Anna sighed deeply, then spoke. "I want you to acknowledge Jake as your father, and so does he, more than you can imagine. But if we marry, it won't be because of you. It will be because we love each other. Very much.''

Leigh couldn't get her breath. She wanted to scream. To cry. To curl up in a ball and forget everything. "If you marry him I won't stay here. I won't! I'll go live with Grandma in California. Or— or Blaire. Or I'll run away. Anything but stay here with you and him!''

She ran out of the house, betrayed and alone, as far away from them as she could get.

JAKE WAS WORKING Slick in the round pen when he felt her presence. He turned around slowly and saw that he'd been right. Leigh stood at the fence, regarding him in stony silence. The brief hope that had sprung up when he first recognized her died. Would she ever look at him again in that same friendly light she had before she knew the truth?

Not bloody likely.

Since she wouldn't speak, he did. "I'll be through in a few minutes, if you want to wait."

Leigh nodded. If looks could kill, Jake decided, he'd be gutted and fried. A short time later, he grabbed Slick's reins to take him out of the pen and walk him to cool him down. Leigh followed without a word.

Their boots crunched in the gravel until they came to a dirt path surrounding the barn area. Reins dangling from one hand, Jake glanced at his daughter, her countenance anything but reassuring. "This is the first time you've come here since you heard the news."

"That's right. And it's gonna be the last."

God, all that energy and emotion expended on hating him. He wished he knew what to say to change her mind. What to say to soothe her pain. "So this must be important."

She strode beside him in silence for a moment. "I came to tell you to stay away from me and my mother."

"Well, that's plain speaking. And does your mother agree?"

Ignoring the question, she blew right by him, her words tumbling over themselves in her haste. "I know your plan. You think you're gonna marry my mom and then you can be my father. Well, you're wrong about that. You go ahead and marry her, but I won't be there. I'll run away before I live in the same house with you.''

"Your mother told you we were getting married?'' That was news to him, since she hadn't shared it with him.

"She didn't have to. I know what you're doing. You're just using her because of me and I want you to stop.''

"You figured that out all by yourself, did you?''

Hunching her shoulders, she glared at him. "I'm not stupid.''

"No one said you were stupid. But you are confused.'' He halted and grasped her arm, hanging on when she tried to jerk away. "No, don't run away. It's time you heard a few things. A few more truths you may not want to hear.''

She said nothing but the mutinous set of her mouth made him certain she wouldn't listen to a word he said. It didn't matter, though. He had to try.

"I don't need to use your mother to get to you. She agrees that I have a right to try to know you. You and I are a different issue from your mother and I.''

"You want to marry her so you can order me around and pretend you're my dad! But you're not! And you never will be. My father is dead.''

God, he needed every bit of patience and understanding he possessed. Tightening his grip on his frustration, he spoke slowly and carefully. "The father who raised you, who loved you like his own flesh and blood is gone. But your biological father isn't.'' Her gaze hardened but he plowed on regardless, determined to say his piece. "I don't want to take your father's place, Leigh. I couldn't. I can't get back the years, even if you'd accept me. I just want a shot at making another place, a different place, for me.''

"You just want to marry Mom because of me.''

His jaw tightened as he struggled with the words. "You're wrong. I want to marry your mother because I'm in love with her. Not because of you. I want a relationship with you, too, but loving her really doesn't have anything to do with that. No matter what your answer to me is, no matter whether you ever accept me or not, I'm still in love with your mother.''

Chest heaving, she faced him, as angry and defiant as he'd ever seen her. "I don't believe you! I don't care! You make me sick, lying and—and acting so nice when you met me. You knew then, didn't you?''

Slick jerked his head at the sudden shouting. Jake soothed him, weighing his answer. But what could he tell her except the truth?

"No, I didn't know. I suspected, but I didn't know for sure.'' Desperate for a way to salvage something—anything—from the mess, he asked, "Look, I know you hate thinking of me as your father. But maybe you could think of me as a friend.''

"No. Because you're not. You're not my friend. You never were.''

"When you first knew me, before all this came out, we were friends. Why can't we be again?"

"Because it's not the same! I'm not the same. I don't even know who I am anymore. And it's all your fault."

She turned and ran, leaving him standing alone with his horse. Slick nudged him, his big head butting against Jake's chest, blowing out a breath as if in sympathy. All his fault. Well, she had that right. So much for the friends approach. Way to go, he thought.

If possible, he'd alienated his daughter even more.

ONE LOOK AT Jake's face when she let him in that evening told Anna he had something serious on his mind. And she had a miserable feeling they were on the same page.

After kissing him hello, she searched his face again. "It's not the rodeo, is it?" she finally asked, leading him into the living room.

"No." Sighing, he rubbed his neck. "As far as I know everything's set for that. Hard to believe it's only a few days away."

"Seems like we've been working on it forever."

"Yeah? Seems like yesterday to me." He gave her a rueful smile. "Remember how mad you were when we first started?"

"Mad doesn't begin to describe it." Her mouth lifted at one corner. "I mellowed, though. Lucky for you."

"It might have been better for both of us if you hadn't."

Her smile faltered. Definitely on the same wavelength. "You don't really believe that, do you?"

"No," he said, his voice so low she barely heard him. He walked to the window, put his hand on the frame and looked out, with his back to her. "Where's Leigh?"

She followed him, laying a hand on his outstretched arm and rubbing it lightly. "In her room. She's about to go to Blaire's for the night. I haven't had the heart to make her stay home." Not when she so obviously didn't want to be there.

He blew out a long breath, then drew himself up and turned to face her. "You know the day you asked me if this was goodbye? And we decided that we'd give it another chance? To wait for Leigh to change her mind?"

Her heart started to pound in her chest. She managed a nod.

"She's not going to, Anna."

Anna couldn't speak. How could she agree?

How could she not?

"You're not arguing," he said, his eyes scanning her face.

She swallowed the lump in her throat and forced the words out. "We had a fight today. She wanted to know if you and I were getting married."

"What did you tell her?"

"The truth. That we loved each other. But that we didn't know yet about marriage."

"And she flipped out."

Anna didn't want to answer, but she owed him the truth. "Pretty much. She threatened to run away."

"Do you think she would?"

Again, she answered with the truth when a lie would have been infinitely easier. "Yes. The instant we made our vows. Maybe before."

"Leigh paid me a visit today, too. After your fight, I guess. Told me to stay away from both of you." He looked away, staring out the window. "We can't do this to her. She's not going to change her mind. She'll never accept me. It's time we faced that."

"I know," Anna whispered. "I've been hoping… But after today I don't believe—I don't believe she'll accept you. No matter how much I want her to, I don't believe she will." She gazed at him, her heart twisting in her chest.

He wrapped an arm around her and pulled her against him, her cheek resting against his heart. She felt him kiss her hair, felt his warm breath flowing over her as he spoke. "The worst thing—it wasn't when she said she hated me. Or when she accused me of only wanting to marry you because of her. But when she said she didn't know who she was anymore, that's when I realized what we've done to her. She has to come first. Leigh matters, Anna. She matters…more than anything."

Anna pulled back to look at him. "I know she does. I know you're right. But, God, Jake, how do we do this? How do we say goodbye again? We love each other. How do we just let that go?"

Despair showed in the lines of his face. But along with that she saw resolve.

"We let each other go because that's what's right for Leigh. It's the best thing we can do for our daughter. We owe her, Anna, and she needs you. She's just a kid. A kid who needs her mother. If we get married it will drive a wedge the size of Texas between you two. We can't do it to her.''

And she couldn't argue with him. She wanted to, oh, so badly. But she couldn't. Tears pricked her eyes. Bitter tears. Useless tears. ''How am I going to stand it, Jake? What am I going to do without you? And how can I see you every day and know—''

''You won't have to. I'm leaving town. After the rodeo.''

''But—your business. You've already started, you can't just quit. Your father. Can you just forget—''

He cut her off with a savage swipe of his hand. Then his hands rested on her shoulders, his fingers gripping her tightly as he looked down at her. ''How can I stay here, Anna? It would kill me to see you day after day and know I could never have you. And to see Leigh every day and know she hates me, know she'll never forgive me. No, it's better I just get the hell out of here. For good this time.''

He plunged his fingers into her hair, tilted her face up to his. ''God, Anna, I didn't think it was possible to love someone as much as I love you. But I can't have you at Leigh's expense. I won't come between you and Leigh. If things are bad now, can you imagine how bad they'll be if we married?''

And again, she couldn't answer. Because every word he spoke was the truth.

''Tell me I'm wrong. Tell me there's a way we can work this out. A way we can be together.'' His voice begged her, but she read the answer in his eyes.

"I can't," she finally said. "We can't be together."

He kissed her then, a rough kiss of despair and longing. She clung to him, tears streaking down her cheeks, her heart literally shattering.

He raised his head and stared down at her. "I love you, Anna. I always will."

She kissed him again, then let him fold her in his arms and simply hold her. Hold her like he'd never let her go, when both of them knew he had to. She heard a sound and turned in Jake's arms.

Across the room Leigh stood in the doorway. Their gazes met but Anna could see nothing in Leigh's eyes, read nothing in her stony expression. From outside a horn sounded.

"Is it true?" Leigh asked. "Is he really leaving?"

Anna started to speak, but Jake's hand gripped her shoulder, holding her silent.

"It's true," he said, and Anna could hear in his voice what it cost him to say it. "I'm leaving town after the rodeo."

"Good."

Frozen, Anna watched as without another word, her daughter turned her back and walked out the door.

CHAPTER TWENTY-ONE

ANNA TORE herself from Jake's arms and ran to the door, yanking it open. "Leigh, wait!"

Hearing the desperation in Anna's voice, Jake was afraid for a moment that Leigh had taken the truck again. But why would she when she'd finally gotten what she wanted? He was out of their lives, for good this time.

Shoulders slumped, Anna turned back to him. "Suzie was waiting for her and she's already taken off. Do you think I should call over there?"

"What's the point? What can you say that both of us haven't said a thousand times? And do you really think she'll want to talk to you?"

Anna bit her lip and continued staring after the departing car. Long moments later, she shut the door. "No, she won't talk to me." Anguished, she raised her gaze to his. "Oh, Jake, I feel so helpless. I've done nothing but let her down."

And he'd let both of them down, starting years ago, before Leigh was even born. "Yeah, well cheer up. You heard her. She's glad I'm leaving. She's probably jumping for joy right now."

Stricken, she gazed at him. "Don't say that. I can't bear to think about it. If only..."

If only Leigh would change her mind, Jake finished silently. If only she would listen. If only miracles would happen. But they never had, at least, not for him.

Anna stretched a hand out to him. "Stay with me tonight. It might be…" Her voice trailed off and she looked at him with her heart in her eyes.

The last night, he thought, taking her hand. The last time he would make love to her, the last time he would hold her in his arms and watch her sleep. The last time he would wake in the morning, still wrapped up in her, drowning in the feel of her soft, silky flesh, the sweet smell of her hair. It might be easier, for both of them, simply to end it now. But he wouldn't take the easy way. Not this time.

"I want the memories," he said, taking her in his arms. "I want tonight. One night that will have to last us the rest of our lives."

She put her arms around his neck, pulled his face down to hers. "Can one night last us for a lifetime?"

Tears streaked her cheeks. He hadn't known she was crying. He wondered who had made it a rule that men shouldn't cry. No fall he'd ever taken, no bruises or broken bones had ever come close to the pain he felt right this instant when he faced the reality of losing Anna.

"No. It won't be enough." He kissed her, tasted the salt of her tears. "But it's all we have."

They walked hand in hand to her bedroom. He turned the lights down low while Anna lit candles. They came together in the middle of the room. He put his hands on her, slipped them beneath her shirt, caressed her gently. He undressed her slowly, his lips tasting her skin, blazing a trail down the column of her throat, to her chest, to her stomach, drinking in the smell and feel of her as each piece of clothing dropped away.

Slowly. As if it were the beginning, instead of the end.

He wanted to taste every inch of her, savor her like a fine wine. Imprint her on his memory, on his senses, for all time. He wanted to remember what it felt like when her hands stroked him, when she followed her hands with her soft, mobile mouth. When she took him to the edge of oblivion, and brought him back just as surely. To remember what she looked like in passion, rising over him like a dream.

So he didn't rush, but he cherished each kiss, each caress, each sigh that came from her parted lips. Each groan she drew from him, each moan he lured from her. When at last she lay naked beneath him, he could wait no longer. Lacing his fingers with hers he said, "Anna, look at me." Her eyes opened, her gaze locked on his as he entered her. She moaned softly with each gentle thrust. Her head fell back and he tasted the pulse racing at the hollow of her throat and his thrusts increased in tempo. Her eyes darkened as they moved together, her body tightened around his with each stroke, reaching for the same sweet oblivion he sought.

At her peak she cried out, strained against him, and he crushed his mouth to hers, drinking in her sweet cries of completion. Then let himself fall.

He held her through the night. They made love again and again, fast and rough and desperate, slow and gentle and haunting. A lifetime of loving, packed into a single night.

They didn't talk much, for what was there to say? Instead they let their bodies speak for them, desperately trying to store up for a bleak future. But late in the night Anna asked him a question.

"Will I never see you again? Does this have to be forever? Maybe with time—"

His arms tightened around her. "Don't, Anna. Don't hope for something that isn't going to happen."

"What about—what about when Leigh is grown? Couldn't we be together then?"

He wanted so badly to say yes. But he couldn't. "She'd still hate me. And it wouldn't be fair, Anna, to either of us, to put our lives on hold. You should—" He squeezed his eyes shut, forced the words out, though it was the last thing he wanted. "You should marry again. To someone Leigh can love, too. Don't waste your life waiting for me."

"It wouldn't be wasted," she whispered, her voice clogged with emotion.

"Yes, it would. You deserve more, so much more than that. You deserve to love and be loved again. I can't ask you to wait. I won't do that to you."

She didn't answer in words, but she lay her head on his shoulder and he felt the heat of her tears.

Later, in the early hours of the morning, he kissed her mouth and said, "I want you again."

She smiled. Her voice was husky when she answered. "Make love to me, then."

He knew she wasn't used to so much lovemaking and guilt pulled at him, but it didn't stop him from wanting her. From needing her. From taking her. His hand slipped over her stomach, caressing the soft flesh, slid down to the curls at the juncture of her thighs. "You must be sore. I don't want to hurt you."

"Oh, Jake." She raised up and laid her cheek against his. "I'm already hurting. Loving you can't make it worse, only better."

He used his mouth that time to take her over, and listened to her sobs as she came.

When the dawn light crept in through the shutters they loved each other one last time. Jake left her at the kitchen door, wrapped in a white cotton robe, her feet bare, her honey-gold hair tousled and streaming over her shoulders, her beautiful mouth swollen from a night of love.

And he prayed for a miracle he knew would never happen.

WES'S EYES weren't as sharp as they used to be, but he didn't need twenty-twenty peepers to recognize Leigh sitting up on her big Appy gelding in his pasture at six-thirty one morning, the day before the big rodeo. Since all the brouhaha he'd only seen her at a distance. He'd figured she didn't have any inclination to see him. Besides, he hadn't known what to say to her. Mary had told him to be patient, that maybe he had a role to play yet and that stranger things had happened than two people who loved each other getting back together.

But Wes wasn't so sure. It looked to him like things were just about as bad as they could be, and God only knew, he had no magic answers. He knew it was breaking Jake's heart to leave town, giving up Anna and his daughter. And this time it would be worse, because he'd know what he was missing. There ought to be a way, Wes mused, to get the little gal to see what *she'd* be missing, if she denied herself the chance to come to know her father.

He kept driving until he drew near her, then stopped the truck to get out and check some of his cattle. A good half of his herd was ready to calve, and he wanted to make sure none of the mothers were in trouble. Nodding at Leigh through the open window, he got out and took a quick look around before walking to the back of the truck.

"No calves this morning," he said, to break the ice. "Unless somebody's hiding one. Did you see any when you rode over?"

Leigh shook her head. Still silent, she dismounted and headed over to the truck, leading her horse. Wes studied her a moment. Way too much sadness for such a young, pretty face. And unless he missed his guess, lots of anger, too. "Heard you came by to see Jake a few days ago."

She shrugged and didn't respond. But her mouth tightened into an even grimmer line.

"Sounded like you were rough on him. Not that he said a whole lot, you understand."

"I hate him. And I hate her, too."

"That a fact?" He underplayed it deliberately, knowing she expected him to take her to task for her words.

All set to defend herself, she popped like a busted balloon at that. "Did you know?" she asked him after a time.

"About you?" He shook his head. "Nope. Didn't find out until the day after you rolled your Mama's pickup and scared the life out of her."

Her gaze narrowed and she stared at him a while. "You really didn't know? You're not just saying that?"

"Knowing and wondering aren't the same thing. I wondered. Through the years, when I'd see you, sometimes I wondered. You look a lot like your Mama, but you've got your Daddy's eyes." He glanced at her and saw the fire shooting from those eyes. "Right down to the expression in them right now."

"Don't call him that. He's not my father."

Wes let that pass, but it hurt him to hear her deny Jake so fiercely.

"Doesn't it even bother you that my mother lied to you, too?"

He nodded. "A bit. But I reckon she did what she thought best at the time."

"That's such a lame excuse."

"Only one we have sometimes." He motioned to the cattle crowding the truck, in search of food. "See these? They're what kept me from seeing my son for sixteen years. Them and my pride."

She stared at him with an expression that seemed to say, *Get to the point, old man.*

"You're wondering what that has to do with you. Take a seat here—" he patted the tailgate of the truck "—and I'll tell you." He sat beside her and looked out over his fields, striving to think of a way to tell her what had happened so long ago. "I don't think Jake left town because of your Mama. I think

he left because of me. Because he had a dream I
just couldn't see.''

"Like my mom and me and the rodeo.''

"Yep. Kinda like that. But I wanted Jake to stay
here and raise cattle. He wanted to raise horses. He
thought he'd win enough on the circuit to make a
starting stake." Wes snorted a laugh. "I told him it
was damn foolishness. I was telling him what I
thought was best, you see. But it was best for me,
not him. Only I didn't know it then.

"I'll always wonder if I hadn't driven him
away..." His voice trailed off and he shrugged.
"Let's say I figure part of this is my fault. So you
can spread some of that mad around to me.''

"It's their fault, not yours. Why did they lie to
me? She and my da—my dad lied to me all my
life.''

He tilted his head and considered her. "So you
wouldn't be upset if they'd told you the truth?''

"I don't know." She sniffed and wiped her sleeve
across her cheek. "Maybe.''

"If you'd known Carl wasn't your daddy by
blood, would you have loved him any less?''

"No! But why did he have to lie to me? Why
couldn't they just have told me the truth?''

Wes rubbed his neck and sighed. "Sometimes
people make a choice and then it seems like they
can't do anything else. Maybe that's what happened
to your parents.''

"I'm never going to lie to my kids. Not like
that.''

He kept his chuckle to himself. "I hope you never
have to." He rose and stood looking down at her a

moment before he added, "They made that mistake a long time ago. Do you want to add on another one now? Is Jake so bad that you won't even give him a chance?"

"I don't know! I thought— At first I thought he was so cool. And now—I'm all mixed up inside." Her hands fisted and she whispered, "I don't know who I am anymore."

"Same person you always were. Nothing's going to change that. Not even finding out you've got two fathers."

She dashed tears away with the back of her hand. "I don't want another father."

"Yep. But you've got one. And I'll tell you something. I lost my son for sixteen years because of stubborn pride. You're young, but I don't think you're too young to understand that can be mighty lonely."

"It's not the same thing."

"Maybe not. But maybe it is. So you think hard on that before you go cutting your mother and Jake clean out of your life."

"Do you think...do you think they really love each other?"

He gazed at the fields, but in his mind's eye he saw his son. His son's face when he'd told him he was leaving. "Yep. I do at that."

"Do you think I'm awful because they're not going to get together? Because of me, I mean?"

He reached out and ruffled her hair. "Not awful. Confused. Nobody blames you for that."

"They do."

"They blame themselves. Not you." They were

both silent for a time then Wes added, ''Jake and Anna made some mistakes, no one's saying they didn't. But they both love you.''

Knowing he wouldn't risk his next words if he looked at her, his gaze returned to the fields. ''And there's an old man right here who loves you, too.''

''Mr. Rollins?'' He looked at her then and saw the solemn expression on her face. ''Could I call you Grandpa?''

A smile spread over his face. ''I'd be proud if you did.''

''This doesn't mean—it doesn't mean I've decided about him. It doesn't mean he can be my father.''

''You'll have to think on that, I imagine.''

He hoped she would. And he hoped like hell their little talk had done Jake and Anna some good. Because if it hadn't… If it hadn't, he might have gained a granddaughter, but he'd have lost his son. This time for good.

CHAPTER TWENTY-TWO

THE DAY OF the rodeo dawned clear and cool, a perfect early summer day. Except it was anything but perfect, Anna thought. The minor problems they'd had to deal with all week turned out to be nothing compared to this morning. Mary called at six-thirty a.m. She couldn't find any of the belt buckles they'd planned on awarding as prizes. What were they supposed to give the winners of those events? Gift certificates?

Anna dressed hastily, settling for her best pair of Levi's and a yoked green satin shirt with mother-of-pearl buttons. Nice but not too fancy. Her place was behind the scenes, anyway, making sure everything ran smoothly. No one would be looking at her.

Except Jake.

Resolutely, she tried to ignore the feeling of grief that had become so familiar recently. Daily, she tortured herself over their decision to end the relationship. Was allowing Leigh, an adolescent running on emotion, the final say in a decision that affected all their lives the right thing to do? Sometimes Anna convinced herself that Leigh could still come around, that she would relent and want to acknowledge Jake. But Jake remained adamant, no matter

Anna's arguments. He refused to let it boil down to a choice between him and her daughter.

And he was right. As much as she loved Jake, she couldn't be with him if it meant losing Leigh. Leigh was her daughter. She couldn't imagine life without her. She truly didn't think Leigh's threats of leaving were idle. So now Anna had to live with the decision she'd made so long ago.

She had lived without Jake before; she could do it again.

Even if it felt like her heart had been ripped from her chest. Even if it wouldn't really be living. Even if she ached for him until the end of her days.

Twenty-five minutes after being startled awake by Mary's call, Anna arrived at the arena and plunged into the myriad details yet to be handled. Such as finding the belt buckles she'd seen herself—last week. Finally, Jake unearthed the missing items, buried in a box underneath another set of prizes. But it had taken all of them an hour of searching before they were finally located. An hour they couldn't really spare.

At nine-thirty, half an hour before the rodeo officially kicked off, Anna decided to check the sound system one last time, just to make certain everything was working.

It wasn't.

Unable to deal with another problem, she spit out an exasperated oath, drawing Jake's attention.

"What's wrong now?"

She smacked her palm against her forehead in frustration. "Oh, this is just great. The sound system doesn't work."

"Sure it does. We checked it last night."

"I know we did. But I'm telling you, it's not working." She waved a hand at the worthless mike. "Try it yourself."

He walked over to where she sat, fiddling with the controls. Clicked a few switches and tested it. Today Jake's method of testing was to sing a Clint Black song into the mike. The night before he'd contented himself with speaking into it.

Anna stared at him a moment, her lips quirking in a smile, for a moment forgetting her woes. Not bad, she thought. A little off-key but not bad at all. "I never knew you could sing."

"I can't. Lucky the system's down," he said and grinned. "Don't worry, I'm sure it's something simple." He began jiggling wires, thumping knobs, squeezing triggers and muttering curses the whole time. Ten minutes later he found a loose connection and fixed it.

"Let's rock and roll," he said and winked at her.

"My hero." Relief washed over her. Disaster averted. Thanks to Jake, again. "What would I do without you?"

As soon as she uttered the words a fist closed around her heart. Her gaze met Jake's. His eyes, so blue she could drown in them, mirrored the pain she felt. "Jake, I—"

"Don't." He cut her off with a savage gesture, his expression as despondent as she knew hers to be. "Don't think about it. Don't talk about it. We have to get through this, Anna. We can't afford to let it get to us."

Not now. Later we can fall apart, but for now we

have to be strong. She heard the words he didn't speak. "I know. You're right." But she couldn't stop herself from watching him as he turned back to his work. And wishing things could be different.

LEIGH SUCKED IN AIR, trying to breathe past the knot in her throat. Always nervous before a race, today she felt even tighter than usual. The things that usually calmed her down—hugging Promise, thinking about both of them in the perfect run, tying their good luck pieces to the saddle—hadn't done a thing to stop the hammering ache in her stomach.

It helped to have her mom around. Her mom always made her feel like the best one out there. And she'd done it today, too, even though she'd been busy working on the rodeo. She had made sure to tell Leigh that both she and Promise looked good and spent some time giving her a pep talk. The way she did before every one of Leigh's races, whether she could be there or not.

But Leigh didn't feel like the best. She felt like a bitch. It didn't take a genius to see that her mother was miserable. And it was all her fault. Every single bit of it.

Leigh thought back to the time before she knew the truth. After Anna and Jake had gotten together her mom had been different. Even though she still worked hard, she seemed happy. She even sang while she worked, which she hadn't done in ages. The last time Leigh remembered her mother singing a lot had been when her dad was still alive. Back then she sang all the time.

But Anna didn't sing anymore. Oh, she tried to

act like things were okay, especially around Leigh, but she was obviously bummed. In fact, she wandered around looking like…like she'd lost her best friend. Because of Leigh. Because she'd told her mom to choose between her and Jake. Anna had picked her, so why didn't she feel better?

Twisting her fingers into Promise's braided mane and leaning her forehead against her neck, she thought about what had happened. Maybe she'd been wrong about Jake. What if Mr. Rollins—her grandfather—was right? Maybe she should give Jake a chance.

Shutting her eyes, she remembered again that day she'd heard her mother and Jake talking. The day he'd told her he was leaving town after the rodeo. Played it in her mind like a movie she'd seen a thousand times, because that's how many times she'd thought about it since.

"I didn't think it was possible to love someone as much as I love you," Jake had said. "But I can't have you at Leigh's expense. I won't come between you and Leigh."

Leigh thought about that, and about what Jake had looked like when he'd told her mom he loved her. She didn't think he was lying, even though she'd wanted him to be. At first she hadn't believed he loved her mother. When she heard he was leaving town she figured she'd won. But the more she thought about things, the more that had changed. Instead of feeling like a winner, she only felt rotten.

Her fingers clenched in Promise's mane. It made her stomach hurt all over again to think about it. Because Jake must love *her,* too. Why else would he give up being with her mom again just because Leigh didn't like it? She knew other kids whose parents had divorced and then remarried. And a couple of them didn't like their new families much, but their parents hadn't asked them how they felt. They'd just gone ahead and done what they wanted.

If Anna and Jake loved each other so much—and they were both sad enough lately to make her sure it was really love—then why were they willing to give each other up?

Leigh knew the answer, no matter how hard she'd tried to deny it. Because they both loved her.

Raising her head, she stroked Promise's neck, soothing her, even though she wasn't calm herself. Every time she thought about Anna and Jake together, about herself and the two of them, she couldn't help thinking about her dad. Carl Connor, the man who had raised her. The man she still thought of as her father. If she told her mom and Jake that she was okay with the two of them, then wouldn't it make her a traitor to her real father? What would her dad want her to do?

She had a hollow feeling in the pit of her stomach that told her she already knew what her dad would say. He'd want whatever it took to make her mom and her happy.

Leigh sighed and jammed her hat on her head, glancing at her watch. Her call would come soon. Was she thinking of the race? Her chance to win, and win big? No, she could only think about her parents and the big fat mess she'd made of everything.

Battling her thoughts, she went through the drill,

checking Promise's girth, making sure the saddle sat right, making sure she had everything just so. Muttering words of love and encouragement in her horse's ear.

She saw her grandfather in the distance, holding hands with Mrs. Gallick. It seemed funny to call her Mrs. Rollins now. Or Grandma. But Mrs. Gallick had told her she could call her whatever she wanted. And Leigh admitted she liked the idea of having grandparents near.

He hadn't said it, in fact he'd seemed to understand how she felt, but Leigh worried that her grandfather wouldn't want to be around her. Not when he thought about it. Because of her, his son was leaving.

Jake walked by just then but didn't look at her. He hadn't tried to talk to her since she'd told him to leave her mom and her alone. Since he'd said he was going away. And though she hated to admit it, she missed talking to him, had gotten used to having him around, making her mom laugh, making her laugh. Nobody laughed around her house now. Especially not her mother. Impulsively, Leigh called out to Jake.

He glanced around and looked totally blown away when he realized who had called him. It made her feel guilty to think he'd been so shocked just because she talked to him. But then lately she felt guilty about pretty much everything.

"Problem?" he asked, walking over.

He looked, she thought, the way her mom did. Depressed. "No. I..." Her fingers curled around the reins as she stood by Promise's side. Promise snorted and pranced until Leigh settled her. "Are you going to watch the barrel race?"

He smiled, chasing away that unhappy look. His eyes—blue eyes the color of hers—crinkled at the corners, just like hers did. She knew because she'd studied herself in the mirror after they'd told her the truth. Trying to prove she wasn't his daughter.

"Wouldn't miss it. Don't worry, you're going to blow them away, kid. My money's on you."

"And Mom? She's going to watch, too?"

Chuckling, he said, "Come on, you know your mom. You couldn't get her out of her seat with a bomb. At least, not until after she sees you race." He studied her a minute before he spoke again. "What's up, Leigh?"

"Nothing." She glanced away. "I guess—" She hesitated, then the words came out in a rush. "I'm sorry I've been mean to you."

"Hey." He laid a gentle hand on her arm and squeezed. "You've had good reason to be upset."

"Yeah. I guess so." She shrugged uncomfortably. "Um, Jake, would you—would you do something for me?"

He looked surprised again, then pleased. "Sure. Name it."

"Would you, um, talk to Promise? You know, like you do your horses?"

"You got it." Leaning forward, he stroked Promise's nose, murmured in her ear. Promise snorted and tossed her head, almost like she understood him. Patting her neck, he grinned at Leigh. "She tells me she intends to win."

Leigh smiled back for the first time since she'd

found out the truth. It felt good. It felt right. "I hope so. Thanks, Jake."

"Any time."

They looked at each other and his eyes clouded as if he'd just remembered he wouldn't be around *any time*. Leigh wanted to say something, but she couldn't get the words out.

He raised his hand like he wanted to touch her, but then he dropped it. "You're a winner, Leigh. No matter what happens in the race, you're always a winner to the people who love you. Remember that." Then he turned and walked away.

LEIGH DREW the last slot. It didn't bother her. In fact, she liked being last. That way she knew the time she had to beat. Still, the waiting got to her. She watched the scoreboard, watched the times, watched the riders. And suffered.

Finally, her turn. Sitting on Promise waiting for the gate to swing free, the sounds of the rodeo threatened to overwhelm her. The beat of the music drumming in her veins. The blare of the announcer giving the results of the ride before hers. The roar of the crowd, restless and talkative. The whinnies and stamping of the horses, the outraged squeals of a bull, kicking its stall. That funny snort Promise always gave before a race.

And the loudest noise of all. Her heart hammering in her chest. She focused, blanking out everything but herself, Promise and the pattern they would run. In her head, she heard her mother's voice, laughing once when they talked about racing. *If you're not scared to death running that first barrel, you're not going fast enough.* And then she remembered what her mother had said earlier today. *Trust your horse. More, trust yourself. You can do it, Leigh. I know you can.*

She cleared her mind, took in a deep breath and sprang forward with Promise as the gate swung open. Made herself one with her horse and felt the breeze in her face, the pounding of Promise's hooves as they raced for the first barrel. The sick feeling of excitement and not knowing gave way to calm. They took the second barrel with a bare brush against it, and she felt it rock. She prayed it wouldn't fall as she and Promise headed for the third barrel and rounded it with a hair to spare. Her heart frozen, her breath lodged in her throat, they thundered down the straightaway and through the final gate.

Dragging on the reins, she twisted around to see the time. 17.22 seconds. A good one, but was it good enough?

And then she heard the crowd roaring and knew they'd done it. They'd won.

THE ANNOUNCER spoke her name in a deep, twangy voice. Leigh sucked in a breath and tried to calm herself. Somehow knowing she'd run the best time hadn't prepared her for actually getting the award. Knowing everyone would be looking at her, watching her, made her want to squirm. Because until the moment they called her name, winning had been only a dream. She'd placed in the top three before, but she'd never won. To win a race like this one… She shook her head, tried to get hold of herself, and started forward.

Slowly, she made her way to the center of the arena, to stand before the famous barrel racer presenting the trophies. She raised her gaze to the stands, searching for two people. She saw her grandfather and his wife, smiling and waving. And then she saw her mother. Anna was wiping tears from her eyes, smiling and looking proud enough to burst. Next to her sat Jake. He winked at her and gave her the thumbs-up sign. And then Jake and Anna looked at each other.

Leigh couldn't describe what passed between them. Pride and joy, sorrow and longing. And then they both turned away as if they couldn't bear to look at each other anymore and for the first time in her life Leigh was able to put a face to heartbreak.

A chill washed over her, then closed like an icy fist around her heart. *They really loved each other.* And unless she did something Jake would leave and never come back.

They gave her the check first, then the huge silver trophy. Her biggest win yet. More money than she'd ever imagined and a trophy that would look great in her room. Suddenly, it hit her. She knew what she had to do.

"I want to dedicate this trophy to someone," she told the lady, stepping toward the mike to make her acceptance speech. "Can I do that?" She'd seen it done at other rodeos, but she wanted to make sure.

"Of course you can," the woman said, smiling. "Someone special, I take it."

Leigh nodded. "Very special." Taking the microphone from her, she spoke into it, careful to keep her voice steady and strong. "There are a lot of people I want to thank for helping me, and two of them are in the stands right now. I'd like to dedicate this win to my mother and father. Anna Connor and Jake Rollins.''

A gasp went up from the audience but Leigh didn't care. She only had eyes for her parents, who sat there with their mouths practically hanging open. She smiled and gave them the thumbs-up, just like Jake had done minutes earlier. Finally, she knew who she was again.

LEIGH DISAPPEARED into the crowd just after the dedication. Stunned, Anna and Jake simply stared at each other. Anna knew her heart was beating, knew everyone around them was talking, but she couldn't manage to say a word.

She laid her hand on Jake's arm and he covered it with his, his eyes scanning the crowd. After a few moments, he turned to her and said, ''She's long gone. Did you know she was going to do that?''

''I had no idea. I still don't believe it.''

''She talked to me before the race. Said she was sorry she'd been mean to me. I didn't want to read more into it than it seemed. I figured it was a good-bye gesture.'' He smiled ruefully. ''The best I could hope for, you know?''

''But this— Oh, Jake, does it mean what I think it means?''

''I don't know. I'm afraid to hope.'' He took her hand in both of his and squeezed it before bringing it to his lips. ''But I am hoping.''

They found her sitting on the tailgate of Anna's pickup, drinking a soda and obviously waiting for them. Her trophy sat beside her, nearly as big as she was.

"Hi," she said as if she hadn't just rocked their whole world. "Did y'all see my race?"

"Sure did. You were dynamite," Jake said.

Anna propped a hip on the tailgate and hugged Leigh. "Great race."

"Thanks. It was pretty cool."

Anna smiled at the understatement. "Leigh, about what you said when they presented the trophy—"

Leigh looked at her warily. "You're mad. Both of you. Because I like, told the world."

Jake said, "Not mad. Surprised. But not mad."

"Well, I knew it was kind of a shock, but I couldn't think of another way to tell you."

"Tell us what, honey?" Anna asked.

Leigh's gaze went from one to the other, her eyes a brilliant blue as they filled with tears. "To tell Jake I don't want him to leave."

Anna couldn't get her breath. She had hoped against hope and now to have Leigh speak what she'd longed to hear… Finally she managed to say, "Do you mean that? Are you sure you know what you're saying?"

Leigh nodded. "I'm sure." She turned to Jake. "I want you to stay."

"You realize if I stay your mother and I will end up married?"

"Jake, we can talk about that lat—"

"No, Anna, let's get it out in the open. We owe her the truth."

Leigh didn't look particularly disturbed. "Yeah, I figured that out."

"Why did you change your mind?" Anna felt driven to ask.

"Well—" She squirmed and looked down at her boot, swinging her leg a moment before she answered. "I thought about things. A lot. About what Mr. R—my grandfather said. About you two loving each other. And about what you both said. That you loved each other and wanted to be together." She compressed her lips. "You were both so depressed, it made me feel crummy. Especially when I figured out that you both loved me and that's why Jake was gonna leave."

"We do love you, Leigh. So much." Anna hugged her tightly. "You've made us so happy."

Releasing Anna, Leigh looked up at her father. "Jake? Do you—am I supposed to call you Dad now?"

He smiled at her and touched her hair. As if he couldn't believe he had the right to do that.

"If you want to. Or you can call me Jake if you'd rather."

"It's not that I don't want to exactly." She turned to Anna. "Do you think Dad would mind? I just—I still love him, you know?"

"I know." A lump formed in her throat. Her heart ached, moved with sadness and with joy. "You're supposed to, Leigh. Carl was your father. And I think…I think he'd understand and want you to do what feels right to you."

Leigh nodded solemnly. "That's what I think, too. He always wanted us to be happy." She looked from one to the other. "So everything's cool?"

Anna's smile widened as her heart soared. "Everything is better than cool."

"Good." She looked suddenly cagey. "Then can I stay at the dance until midnight?"

"What? Of course not. You know your curfew is eleven."

"Thought it was worth a try," she said, grinning. "Since you're in such a good mood now."

She hugged Anna, then hugged Jake. At the sight of the two blond heads together, Anna teared up. She'd never thought to see the two together like that. And she'd never seen a man look as happy—and bewildered—as Jake did just then. She would keep that picture in her heart forever.

"Hey, there's Blaire," Leigh said, turning him loose. With typical youthful zeal, she hopped down off the tailgate. "Will y'all watch my trophy? I need to tell her something." Without waiting for an answer, she ran off.

"If I'm dreaming don't wake me up," Jake said, staring after her.

"I know what you mean." She grabbed Jake's arm and squeezed it, to reassure herself he was real, and that she hadn't imagined the whole thing. They both fell silent, watching their daughter in the distance.

"We took a big risk," Anna said after a moment. "Loving each other again."

"It was worth it," Jake said. "Look what we gained. A family." He took her in his arms and smiled down at her lovingly. "Which reminds me, I never have officially asked you again."

"Asked me what?" she said, returning his smile and winding her arms around his neck.

"I love you. Will you marry me, Anna? Grow old with me? Have more kids with me?"

"Yes." She kissed him deeply. "To all of the above."

HEART OF THE WEST

Every Man Has His Price!

Lost Springs Ranch was famous for turning young mavericks into good men. So word that the ranch was in financial trouble sent a herd of loyal bachelors stampeding back to Wyoming to put themselves on the auction block!

HARLEQUIN®

Makes any time special ™

Visit us at www.romance.net

PHHOWGEN